COLTON'S
COWBOY CODE

BY
MELISSA CUTLER

MILLS &
BOON

Published in Great Britain 2015
by Mills & Boon, an imprint of Harlequin (UK) Limited,
Eton House, 18-24 Paradise Road, Richmond, Surrey, TW9 1SR

© 2015 Harlequin Books S.A.

Special thanks and acknowledgement are given to Melissa Cutler for her contribution to the Coltons of Oklahoma miniseries.

ISBN: 978-0-263-91545-7

18-0715

Harlequin (UK) Limited's policy is to use papers that are natural, renewable and recyclable products and made from wood grown in sustainable forests. The logging and manufacturing processes conform to the legal environmental regulations of the country of origin.

Printed and bound in Spain
by CPI, Barcelona

Melissa Cutler is a flip-flop-wearing Southern California native living with her husband, two rambunctious kids and two suspicious cats in beautiful San Diego. She divides her time between her dual passions for writing sexy, small-town contemporary romances and edge-of-your-seat romantic suspense. Find out more about Melissa and her books at www.melissacutler.net, or drop her a line at cutlermail@yahoo.com.

To my husband, who's the most amazing father
I've ever seen. The kids and I are so lucky
to have you as the rock of our family, my darling.

Chapter 1

In Brett Colton's ears, in his mind, the shrill keening of tornado sirens eclipsed all other sound, despite that he and Outlaw were too far into the backcountry for the sirens to be more than a figment of his imagination—his intuition warning him that this mission was a really stupid plan because there were a hundred ways to die in a storm this angry.

There was no fury in hell or on earth that compared to an Oklahoma thunderstorm when it decided to unleash a twister. The clouds above Tulsa churned, glowing gray green. Golf-ball-sized hail pelted Brett's Stetson and the back of his oiled leather duster. He folded forward, shielding Outlaw's neck and mane from the brunt of the hail's force as best he could, though neither man nor steed were strangers to the elements.

One of these days, Brett's guardian angels would give him up as a lost cause, but, God willing, it wasn't going to be today. Not with so much on the line. Not after everything his family had been through in the past month or the sharp edge of disappointment in his father's and brother's eyes when Brett had broken it to them about the downed fence and the missing cattle. As if Brett had let the herd loose on purpose. As if he was still the same reckless punk he'd been four months ago.

Then again, maybe Brett hadn't completely vanquished the recklessness from his blood, because here he was, racing across the rolling plains of the Lucky C ranch's backcountry, straight toward the deadly funnel forming in the distance. Any minute, a flash flood might come rocketing through, if lightning or a twister didn't hit down first, but he refused to return to the Lucky C homestead without the half dozen pregnant cows that had escaped.

The downed fence was a mystery that Brett would have to contemplate later. He'd checked that line himself the week before. All he knew was that the ranch that he'd once thought of as a fortress was no longer an impenetrable haven for his family, and the decades of peace and prosperity that the Coltons had enjoyed had been shattered beyond repair.

Brett had followed the tracks of the six stampeding cows southwest, keeping them in sight through the rain and the darkening sky, right up until the clouds had let loose with hail. With zero visibility and the cows' hoofprints lost in the churned-up ground and melting balls of ice, he was riding with nothing to guide him but the hunch that the cows had headed toward Vulture Ridge, as the stock on the ranch had done so many times over the years. As long as they'd had enough sense to stop at the ridge instead of going over the edge—*Lord, please don't let them have gone over the edge*—Brett would find a way to get them back to the Lucky C before the twister touched down.

Outlaw expertly cut around scrub trees and boulders without losing speed until Vulture Ridge came into view.

"Gotcha," Brett said, though his words were lost in a crash of thunder.

Four of the cows crowded at the edge of the infamous gully, their hind hooves pawing at the muddy, disintegrating ledge and baying, clearly terrified. Brett slowed Outlaw to a trot and instead of closing in on the cows head-on, guided the horse in a wide arc. Then he rode along the ridge and came up on the cows from the side. Outlaw knew the drill, imposing his authority to the cattle, crowding and nudging them away from the edge.

Once they complied, Brett craned his neck to scan the expanse of prairie land for the remaining two cows. One, he spotted immediately, huddled against a boulder, but the other was nowhere to be seen. Fearing what he'd find, Brett turned his focus to the gully below Vulture Ridge that had been carved out by centuries of flash floods. The missing cow's ear came into view first, tagged with a green tag that meant she was a heifer—a young first-time mom who was probably beyond freaked out at the moment.

He dismounted and got closer to the edge. The heifer

was perched on a narrow outcrop of dirt and rock ten feet below the lip of the ridge, lying on her side, propped against the ridge wall, her massive round belly undulating. She was in labor, and the way she was angled, when the calf was born, it would fall the additional ten feet or so into the gully's basin. That is, if the ledge didn't crumble and the heifer didn't fall herself, first.

This time, Brett's curse was loud enough to be heard over the storm. An older, seasoned cow might have been amenable to Brett's efforts to get her standing and help her pick her way out of the gully, but he already knew this heifer wasn't going to make his life easy like that. He was standing next to Outlaw, debating his options, when a thunderclap sounded so loudly that Brett's teeth rattled. The four cows they'd gathered immediately spooked and took off along the gully ridge.

Brett swung up into the saddle again. Shaking away the water and ice from his face, he set his teeth on his lower lip and whistled in the same tone he used on the livestock around the ranch, the one that often worked—in normal conditions, anyway—as a command for them to stop. These particular cows weren't interested in commands. If anything, they picked up their pace.

He gave another, different toned whistle command to Outlaw and the horse surged toward the cattle as Brett reached for his lasso. Throwing it in this weather would be a crapshoot at best, but he had to try. He secured the rope in his hands, then drove Outlaw faster, getting in front of the cows and cutting them off.

He waited until they were right up on the beasts to

throw the lasso. It caught the neck of the farthest cow, just as it was supposed to, so he cinched it nice and tight and brought all four cows crowded between the lassoed cow and Outlaw's body.

"Thataway, Outlaw," he called over the wind and hail, stroking the gelding's neck. "Thataway."

They maneuvered the cattle to a cluster of shrubs not too far away from where the fifth cow was still huddled by the boulder. Brett swung off the saddle, then looped the other end of the rope around the neck of a second cow. He tied another rope around the necks of the third and fourth cows and hooked all the ropes into the branches of the sturdiest scrub tree. It wasn't all that secure, should another thunderclap spook them again, but it was the best he could do for now.

He left Outlaw standing near them, but refused to tie him to the tree, even if it meant Brett getting stranded should the gelding take off. Because what if the horse needed to flee with good reason? What if Brett didn't make it out of the gully alive? Brett would rather chance getting stranded than put his horse in any unnecessary danger, which was a vital part of the cowboy code he lived by.

Brett threaded his head and an arm through his last bundle of rope from his saddle bag, then stroked Outlaw's neck and got close to his ear. "You stay with the stock. Keep 'em calm for me until I get back." For all he knew, Outlaw understood every word. He liked to imagine that bit of magic, anyway.

It wasn't until he was slogging to the edge of Vulture Ridge that he realized how soaked-to-the-bones he was.

The muddy ground sucked at his boots, and his jeans felt as if they weighed twenty pounds. He flapped the tails of his duster around his body, then checked the collar to make sure it was standing on end, but still, bits of hail wormed their way between his collar and his hat to melt against his neck. Sniffing, his eyes downturned and marking each labored step, he put his shoulder to the wind and pressed on.

The heifer was lying on her side still, but didn't seem to have given birth yet. Her hooves hovered in midair over the gully that was rapidly filling with water. The path she'd slid down was steep, but wouldn't be impossible for her to traverse back up over the ridge—if he could get her standing again.

He was debating the merits of risking his life for a single livestock, when the heifer brayed, a pained, fearful cry. Then one of her hind legs and her tail lifted. The water sac was visible already.

"Holy day…" Brett muttered.

The calf was coming.

He slid down the mud wall following the same path the heifer had. There wasn't enough room on the ledge for both of them to fit comfortably. His boot heels cut into the dirt wall as he skirted her body to reach her tail. The calf's tail was crowning first.

"Damn it. This baby's not making it easy on you, is it, girl?" Brett wiped his muddy hands on his coat, then pushed the calf's rump back in. Working by feel, he located the hind legs and positioned them one at a time in the birthing canal.

The heifer brayed and kicked out. If they were at the

ranch, Brett would've secured her in a head gate and
called for help. All he had now was luck, a single rope
and his wits, and he was going to need all three to birth
the calf before it died.

He took off his coat and draped it over the heifer's
face, hoping the reduction of stimulus from the rain
and storm would calm her down. No luck. She kicked
harder, and before Brett had gotten back in position near
her tail, she tipped over the edge of the outcropping and
slid into the rapidly-filling gully.

Brett followed, his rope in his hand. The water was
three feet deep and rising. The rain and hail beat down
relentlessly as the wind whipped up. Time to get this
calf birthed and get the hell out of there before they
all lost their lives. The cow, on her side in the gully,
strained to keep her head above water. Brett slogged to
her backside again, the water and mud caking his legs
and seeping into his boots. He wrapped the rope around
the calf's legs once, twice, three times.

He wiggled his boots into the riverbed, bracing himself, then got a firm hold of the rope and pulled, growling with the effort. The calf slid another four or five
inches out. Panting, Brett adjusted his grip on the rope,
then pulled again. This time, the calf came. Brett fell
backward in the water, the calf on his chest.

With a laugh of triumph, Brett cleaned the calf's nose
out with his finger, then tickled its ear to get it breathing. Then a golf-ball-sized piece of hail smacked Brett
hard on his cheek, killing his awe over the miracle of
helping birth a new life and reminding him of the danger all around them.

He pushed to his feet, bringing the calf up in his arms. He worked to untie the rope from the calf's hind legs with one eye on the steep side of the gully. The water was above Brett's knees, sloshing at his groin. He couldn't get the rope around the mama cow and keep his hold on the wiggling calf, so he'd have to come back down for her.

He'd pulled himself and the calf a good five feet up the gully wall when he heard it, a roar like no other he'd heard before. Not thunder, not a twister. Something otherworldly that got louder, closer. The gully walls vibrated with the force. A flash flood. Had to be.

In full panic mode, Brett hauled himself to the ledge that the cow had originally slid onto. He grabbed his duster from where the cow had tossed it away from her face. He threw it up to the top of the ridge, then hauled himself and the calf the rest of the way up, his fingers and boot toes digging into the muddy wall, pushing the calf up in front of him with his chest. He heaved the calf over the top of the ridge as a wall of water appeared in the gully, bearing down on their location.

Brett scrambled to safety and got on his knees. As fast as he could, he wound the rope back and set the lasso loop down to the mama cow. Maybe he could anchor her there so she wouldn't get swept away. Maybe the floodwaters weren't as high and fast as they looked.

The flash flood hit her hard, rolling her under. The rope pulled on him as though he was playing tug-of-war with a whole football team. There was nothing to do but let go. He'd heard too many accounts of ranchers getting swept into floodwater and drowning because they were too stubborn to lose their livestock.

Brett's legs were shaky and weak with an adrenaline crash as he stood, following with his gaze the glimpse of the cow's head in the water until she disappeared. The floodwaters gurgled and spit at the edge of the gully wall. He stared at the water, trying not to think of the loss as a failure. After all, he'd saved the calf, five pregnant cows and his own life.

He swung his attention to the boulder where he'd left the other cows and Outlaw. Outlaw was still there, but none of the cows. Damn it.

He pulled his drenched, muddy coat on, then lifted the calf into his arms again and trudged to his horse, his eyes on the storm front that looked to be moving away from them. At least one thing had gone his way today.

Outlaw nuzzled his cheek.

"Thanks for waiting for me," Brett said. "Happen to see which direction those cows went?"

Could've been his imagination, but Outlaw snorted in reply.

He scratched the horse's neck. "Good. How about you lead me to them so we can call it a day?"

He lifted the calf onto the saddle first, then hoisted himself up, the weight of the water and mud making him feel a good fifty pounds heavier than he had when he'd left the stable. The orphaned calf looked up at him, helpless and trusting. Brett usually didn't think of the livestock as cute, but this one surely was, with long lashes, a soft buttercream-colored coat and a pink nose. He wrapped his coat around it and held it close.

"We'll get you home soon and make you up a bottle as soon as we find your mama's friends. I do believe we're gonna name you Twister. How does that sound?"

The calf's tongue came out to lick a pebble of hail from its nose, the cutest thing Brett might've ever seen besides his nephew, Seth.

Jack, Brett's oldest brother, was going to be furious about the loss of the cow. Already, he didn't trust Brett, and this wasn't going to help. But Brett was tired of working under his brother like some hired hand, getting his butt chewed for every perceived misstep. He was ready to redeem his reputation and earn his slice of the Colton legacy—and he had just the plan to make it work. All he needed now was to hire a financial whiz to help him crunch the numbers and profit projections he'd need to help Jack see his point of view.

With a whistle and a nudge of Brett's boots, Outlaw burst into motion back through the storm toward home while Brett's mind churned, plotting and planning his next move to seize a hold of his bright future once and for all.

Being a poster girl for the perils of sin had gotten Hannah Grayson nowhere fast. For as much mileage as her family's church had gotten out of using Hannah's accidental pregnancy as a cautionary tale, they could have at least provided her with a small stipend to ease the sting of being disowned by her parents, fired from her job and evicted from her apartment, all while battling a nasty case of morning sickness.

From her pocket, she withdrew the help-wanted ads

she'd printed from *Tulsa World* newspaper's online classifieds. Every lead on the papers but one had been crossed out as a dead end. She'd been counting on her newly minted accounting degree from Tulsa United On-line University to help her land on her feet, but every employer she'd met with had taken one look at the now-obvious swell of her belly and decided she wasn't qualified for the job.

With her meager savings running out, she'd made a deal with herself to explore this one last lead before giving up on accounting in favor of a retail or a fast-food position, but it was a long shot at best.

> *Tulsa businessman in need of an accountant for a temporary project, discretion a must.*

No name or company name given, no phone number or address. Just a generic email address of "okla-homa45678" that could belong to anybody. Including a psychopath. Which was why she'd created a new, generic email address of her own to reply to the ad and had refused to give out even her name to the individual when she agreed to meet him at a window booth in the Armadillo Diner & Pie Company.

Replacing the classified ad in her purse, she paused at the window of the Fluff and Fold to check herself in the window reflection. Wisps of her pencil-straight black hair lifted in the wind that had hung around Tulsa since the previous week's storm. She smoothed them into place and used the pad of her thumb to sharpen the line of her light pink lip gloss on her bottom lip.

The gray slacks were a clearance-rack find from a couple months earlier, when they'd been a loose fit. Now, the waist sat below the swell of her belly, which she'd covered with a form-fitting pale pink blouse. She could have de-emphasized the evidence of her pregnancy with another outfit, but all that had done in the past was delay the inevitable disinterest from the prospective employers that came when she disclosed the truth, and wasted everyone's time. Better to put her condition out in the open right up front, before a single word was exchanged.

With her eyes on her reflection, she stood tall and proud, rubbing a hand over her belly. "Something's going to work out, little guy. Or girl. If this opportunity isn't it, then we'll keep trying. I'm not going to let you down."

She squared her shoulders and strode toward the diner door, harnessing her pride and owning her power. She was a terrific accountant and a good person. That had to count for something. Maybe Mr. Anonymous Businessman would be the first person to see her for the workplace asset she could be.

Inside the Armadillo, the smell of old, burned coffee and cooking eggs rushed up on Hannah, making her stomach lurch. She ground to a stop in the waiting area. Hands on her hips, she raised her face to the ceiling and breathed through her mouth as the wave of nausea passed. When she'd selected the diner as a meeting place, she'd been hoping for a free meal, not the possibility of the diner smells triggering her morning sickness.

"You okay, darlin'?"

Hannah lowered her gaze to see a middle-aged wait-ress eyeing her with concern from behind blue-tinted eyelashes, tapping a laminated menu against her palm.

"I think so. Food smells, you know?" She rubbed her baby bump and offered a smile to Janice, or so the waitress's name tag read.

"Oh, I know. Try working here while pregnant, with the omelets in the morning and the liver-platter special at dinner. I spent the first half of each of my pregnan-cies serving the food, then running to the can. How far along are you?"

The mention of eggs and liver had Hannah raising her face to the ceiling again. "Nineteen weeks."

"Ah. Well, the worst of it should be about over. You want a table near the air vent, I bet."

After another fortifying breath through her mouth, Hannah lowered her face and smiled at Janice. "Actu-ally, I'm meeting someone here. Job interview."

Her curiosity about Mr. Anonymous's identity had her shifting her gaze from Janice to the row of window booths. There was only one man at a booth by the win-dow. Brett Colton, and he was standing up next to the table, his napkin in his hand, nailing her with a gaze of utter shock.

Gasping, Hannah wrenched her face away. *Crap on a cracker. This can't be happening.*

Janice's voice floated over the air as though from a great distance. "Well, bless your heart, looking for work in your condition. What does your baby daddy have to say about that?"

Her baby daddy was about to say a whole lot because, judging by his expression, he'd heard the whole exchange with Janice and was really good at doing fast math in his head.

"Excuse me," Hannah muttered. Then she pivoted in place and marched back out the door.

She paced the sidewalk in front of the diner, garnering her courage because she knew with 100 percent certainty that Brett was going to follow her out and demand the answers he deserved. Over the past few months, she'd played this moment in her head a dozen different ways, but it never looked anything like this. She never planned to leave him in the dark about the baby. All she'd wanted to do was hold off on telling him until she had a job and a permanent place to stay.

"Anna, wasn't it?" The growl of Brett Colton's sexy-as-sin voice had her freezing in her tracks. She squeezed her eyes closed as mortification set in that the father of her child didn't even remember her name correctly. Then again, what did she expect from Tulsa's most notorious playboy? She bet he seduced a different girl every night of the week, or so the rumors would have her believe.

She fluttered her eyes open and caught sight of her reflection in the Fluff and Fold window again, surprised at the sight of a meek girl hanging her head, dread and guilt etched in her features. What happened to the proud, confident woman she'd been only a few minutes earlier? She'd done nothing wrong and broken no rules. There was no official timetable on telling a man you were pregnant with his child.

Clinging to that truth, she straightened up, smoothed her features, and then spun to face Brett. "It's Hannah, actually."

He winced at that, and then those soulful green eyes turned sheepish—a reaction that Hannah found absurdly comforting. "Sorry. Hannah." He closed and opened his mouth, his eyes flitting from her belly to her face, as though he was in the same clueless state of communication as she was. "I, uh…you're, um…nineteen weeks. That's about when we, uh…"

"Yes. I know. It's yours," she blurted. And cue her turn to wince. So much for breaking the news to him gently.

The sheepishness vanished from his face, along with the color. "That's impossible."

She schooled her features to mask a sudden flare of irritation. "Really? Ya think?" Okay, so maybe she hadn't done that terrific a job concealing her feelings.

"We used protection, so how is that possible?"

She'd asked herself that same question a million times. "Yes, we did. We used protection that you supplied, in fact. So maybe you should be the one explaining to me how it happened."

His eyes narrowed. "Moving on. You're going to have to work pretty hard to convince me of the reason you kept this from me. When were you planning on telling me, anyway? Or did you?"

The accusation dripping from his words got her back up. "So you didn't remember my name correctly, yet you expected me to remember yours and know where to find you? Narcissistic much?"

His mouth fell open at that and the color returned to his face in full force. "I'm sorry. You're right. I…"

He looked so abashed and sincerely apologetic that all the fight rushed out of her. "That wasn't fair of me. I'm sorry. The truth is, I did remember your name and I fully planned to tell you. I was looking to get my life in order first."

The ranching community of Tulsa was an *everybody's in everybody's business* kind of town, and Hannah couldn't bear for her baby to be born under a cloud of suspicion and rumors that his or her mother was a gold digger, getting pregnant on purpose to get at the Colton fortune. It would be bad enough for her baby having its mama's reputation run through the mud in the church community.

His mouth screwed up as though he didn't buy what she was selling. "By answering a sketchy classified ad for temporary work? I've been in your car and to your apartment. Your life is the opposite of screwed up. Try again."

She smoothed a hand over her stomach out of habit. If he wanted to hear the whole pathetic story, then who was she to deny him?

"That's the truth, whether you believe it or not. When my parents found out I was pregnant, they relieved me of the burden of being their daughter, which included firing me from managing the feed-supply store they own. And, because I'd sunk all my money into getting my accounting degree, I had nothing in savings. So I sold my car to pay my doctor bills, which then got me evicted from my apartment.

"I'm trying to get my life back on track, but nothing I've tried is working. I can't just snap my fingers and fix my life. All I wanted to do is land on my feet before coming to you. A job. And a place to live." She'd wanted to tell him truthfully that she was doing fine and didn't need his financial support or—God forbid—a mercy proposal of marriage. She'd seen enough of her parents' own unhappy marriage to know that wasn't the life she wanted for her or her child.

"The only trouble is," she continued, "who's going to hire a pregnant lady for any kind of real job, with health insurance and maternity leave? Nobody, as it turns out, because I've looked. I've scoured this whole darn city looking for work that would help my baby—" Emotion tightened her throat. She was exhausted and nauseous and so tired of being judged unfairly. She swallowed and took a breath. "I've been looking for work that would help my baby have a good life."

Grimacing, he wrenched his face to the street, his hands on his hips, his eyes distant.

Hannah did a whole bunch more swallowing, reining in her hormone-fueled emotional fireworks as she studied his profile. He really was a stunning specimen of a man—his face perfection with those masculine cheekbones and that fit cowboy's body that had brought her so much wicked pleasure that night. He kept his light brown hair disheveled just so, adding a rakish quality to his charm. No wonder he turned the head of every woman in Tulsa when he walked down the street.

He deserved better than to find out he was going to

be a father on the side of the road outside a Laundromat, not with a woman he loved, but with a virtual stranger.

When she was sure she could speak calmly, she said, "I'm not trying to get at your family's money, Brett."

He jerked his face in her direction, his face a stone mask now. Gone was any trace of the smile he'd wooed her with nineteen weeks ago at the Tulsa club where she'd decided to let her hair down after her college graduation.

"You still need to pay your bill, hon," called a female voice.

Hannah and Brett both turned to see Janice standing at the Armadillo's door, waving a slip of paper.

"I'll be right there," Brett called to Janice, his voice tight with harnessed emotion. To Hannah, he added, "I need to take care of this, and then we're going to go somewhere private to talk."

Hannah nodded, even as her stomach ached, empty. She'd been counting on the interviewer's promise in his email to buy her breakfast. She wrapped her arms around her ribs and battled a fresh round of pathetic tears. "I'll wait here."

He huffed, his hardened, distant expression not really seeing her when he looked her way and took her arm. "I don't think so. You're coming inside with me while I pay the bill. I don't want you disappearing on me before I get some answers. I don't even know your last name." He swept his hand in front of him. "After you."

Chapter 2

Brett was pretty sure he'd never been so blindsided by anything as seeing the woman he'd slept with a few months earlier appear at the diner where he was waiting to interview a temporary accountant—and learning that she was pregnant with his child.

His child. Good God, what had he done?

He'd already come to think of that bender of a weekend as life-changing because he'd nearly gotten himself killed, not because he'd knocked up the girl he slept with, the one whose last name or phone number he hadn't even bothered to ask, he was so drunk and self-destructive. He was lucky he remembered her face at all, given the state he'd been in, but she held the dubious honor of being his last conquest before he'd gotten right with himself and had given up partying, drinking and women cold turkey.

He held the diner door open for Hannah, who marched past him, her feathers clearly ruffled. "I know you're upset, but you don't get to treat me like a criminal."

He wasn't trying to, but he also wasn't taking a chance on her sneaking away before he got some answers. All he had was the email address she'd contacted him with about the job, and he doubted that was anything but a shell account. He didn't even know her last name, and hadn't even recalled her first name correctly. Didn't that just say it all about how severely he'd screwed up his life?

At the hostess desk, he paid for his coffee and left a generous tip. That's when he heard it. Hannah's stomach growled. Loudly.

He froze, his change halfway in his wallet.

"Shoot," she muttered. "You didn't hear that."

In his periphery, he watched her arms wrap around her middle, protective and proud. His attention slid to the scuffed black flats she wore. They were old, worn. The edges of the material fraying. Yet she'd worn them to the job interview so they had to be the best pair she owned. She'd lost her job, her car and her apartment. Where was she living now? Was she getting the medical care she and the baby needed?

That's when it hit him that the answers to those questions didn't matter yet. All that mattered at that moment was that she was clearly hungry. She was also too thin, now that he thought about it. Hungry. Jobless. Homeless—and she was having his baby. Damn.

"Change of plans." His words came out as a croak. He cleared his throat, then met the waitress's confused gaze. "Could you seat us again? Turns out I'm hungry for breakfast after all."

Hannah stiffened. "I don't need your charity."

Judging by her growling stomach, she did, but she was far too proud to accept it. She hadn't come to him for help when she first found out she was pregnant or when she'd lost her job. She'd made of point of telling him that she wasn't after his money. Other than her dancing skills—both of the club variety and the horizontally-in-bed variety—her sense of pride and honor were just about all he knew about her. That, and the fact that she was an accountant, which he would have never pegged her as.

Proud, dancing Hannah the accountant didn't follow the waitress, but stood stock-still, giving him a stink-eye that even his mother would admire. She didn't want help or charity and didn't seem to trust his breakfast offer, but Brett did have one thing he could offer her that he bet she wouldn't refuse.

"You came here today to interview for a job and I need an accountant, so I say we get on with the reason for our appointment."

She held him with a searching gaze as though testing his intentions, then gave a terse nod.

He fought against letting his relief show on his face as he ushered her ahead of him to follow the waitress to a booth.

The waitress handed them menus. "I'm glad you

came back for some food, darlin'. I was worried that your morning sickness got the better of you."

Hannah offered the woman a warm, genuine smile that held Brett riveted, his memory jogged. He remembered that smile from the night they'd hooked up and what it felt like to have it directed at him.

"Wait," he said as the waitress turned to leave. "Janice, I'm really hungry. I think we'd better get that food on order right now. Hannah, you ready?"

"I'll have the oatmeal and a fruit cup."

That wasn't enough. Not nearly. When his brother's now ex-wife had been pregnant, she ate her weight in food every day. "I'll have the Paul Bunyan flapjack stack, the sausage omelet with the cheese grits, and a side of bacon." He winked at Hannah, whose eyebrows were pinched as though she were onto his plan. "Working on the ranch builds up quite an appetite."

When the waitress left, he folded his hands on the table. "Let's get right to this interview. Lucky C—that's the name of my family's ranch—needs a new accountant."

"I know what your family's ranch is named. Everybody round these parts knows the Coltons, which is why it doesn't make any sense for you to post the help wanted ad the way you did, anonymously, discretion required."

On top of everything else, she was smart as a whip. Smart, proud, stubborn and a great dancer. Her list of attributes was getting unwieldy.

"What are you smiling about?" she asked.

He shook his head. "You're quick. I can already see you'll do a great job for the Lucky C."

She frowned at his compliment. "You're patronizing me. You don't even know my qualifications." From her massive purse, she pulled a page of substantial, pricey stationery from a folder. Her résumé.

"I'm not patronizing you. I put the ad in the classifieds because I need an accountant. You answered the ad and I'm a pretty good judge of character. Something tells me that you're perfect for the job."

"I am, but first, tell me why you did what you did, with the anonymous classified ad. Your family's ranch is huge and prosperous. If you need an accountant, you could have the best in Oklahoma, none of this cloak-and-dagger baloney."

He could tell she wasn't going to let him off the hook. "My father's getting up there in years and his memory isn't what it used to be. I've done what I can to help him—we all have—but it's time we bring in a qualified professional. I made the ad anonymous because my father's in denial about what's happening to him and I didn't want to alert the Tulsa gossip hounds, not after everything our family went through last month."

That was only a half-truth, but the real reason he'd wanted to hire an accountant wasn't going to cut through her pride, so he had no remorse for feeding her a line, not when her and their baby's well-beings were at stake. The real reason he'd put the anonymous ad in the paper was because he'd been planning to hire an accountant to take a look at the ranch's books on the sly, without his father and brothers' knowledge, and to help him crunch the numbers for the horse breeding business plan he was going to lay out for his family to consider investing in. But Hannah needed more than a part-time temporary job on the sly.

She set a hand on his forearm, her face pinched with worry. Her nails were trimmed to a short, practical length but were well-manicured and glossy, as though she'd used clear polish on them. "What happened last month? Is everyone okay?"

That surprised him all over again. The local news had done a thorough job raking his family through the public eye. "You mean you didn't hear?"

Her concerned look deepened, darkening her eyes. "No. Last month was the worst of my life. I was just trying to survive."

She was just trying to survive. He gripped his knees hard, holding himself back from scolding her. *You should have contacted me. I would have taken care of you. I would have taken care of everything.*

Brett wasn't ready for fatherhood, and truth was, it'd take some time for that change in his life to sink in, but nothing was going to stop him from doing the right thing by Hannah and the baby. That's what Colton men did and that's what Brett was going to do—for the rest of their lives.

Marriage? Maybe. If that's what Hannah wanted, what she needed in the long run, then his code of honor depended on making that offer to her. But not yet. Not when he wasn't sure she'd even agree to come live at the ranch once she heard what happened there the month before. He'd just have to find a way to convince her despite everything, because there was no getting around the truth about the trouble at the Lucky C. She'd find out soon enough. "Our house was robbed and my mother was attacked."

Hannah gasped. Her grip on his forearm tightened. "Is she...?"

He set a hand over hers and squeezed. "She's alive. In a coma. The doctors aren't sure she's going to make it, but we have to hold out hope."

Brett's relationship with his mother was the most complicated in his life. They'd never seen eye to eye and clashed more often than they were at peace. His deepest regret was that their last words to each other were angry, cruel. She wasn't an easy person to love, but she was the only mother he had and the thought of losing her hurt him something awful.

Hannah turned her hand over and threaded her fingers with his. "I'm so sorry. Did they catch the man who did that to her?"

"Yes. They have a suspect in custody. If you accept my job offer, and I sincerely hope you will, I want you to know that the ranch is safe. You don't have to worry about that." God, he hoped that was true. But there was no need to worry Hannah with his private doubts that the police had captured the man responsible for the assault, not when there was no evidence beyond his gut telling him that there was more to the robbery and attempted murder than everyone else thought.

Mistrust—or was that her pride rearing its head again?—pushed through her worried expression. "I don't remember you making me an official offer yet."

Their food arrived in a clatter of plates on Janice's massive serving tray, the smell so delicious that Hannah's stomach gurgled like crazy.

"I was just about to. Come work for the Lucky C, Hannah. It's what the ranch needs, and it's what you need, too. I'm prepared to compensate you with a competitive salary, health insurance, housing—"

"Housing? Isn't that a little unusual?"

She was a hard nut to crack, this one. Far harder than her sweet, soft voice and kind smile suggested. He summoned his most charming smile onto his lips, hoping that a little buttering up would help his cause. "Maybe, but then again, I've never met an accountant as pretty as you, so I'd say this situation is mighty unusual any way you cut it."

Sure enough, the mistrust in Hannah's eyes softened. And was that a hint of a smile on her lips? She poked her spoon through the air in his direction. "You can't flirt with me if you're going to be my boss."

"Then you're accepting my offer?"

"I said *if.*"

He slid the plate of bacon toward her. When charming failed, bacon often had a way of coming to the rescue. "Eat."

Desire shone in her eyes, jogging another memory of the lust he remembered seeing on her face that night at the club, then later, at her apartment. He remembered the way her every emotion played on her face without artifice or pretense. At the time, he'd appreciated that quality of hers only because it had made her easier to seduce, then easier to bring pleasure to in bed. He supposed what he was doing this morning still counted as seduction, but now, he was wholly focused on her needs instead of his.

To his relief, her fingers closed around a crispy slice of bacon. "I wasn't going to eat your food, given your enormous rancher's appetite, but that smells too darn good to resist. One little piece…" She crunched into the bacon, her eyes closing with the bliss of it.

He watched her face, riveted anew by the ever-shifting nuances in her expression.

Yet he forced his wayward thoughts aside. There would be time enough to marvel over Hannah, but he was a man on a mission, and he would not be deterred for anything. "Our chef cures and smokes her own bacon, harvested from our ranch's livestock. I wake to the smell of it frying in the kitchen every single morning. You could, too."

Her eyes jolted open. "I'm not moving in with you."

Time for the next step in his seduction. He liberally spread butter on his stack of flapjacks, then drizzled it with warm maple syrup. He sliced off a hearty wedge, then held his forkful across the table for her.

She backed her face up, eying the flapjack bite suspiciously.

"When was the last time you had pure maple syrup and real butter?" he crooned.

She reached a finger out to his plate and swiped at a drop of syrup, then brought it to her tongue.

Mercy. Just like that, Brett felt every one of the nineteen weeks of his self-inflicted abstinence.

"You, Brett Colton, are as slippery as a snake-oil salesman."

He brandished the fork under her nose. "I prefer to think of myself as stubborn and single-minded. Not so different from you."

The suspicion on her face melted away a little bit more. She guided his hand toward her and closed her lips around the fork in a way that gave Brett some ideas too filthy for his own good.

He cleared his throat, snapping his focus back to the task at hand. "When my parents remodeled the big house, they designed separate wings for each of their six children, but I'm the only one of the six who lives there full-time. Me and my father. My younger sister passes through sometimes, but you would have your own wing, your own bathroom with a big old tub, and plenty of privacy."

For the first time, she seemed to be seriously considering his offer. Time to go for broke. He handed her another slice of bacon, which she accepted without a word.

"Where are you living now?" he said. "Can you look me in the eye and tell me it's a good, long-term situation for you and the baby?"

She snapped a tiny bit of bacon off and popped it into her mouth. "It's not like I'm living in some abandoned building. I'm staying with my best friend, Lori, and her boyfriend, Drew. It's not ideal. Actually it's far from ideal—I mean, I'm sleeping on the sofa—but with the money from this job, I'll be able to afford my own place."

"And until that first paycheck, you'll live at the

ranch." He pressed his lips together. That had come out a smidge more demanding than he'd wanted it to.

Their gazes met and held. "Are you mandating that? Will the job offer depend on me accepting the temporary housing?"

Oh, how he wanted to say yes to that. "No. But you should agree to it, anyway. Your own bed, regular meals made by a top-rated personal chef, and your commute to work is down a set of stairs and along a short dirt road to the ranch office. The only traffic you might run into would be some overly excitable ranch dogs."

She popped the rest of the bacon slice into her mouth, then washed it down with orange juice. "I know why you're doing all this, and I still don't fully believe you about the reason you're hiring an accountant on the sly, but I really am grateful for all you're offering—the job and the accommodations. In all honesty, this went a lot better than I thought it would."

"The job interview?"

"No, telling you about the baby. I thought you'd either hate me or propose to me."

Brett didn't miss a beat. "I still might."

"Which one, hate me?"

Leaning forward, he gave her a look full of commitment and honor. "Ask you to marry me. I haven't taken that option off the table yet, either." At the flush of pink to her skin, he added with a knowing smile, "For the record, I don't think there's a person on the planet who could hate you."

"There's a whole congregation of them over on Grand Avenue and Fourth Street."

"That's your church?"

"The Congregation of the Second Coming. My parents' church, not mine. And it's more like a cult than a church, truth be told. Even before they excommunicated me because of the pregnancy, I was done with that place. I'm still a Christian, but I doubt there's room for that church's closed-minded judgment in the kingdom of heaven."

"Then you're better off without them."

She drew herself up tall. "Thank you. Yes, I am."

"Take my offer, Hannah. Let me take care of you." He clamped his teeth together, cursing himself for adding that last part. A strong, proud woman like her would chafe at such an old-fashioned notion.

She picked up her butter knife and made swirls in the bottom of her oatmeal bowl. Brett held his breath, watching her.

"I accept the job and the housing, even though 'Pregnant with the Boss's Baby' sounds like a bad soap opera plot." A conciliatory smile graced her lips.

Relief swept through his system with the force of last week's flash flood. "I don't know, I think it has a nice ring to it." Even as he said that, the truth in her jest hit him with a fresh dose of clarity. He was going to be a father. His future was going to include diaper changes, first steps, scraped knees and sleepless nights. Everything in his life was about to change, and he and Hannah would forever be linked by the life they'd created together.

His attention raked over the mother of his child, who

was worrying the edge of her napkin. "What's bothering you now?"

"What about your family?" she said. "You took all this so well, but what if they hate me? Or worse, what if they think I got pregnant on purpose to get at your money?"

As much as he wished that her worry had no merit, she'd brought up an excellent point, because his family had no shortage of closed-minded judgmental attitudes, too. He'd been fighting for months to get them to see him in a new light, to prove to his brothers and father that he had turned over a new, more responsible leaf, so that they'd finally support the big plans he had for the family business. The last thing Brett needed was to add fuel to his brothers' and father's belief that he wasn't fit to help run the Lucky C, and nothing said *screwed-up, irresponsible rich boy* better than getting a girl pregnant during a one-night stand.

But facing the consequences of his misspent years and terrible choices was his problem, not Hannah's, so he squelched the grimace he felt coming on at the thought of breaking the news to his father and siblings. "Leave them to me."

Chapter 3

Brett stood at the edge of Vulture Ridge, at the very place where he'd watched the cow get swept away in the flash flood, his gaze absorbing the land that he loved, despite Mother Nature's occasional cruelty. Today the sky was clear, but they'd had afternoon thundershowers every day lately, and this afternoon's forecast was no different. Even now, at a few minutes to noon, the clouds were stacking up on the horizon.

His eyeballs ached from a sleepless night of self-torment, with his conscience replaying every mistake he'd ever made. Every whiskey-soaked night, every morning of work he'd slept through—his past was littered with so much waste of money, time and opportunity that he could hardly believe that he kept being given more chances to get it right. That same life-changing bender of a weekend that had resulted in his car accident was now changing his life all over again. From this point forward and for the rest of his days, he would be beholden to a woman and, soon, a child. Somehow, he was going to become a man worthy of the charge—that he knew with absolute certainty.

Before dawn, he'd walked out of his house determined to stop looking back, ready to face his future with eyes wide-open. With a straight spine and determination coursing through his veins, he'd saddled Outlaw and had taken off to the backcountry, long before Jack and the ranch hands had arrived for their workdays.

He'd watched the sun rise over the prairie with an appreciation that reminded him of how he'd felt returning to the ranch after being released from the hospital after his accident—full of gratitude and hope. The longer he soaked in the views and scents of the backcountry, the land he adored, the more at peace he became with the new direction his life was going. Becoming a father was going to change a lot, but it wasn't going to change everything. He would always have this land, this Colton legacy. And now he had someone to pass it to. The realization brought a smile to his lips.

The irony wasn't lost on him that the very reason he couldn't give up fighting for his rightful place in the Colton legacy was the very reason he was about to be back to square one with his family on that very topic. When his dad and brothers learned about Brett's impending fatherhood resulting from a one-night stand, he was going to lose their trust all over again, along with whatever leverage he'd fought for over the past four months.

When the alarm on his phone chimed, alerting him that it was almost time for the family meeting that his older brother Ryan, a detective with the Tulsa PD, had called in order to share the latest developments in their mother's assault case, Brett's resolve faltered for a split second. Nerves settled in his gut like stones. Ryan wasn't the only one with news to share.

A click of his tongue and a slight wiggle of a rein was all the direction Outlaw needed to turn away from the ridge and trot in the direction of the ranch buildings. Brett urged him faster, relishing the feel of unadulterated power in Outlaw's muscles and stride. Brett knew that Outlaw loved this part, too, the wind in their faces and the open range at their feet as they shot across the plains, the sensations of speed and freedom potent enough for Brett to almost imagine it possible to outrun his past and his reputation.

The circular driveway in front of Brett's family home—the Big House, as it'd been called since long before Brett's birth, and where now only he and his dad lived, and his mom before her attack—was crowded with vehicles, including his half brother Daniel's truck and the farm truck that Jack's fiancée, Tracy, liked to drive around the place. Even his brother Eric had deigned to make a rare appearance, by the looks of it. Greta, they'd already been informed, couldn't break away from her job until the next day, when she planned to swing through the Big House for a short stay.

Brett walked around to the back of the house, then

climbed the four steps up to the wraparound porch. The stones in his stomach that had been sitting there since seeing Hannah yesterday seemed to double in size with every step. He swallowed hard, then opened the door and entered through the mudroom attached to the kitchen.

The aroma of onions and garlic and roasting beef wafted past his nose as he removed his hat and boots. Maria, the chef, must be slow-cooking a roast for supper, if he had to hazard a guess. For Hannah's first meal there, he'd requested something hearty and homey that showcased the ranch's prized steer, and judging by the mouthwatering smells, Maria was going to knock it out of the park.

A smile worked its way onto his lips at the sudden vision of the look on Hannah's face when she'd crunched into that first slice of bacon the previous morning. Oh, man, he couldn't wait to watch her reaction to Maria's cooking. The anticipation of it was almost enough to quell his nerves over coming clean to his family about the many ways his life was about to get turned upside down.

From the kitchen, he crossed the foyer to the living room on the east side of the house, where a collection of male voices could be heard. As opposed to the kitchen, the foyer invariably smelled of fresh flowers from the arrangement that graced the circular marble table at the center of the grand entrance, which his mother insisted on having delivered weekly. To her warped way of thinking, the flowers were a display of power and wealth, but since Brett's brush with death, he'd come to think of the arrangements as reminders of how beautiful and fragile life was.

Even after his mom's attack, Edith had maintained the fresh flowers in the house. The only change was that the smaller arrangements that used to grace his mom's room got sent to her room at Tulsa General Hospital.

He'd taken no more than three steps through the foyer when a blond ball of little-boy energy bounded toward him, squealing his name. Despite Brett's nerves, he felt another grin coming on. Nobody made Brett feel like a rock star more than his five-year-old nephew, Seth, Jack's only son. The two were fast friends, and had been since the day Brett first held Seth in his arms when he was nothing more than a red-faced potato head wrapped in a hospital blanket. He opened his arms as Seth launched himself into them.

"Hey, cowpoke."

"Hiya, Uncle Brett!"

"Wait, what's this in your armpit?" With that, Brett dug his thumbs into Seth's prime tickle spot under his armpits. Seth squealed with delight, writhing and arching.

Brett redoubled his efforts. "Just a sec, I think I've almost got it," he teased. "Lemme just dig in there a little deeper."

Seth's legs kicked out, and one of his feet accidentally nudged the marble table. The flower arrangement's vase wobbled. Brett lunged for it as best he could while being careful not to drop Seth, but Jack was quicker.

Jack steadied the vase, casting his signature stern look at Brett that got right under his skin, as it always did. "Careful, you two. Edith works too hard to keep this place up to have you messing it up by roughhousing."

As though Brett needed to be scolded like a child. He was about to say as much when Tracy appeared. She wore her dark blond hair pulled into a ponytail and a dark shirt and jeans that emphasized her pale, slim figure.

"Oh, now, Jack, they were just having a little fun. No harm done." She rubbed his shoulder and offered him a sweet smile. Jack instantly relaxed, a phenomenon that Tracy got full credit for cultivating. Truth be told, Brett was fascinated by the soothing and centering effect she'd had on Jack since coming into his life the month before.

"Seth, why don't you go outside and play so the grownups can talk?" she said to her soon-to-be stepson. "See if you can find your kitty friend, Sleekie, in the barn."

Brett managed to ruffle the little guy's hair before he bounded outside, half skipping and half jumping.

Brett followed Jack and Tracy to the living room that doubled as a library of sorts. When he'd been a kid, this had been a place of fascination for him in the house, the one room his parents had forbidden the kids from entering, not just because of all the breakable trinkets and pieces of art, but because it was where they retired with their guests for cocktails after the occasional dinner parties his dad was so fond of hosting.

His dad, Big J, was seated in his usual chair near the fireplace, chatting up Brett's older brothers Ryan and Eric. Daniel sat apart from the others, bent over his smartphone and keeping to himself as usual.

Dad was still fit and youthful, even after a lifetime of working the ranch and raising six kids, largely on his own when Brett's mother, Abra, decided to check out and skip town, which was a lot. Brett saw a little bit of all his siblings in Dad. They shared the same nose and same shape of their face, but Brett was the only one of the Colton kids who'd inherited his dad's boisterous laugh and love of good times, or so Edith, their housekeeper, was fond of saying.

Dad gave Brett a wave and his signature beaming smile. "I saw you race out of here this morning before dawn. You get some kind of sticker in your paw about something?"

Brett most certainly did have a sticker in his paw, but his big announcement could wait until after they learned more from Ryan about the search for his mom's attacker. He dropped into the center cushion of the sofa between Eric and Ryan. "Checking the fences. Can't be too careful after that one was tampered with during last week's storm."

Dad harrumphed as though he didn't buy Brett's pat response. Brett just smiled serenely at him.

"Losing one pregnant cow was enough for a lifetime," Jack grouched.

"She wasn't pregnant when she was swept away in the flash flood," Brett corrected.

"Yeah, what'd you name that calf you birthed in the gully?"

"Twister, and she's doing just fine, thank you very

much. And now that you mention it, what do you say we focus on Twister and the five pregnant cows I saved, rather than the one we lost, Jack? Maybe you could take a hiatus from busting my chops all the damn time."

Jack scowled at him. "Maybe you could start giving me reason to trust you."

"All right you two, that's enough. Don't forget that your mother is lying unconscious in a hospital bed," Dad barked. "Ryan, let's get to it. What's the latest on the investigation into her attacker?"

"Right, okay," Ryan said, scooting to the edge of the sofa. With his elbows propped on his knees, he flipped through the small notebook that was an ever-present accessory of his shirt pocket. "I don't know an easy way to break this to y'all, but you know how some of you were doubting that the hit man who tried to kill Tracy last month was the same perp who attacked Abra and robbed her room? Well, those same doubts have arisen among my investigative team. And we have some proof of that."

Brett had been among the earliest to voice his doubt that the hit man had also targeted their mom, but convincing the police to drop that lead and concentrate their efforts on an unknown perpetrator had been like trying to herd a group of pregnant cows in a thunderstorm—which he knew since he'd had the honor of attempting both feats. "What kind of proof?"

Ryan gave a look around, as though some interloper might be eavesdropping on their meeting. Not that there were interlopers to be found, but he still lowered his voice. "The gold locket with Greta's picture in it that was stolen on the night of Abra's attack turned up at a pawnshop. Greta's picture had the eyes gouged out, making her likeness unrecognizable, but the inscription on the back was a dead match."

Dad cursed under his breath. Jack scrubbed a hand over his chin, his eyes narrow and his expression distant.

"Pawnshops have security cameras, right? So this is great news," Brett said.

"Yes and no. We were, indeed, able to identify the suspect using the pawnshop's external security camera to identify the man's car's license plate, and we brought him in for questioning last night."

"And this is the first we're hearing about it?" Dad grumbled.

"Who is he?" Eric asked.

"A dead end. The guy's name is Dell Cortaline, a small-time oxy addict we've seen before. He's not our guy, though. There's no way. He's not smart enough to get in and out of this house without leaving fingerprints or some other trail of evidence."

"Then how did he get the locket?" Brett asked.

Ryan rolled his tongue around the inside of his bottom lip. His gaze locked onto Dad. "He claimed to have found it in the bushes outside Tulsa General Hospital."

Brett leaped to his feet before he knew what he was doing. "What? That's…"

Jack stood and joined Brett behind the sofa to pace. "What that is is a new threat. Someone's trying to get at Mother in the hospital."

"That was my thought, too," Ryan said grimly.

"I'm assuming your boss agreed to put an armed guard outside her room? To make sure she's safe?" Dad said.

Ryan rubbed the back of his neck. "That's easier said than done. This isn't a big enough red flag to justify putting an armed guard outside her hospital room door 24/7, but I have put the hospital on alert. Abra's in intensive care, which is highly monitored by the staff, anyway, both with door locks and cameras. Visitors don't have easy access to the rooms in the ICU. I really believe she's safe in there."

"I'm there a lot, too," Eric said. "I'll keep a closer eye. But I agree with Ryan. The ICU is practically impenetrable."

Dad shook his head. "I don't understand. Abra wasn't the kind of person who'd have a target on her back. But if her attacker went to the hospital where she's at, then that makes it personal, doesn't it?"

"Maybe, maybe not. It's possible that Abra saw the perp's face and he's afraid she'll be able to identify him. Could be that when he discovered how difficult it would be to get to her inside the ICU, he abandoned his plan and tossed the jewelry. That theory leaves me with more questions, but that's one of the more solid theories we're considering at this point."

"Any news about the possible DNA the police tech found under Mom's fingernails from the attacker?"

"Detective Howard is doing her best to expedite the results, but DNA testing is notoriously slow. As soon I know, I'll let y'all know, and that's a promise."

"This is an attempted murder case," Dad said. "It's

got to count for something that we might have an attempted murderer on the loose in Tulsa. Can't you push them harder?"

Ryan pocketed the notepad again. "No, I can't. I know we're all in a hurry, but this isn't the only unsolved violent crime the Oklahoma State Bureau of Investigation is running DNA tests on. I'm doing the best I can. As far as we can tell, the ranch is safe."

"It is if you don't count the downed fence lines. Last week was the third occurrence since Mother's attack of our fences being tampered with."

"Maybe that's the ghost that Maria keeps swearing she sees walking the fields at night," Jack said, a gallows humor grin on his face.

With a huff, Dad shook his head. "I swear, Maria is the most superstitious person I've ever met."

"Even still," Daniel said, "I think Brett's right. And I think we need to take action."

Being that this was the first time Daniel had seen fit to open his mouth that day, the chatter in the room died instantly as everyone gave him their full attention.

Jack dropped back down to the sofa. "What do you propose?"

"While the police do their thing, we circle the wagons. No more vandalism. No more hit men or violent robberies. We need to protect the ranch and the people in it."

"Agreed," Brett said. He'd promised Hannah that she'd be safe here, and he planned on delivering. "I vote for nightly patrols in groups of two."

"That works for me," Daniel said. "And we should

consider installing alarm systems to every house and motion sensor lights in the yard, and running background checks of every Lucky C employee."

"This ranch employs a lot of people," Dad said. "We can't account for everyone, all the time."

"Well, we sure as hell better start trying," Brett said. "Daniel's right. It's time to cowboy up and take care of our own. No one hurts the Coltons and gets away with it."

"I'll help as much as I can," Ryan said. "Meanwhile, my theory is that since we found one piece of Abra's jewelry, there's got to be more. I'll get some uniforms in our department to search local pawnshops again. I've already got a techie going through the hospital's external security footage."

"I'll take first patrol tonight," Jack said.

Dad stood. "I'll join you. This old house is too quiet these days without Abra."

Nobody argued with that, even though their mother was a nonentity in the house most days. She and Dad hadn't slept in the same quarters as long as Brett could remember, and she rarely left her bedroom suite, especially in the evenings.

In the awkward silence that descended over the room, Daniel stood and set his empty coffee mug on the tray. Eric followed suit, busing his mug then checking his phone.

Brett drew a deep breath. The mood wasn't even close to relaxed and jovial, but it was time to get this next conversation over with. "Wait, everyone. Eric, Daniel. I have something big I need to tell you."

"You're gay," Daniel deadpanned under his breath, quiet enough that Brett was probably the only person who heard him.

"What? Yeah. Exactly." He slapped Daniel on the back. "Way to call it, bro."

Daniel shrugged, flashing a hint of a devilish smile that was gone just as fast. He might be Brett's funniest sibling, if only he'd let his guard down around the rest of the family.

Jack released a deep sigh. "This better not be any more of your harebrained schemes to make changes around the ranch. I already agreed to purchase a stud horse, so don't push your luck."

"It's not about the business. Well, I mean it is, but not like that." He bit his lip to stop his blathering while everyone resettled.

Edith chose that moment to bustle in and beelined for the coffee service. "Are you done with the coffee, everyone?"

"That depends," Dad said. "Brett, is this going to be quick or should I pour myself another cuppa?"

Brett checked the time out of habit. He was scheduled to pick Hannah up in ninety minutes, give or take. "Have another cup, Pops. And Edith, you might as well stick around to hear this, too."

In no time, all eyes were on him. Last night and that morning, he'd visualized broaching the topic of his impending fatherhood from dozens of different angles, but the only conclusion he'd reached was that there was no good, easy way to reveal the news.

"I hired an accountant for the ranch." He shook his

head and nearly smacked it. *What the heck was that, stupid? That's how you're going to tell your family you're going to be a father?*

Jack scowled at him, his mouth agape. "How do you figure you have a right to make a decision like that without consulting us?"

No backing down now, especially with Jack in full jackass older-brother mode again. "Number one—because we could use the help. Pops, you spend half your time at the hospital tending to Mom, as you should be, and you have enough to worry about without messing with a bunch of ledgers and spreadsheets."

"That's my call," Dad said. "Don't tell me what I can and can't handle. I'll retire when I'm good and ready, and I'm not expecting to anytime soon. I'm with Jack. What were you thinking, making such a huge decision like that on your own?"

A wave of panic hit Brett. He'd expected his dad to stubbornly cling to his job, but not to be so fundamentally offended by the idea of Brett hiring help. A part of him had held out hope that his dad would be relieved to have the burden taken off his shoulders.

"With all the new tax laws and corporate regulations this country is levying on small farms, the ranch's books have become a helluva lot more complicated than simple addition and subtraction," Brett said. "If we want this ranch to thrive in the future, then we have to modernize every aspect of the business in a competitive, forward-thinking way—our breeding programs, our business model and our financial plan."

Jack groaned. "Here we go again. I thought you

agreed to lay off the 'futuristic business' talk until we see how that goes."

"I know, and you'll see that I'm right, but hiring an accountant is different. Tax planning, retirement planning, workers comp insurance," Brett enumerated on his fingers. "Pops, you don't want to have to deal with all that, do you? Furthermore, you're not qualified to. None of us are."

Jack set his mug on the coffee table hard enough that the spoons on the tray rattled. "I'll give you that, but I still don't understand why you saw it as your right to go behind our backs to do the hiring. Even if you are right about us needing a full-time accountant."

Brett squelched a look of utter shock. Jack conceding a point to Brett? It was inconceivable. He was afraid to look outside, lest he see the ranch's hogs taking to the skies upon wings. "You won't regret it. She's highly qualified."

Ryan and Jack both threw up their hands as though they'd choreographed their disgust. "She. Okay, I get it now, hotshot," Ryan said. "So by *highly qualified* you mean she's young and hot."

Hannah was young and hot, but he kept that part to himself.

Jack stabbed the air with his index finger. "We are not—I repeat, *not*—hiring your good-timing girl of the week to be responsible for our ranch's financial health. Deal off."

Well, this is going about as well as I expected, Brett thought grimly. *Time to solidify their stellar opinion of me.* At least Hannah wasn't around yet to witness the ass chewing he was about to get.

He slid her résumé onto the table. "She's not my good-timing girl of the week." She had been exactly that give or take nineteen weeks earlier, but that was beside the point. "Her name is Hannah Grayson. She has a bachelor's degree in accounting from Tulsa United's online program, from which she graduated summa cum laude."

Dad slid his glasses on and took a closer look at her résumé. "This looks reasonable. She seems to have quite a head on her shoulders and, since she's a new graduate, we could hire her at an entry-level salary, which would be affordable enough. Make her part-time so we don't have to pay benefits and I'll agree to it."

Brett barreled ahead, suddenly eager to get to the real point of his announcement. "I already offered her a full-time position with benefits and a competitive salary because she's pregnant."

Jack's whole face turned red, his head of steam going like gangbusters. "You just keep pushing and pushing, don't you? The Lucky C isn't a charity organiz—"

"With my child," Brett added, cutting him off. "I'm going to be a father in about twenty weeks, give or take."

Chapter 4

The room went dead quiet. Dad stared at Brett, disappointment dragging at his features. Jack's mouth flopped open while Tracy rubbed his arm. Eric and Daniel stared out the window, their expressions shuttered.

Brett sipped his coffee, though he couldn't even taste it, giving them time to get over their shock.

In the gaping silence, a hard, patronizing laugh burst out of Jack. "You really did it this time. How in the world did you get yourself into a mess like that?"

Jack's laughter, even more than the disappointment in the rest of his family's eyes, snapped Brett's patience. He was done with being a whipping boy. "Let me see if I can spell it out for you. When a man and a woman are attracted to each other, sometimes they express that attraction by doing a mommy-and-daddy grown-up dance with all their clothes off—"

Jack sneered at him. "And you wanted me to give you more responsibilities around here. Unbelievable."

Dad scrubbed a hand over his mouth and chin. "Like I always say, the apple don't fall far from the tree," he murmured, his eyes shifting briefly to Daniel.

Just once, Brett wanted his father to tell him that with pride in his voice instead of disappointment. Just once in his damn life. Brett had grown up idolizing his dad, from his larger-than-life presence and joviality that made him the life of every party to the bullheaded conviction that had led him to forge the Lucky C ranch from the earth and transform it into a profitable enterprise.

On the surface, yes, Brett's getting a girl pregnant out of wedlock seemed similar to his dad's screwups, but the situation with Hannah wasn't at all like the extramarital affair his dad had that resulted in Daniel's conception. Brett hadn't broken any marriage vows. Not that Brett or any of them would point out the differences aloud and risk making Daniel uncomfortable. He might only be their half brother by blood, but he was a full brother in their hearts—the only place it mattered.

He didn't think Dad meant to be callous with the comment. Over the years, his dad had made it clear that he'd separated in his mind the sin of his affair from the love he felt for the son he'd gained from it. Still, Brett chanced a look in Daniel's direction to see him staring out the window, as though he'd shuttered himself from the conversation.

Brett wished his sister, Greta, had been there. She

had the kindest and most forgiving heart of all of them and, because of that, been the glue of the family since she'd been a child. She would've known what to say to ease the tension in the room and remind Daniel that their dad didn't mean any harm.

With his eyes on Daniel's profile, Brett cleared his throat and tried to imagine what Greta would've said had she been present. "Then it's a good thing we grew up understanding that family is family and that a baby is a blessing, no matter what."

Edith gave Brett an affectionate rub on the back. "Well said."

Eric refilled his coffee mug. "I'm with you on that sentiment, but this is a lot to take in. I'd like more details about what happened. Forgive my bluntness, but I've gotten the impression that you've slept with plenty of women over the years, and you managed not to knock any of them up—I feel safe in saying. So how did a mistake like this come about? I mean, assuming it *was* an accident and she didn't do this on purpose to get at our money. Because something smells fishy to me."

Brett looked from Eric to Ryan and the rest of the family, all of whom wore expressions of surprise and concern and, as opposed to his dad and Jack, they looked as if they were ready to listen to what Brett had to say instead of merely pelting him with insults. Even Edith perched on the edge of a chair, her arms crossed and a sympathetic smile on her lips.

Brett shifted toward them, putting a cold shoulder to Jack. "She's not trying to get at our family money, and you're just going to have to trust me on that until you meet her." Behind him, Jack chuffed, but Brett pressed on. "Here's what happened. You remember that day, four months ago, when I wrapped my truck around the tree? That was the moment that made me turn my life around and get a clue about the kind of man I wanted to be and the kind of life I wanted to lead."

"Of course we remember that," Ryan said. "You tattered that truck and you're lucky to be alive."

"I am. I know. Leading up to that moment, I'd had a hell of a weekend, a real bender after Mom and I had argued. About what, I can't even remember. Anyway, I'd gone out clubbing the night before the truck accident, which was where I met Hannah and slept with her. We used a condom—" Eric opened his mouth, probably to suggest that Hannah had sabotaged the condom, so Brett held a finger up to quiet him and added, "A condom that I provided, so get that out of your mind. Yesterday was the first time I'd seen her since that night. Needless to say, we had a long, serious talk. Neither one of us has any idea why the condom didn't work."

Jack templed his hands in front of his mouth. "Wait. She's nineteen weeks pregnant, yet she didn't tell you until yesterday? I'm with Eric. Something smells fishy to me."

"Hate to beat a dead horse," Ryan said, drumming his fingers on his knee, "and maybe you're right and our suspicions will be laid to rest when we meet her, but this wouldn't be the first time a desperate, misguided young woman tried to get at our family money. And with your less-than-monogamous lifestyle, you'd be the perfect target for a scam. My advice is for you to get a paternity test before this goes any further."

Less-than-monogamous lifestyle. That would have been the understatement of the century a few months ago. Nevertheless, Hannah had called it correctly. On the surface, her being desperately hard-up for money and pregnant with a Colton's child looked bad from every angle—except one. "No paternity test necessary. I'm going to take her word for it that I'm the father, and when you meet her, you'll take her word for it, too."

Dad snickered. "She's that homely?"

"What? No. She's that honest. Honest and smart and stubborn to a fault. You'll see." Because he knew that everything would change in their minds the moment they laid eyes on her. She'd win them all over with a single smile, of that he was certain.

His family still looked unconvinced, so Brett continued. "The reason she waited so long to tell me about the baby was that she wanted to get back on her feet first. Because she knows exactly how suspicious this looks from the outside. Hannah's parents disowned her and fired her from their family business when they found out she was pregnant. She spent the last of her savings on medical care for her pregnancy and has been crashing on her friend's sofa ever since. This solution, her moving here and working for us as an accountant, was my idea. And believe me, it took some convincing."

"Wait, she's not only going to work for us, but you're moving her in here, without a paternity test, background check, nothing?" Jack said.

"I'll run a background check on her, no problem."

Ryan whipped his phone out and peered at Hannah's résumé, mouthing the letters of her name as he typed.

Brett grabbed the résumé away from Ryan's gaze. "Not necessary. I went by her family's store yesterday after I dropped Hannah off at her friend's house and I talked to her parents. I didn't tell them who I was or why I was there, but I asked them where Hannah was and congratulated them on her pregnancy, and let me tell you, they're even nuttier and filled with more hate than I expected."

Just picturing the fury in their expressions when they told him their heathen daughter was dead to them put Brett in a fighting mood. "What's more, Hannah hadn't told them I was the father. I don't think she's told anybody. Does that sound like the actions of someone trying to scam me?"

"A background check still wouldn't hurt," Ryan muttered.

Brett shook his head, ignoring Ryan, his attention on Jack. "So, to answer your question, yes, I am moving her in here. She's homeless, jobless, out of money—and she's having my baby. And she's too stubborn to agree to anything that has the whiff of charity, which was why I offered her a job. Full-time with benefits so I can make sure she and the baby get the proper health care they need."

He could tell he was breaking through their judgmental walls because they'd started to squirm, their eyes averted. Time to drive the nail the rest of the way in. He stood and tossed his napkin on the table. "Y'all keep banging on me about being irresponsible, and I'm the first to admit that I used to be. But even if you can't see it, I've changed. This is me being responsible, doing the right thing and living up to our family's code of honor. Ask yourself—what would you do if you were in my shoes?"

That shut them down, all but his dad. "Did you at least offer to make her an honest woman?"

The head of steam Brett had built up diffused a little. If they were moving on to questions like that, then perhaps his family was ready to accept Brett's new reality. "This is the twenty-first century, Pops. A woman doesn't have to be married to be considered honest."

Dad chuffed at that, clearly a nonbeliever in that vein of modern-day feminism. "When's this Hannah woman coming to the ranch?"

"I'm going into town to get her as soon as we're done here."

A car engine sounded outside. Everyone craned their necks to look out the windows. Brett took a few steps in that direction in time to watch a yellow taxi disappear along the road leading away from the house.

"Something tells me Ms. Hannah Grayson has saved you from having to make a trip into town," Ryan said.

Jack clapped his hands together as he stood. "Let's get this introduction over with."

The somber resignation in Jack's tone set Brett's teeth on edge again. He whirled around, a warning on his tongue for everyone to behave themselves and show Hannah the respect she deserved, but Edith saved him from it.

"I have a better idea," she said brightly from the doorway, where she stood with the rolling coffee cart in front of her, blocking passage. "Let's give our new houseguest a chance to settle in first, before she has to contend with a household of grouchy men. Let Brett help her get acclimated first. Greta will be here tomorrow, and I can't think of a better way to celebrate a new baby than with a big family dinner."

Thank you, Edith. She was a commanding force in the house, not because she was pushy or overbearing, but because of her kindness and levelheaded management of the household since before Brett was born. The family respected her too much to defy her will. It was all he could do to keep himself from throwing his arms around her.

"That's a perfect idea," Brett said. "Hannah's skittish enough about being here."

Dad pushed himself out of his easy chair. "I like that plan. That'll give me some time to get used to the idea."

"You can eat at our house tonight, Big J," Tracy said. "We can let Brett and Hannah have a private dinner together. It sounds like they still have a lot to talk about, if they just connected yesterday."

That was a perfect idea. He'd have to talk to Edith about arranging for a multicourse dinner for the two of them, a meal they could really linger over while they got to know each other. "Thank you, Tracy."

Eric rattled his car keys and inched toward the exit that Edith was still blocking. "I'll try to make it tomorrow night, but I have a late shift at the hospital." In other words, he was begging out of the event, as usual, because there was no way he drew so many short straws for late shifts at the hospital, coincidentally any time the rest of the Coltons planned a get-together.

"If we wait until tomorrow, then Tracy and Seth can meet Hannah at the same time, too."

"I'll plan a big dinner. Brett, you figure out what she likes and dislikes. Maybe there's something she's been craving."

"Thank you," Brett said. So relieved.

She stepped to the side and swept her hand toward the rear of the house. "Out the back entrance, all of you. No sense in intimidating her in the first five minutes she gets here with a big group of strapping, foul-tempered cowboys."

"Yes, ma'am," Ryan mumbled in an exaggerated drawl. He kissed Edith's cheek as he passed, as they each did, in a show of respect to the woman who'd played a fundamental part of their upbringing and daily lives for decades.

When the last of them had filed out of the room, she smiled lovingly at Brett. "I'll talk to the staff and make sure you get the space you need to do this your way. And I'll send Mavis up to the guest suite next to yours and have it fixed up for Hannah in no time. Fresh linens and the works."

He gathered all hundred pounds of her in a tight hug, lifting her off her feet. "You're a lifesaver. How do you always know the exact right thing to say?"

She blushed and swatted her hand through the air, dismissing the praise. "Hush, now. Go on and find Hannah before she gets cold feet and calls that taxi back."

* * *

Hannah crept along the wraparound porch of Brett's massive house, away from the window where she'd been eavesdropping. Not that she'd set out with the idea of listening in on Brett's family's conversation, but once she'd stumbled into hearing range, she'd been power-less to resist.

A case of cold feet had compelled her to ask the taxi driver to wait there until she gave him the all-clear to leave, just in case she had a change of heart or she'd accidentally come to the wrong house or she'd misun-derstood Brett's desire for her to move in that day. The driver hadn't been too keen on waiting, but she'd prom-ised him he could leave the meter running and after a bit more begging, he'd acquiesced.

After climbing the tall staircase leading from the cir-cular driveway up to the mansion sitting on the highest and most central part of the ranch, she'd knocked and pressed the doorbell, but no one had answered. The lon-ger she stood there, the more nervous she got and the more she doubted her decision to show up early.

Thinking that the house was so big that it was en-tirely possible that no one had heard the doorbell ring, she'd followed the porch around to the side of the house, which was when she'd heard voices. More specifically, she'd heard one of the men in the room explain his the-ory that their mother's attacker was still on the loose and, potentially, had been lurking around the ranch.

Wait, what? That wasn't what the local news had been reporting. Last night, she'd used Lori's computer to research Brett's mother's attack. What she'd learned had made her heart break for Brett and his family. His mother had been attacked in her bedroom and left for dead, her belongings ransacked and her jewelry stolen by—according to the news report—a hit man who'd been hired to off Brett's older brother's fiancée. The main suspect had been gunned down, or so the police and the newspaper had indicated.

She continued to listen to Brett's family talk, justifying the eavesdropping because she deserved to know if she was safe at the ranch or not, or if Brett had glossed over his family's troubles in his fervor to get her to agree to his plan. If there was any chance that she was in danger at the ranch, she could turn right around and leave.

But the more she listened, the more affected she was by the hurt in each man's voice over their mother's assault and their frustration that her investigation had stalled. And then, one minute turned into the next, and before she knew it, she was listening to Brett tell his family that he'd hired an accountant.

She was touched by his approach, and that he'd opened the conversation with a discussion of her accounting skills. For whatever reason, that mattered to her. A lot. He'd stood up for her, and complimented her abilities and qualifications. She'd been held entranced by his praise…right up until one of the other men in the room had labeled her as Brett's good-time girl of the week.

She'd winced at that, even though she agreed with the term, if not the negative judgment implied by it. She'd been Brett's good-time girl as much as he'd been her good-time guy for the night. While she refused to be shamed for enjoying her sexuality, even if Brett's family turned out to judge her as harshly as her own family had, it still smarted to realize that, as she'd expected might happen, Brett's family assumed she was trying to get at their money. It wasn't a shock that they didn't trust her. The surprise was that they didn't seem to trust Brett, either. And that frosted Hannah something fierce because she'd suffered the same mistrust at the hands of her own family.

Probably, her relationship with Brett's family would go a lot more smoothly if she weren't aware of their candid feelings about her and Brett, because those assumptions didn't matter in the grand scheme of things. All that mattered was that she believed in herself and knew in her heart that she was a good and honest person. Which meant it was high time for her to get the heck out of earshot again.

She tiptoed back to the front of the house and down the stairs, her eye on the taxi. Nothing was stopping her from jumping back in it and taking off. Except that there kind of was, now that she was considering it. Brett was being judged by his family same as she'd been by hers. They were about to become parents together, and if she stayed with him, if she gave him a chance, then she would spare him from her same fate of having to face his family's negativity alone.

And Brett had told her the day before that his father was slipping mentally. Not only that, but Brett's dad shouldn't be working so hard around the ranch when his wife lay in a coma. Brett's father deserved better and the ranch deserved better, too, because Brett was also right about them needing an actual financial specialist to help them with long-term tax planning, one of her specialties. No matter how negatively Brett's family judged her for getting pregnant, her conscience couldn't just walk away from that situation.

Her two measly pieces of luggage sat in the driveway next to the cab. She'd packed light because, one, she had no idea how long she was staying, and, two, she didn't actually own that much stuff anymore, having sold most of it to afford the business of living. She navigated around the suitcases and handed the taxi driver his rate plus a generous tip through the open driver's side window. "Thank you for waiting. Have a nice—"

"Back up so I can turn around."

Gee, what a sweet guy. So deserving of my last bit of cash as a tip—not. She stepped back and tripped over her suitcases, planting her rear end hard on the one she'd knocked over.

Her face growing hot with embarrassment, she took a furtive glance around for witnesses. Not seeing any, she stood and brushed off her dress in time to watch the taxi hauling butt in a cloud of dust as it disappeared along the dirt road.

She took a moment to catch her breath, marveling at the endless string of awkward moments that her life had become since graduating from college. What was her next move? Should she try knocking again? Call Brett's cell phone? Settle in on the porch and wait for Brett's family to find her after they finished their meeting?

"If you're here looking for a handout from Mr. Colton,

then you'd best be leaving before I call the police," called a female voice.

Hannah turned to see a familiar, if unexpected, face. Her defenses immediately went on red alert, as they did every time she saw someone from the Congregation of the Second Coming. "Mavis?"

Mavis Turnbolt was dressed in what could only be described as a maid's uniform. Her brown hair was constrained in a tight braid that had been coiled into a bun from which no wild hairs had escaped. She was only a year older than Hannah, and over the years, their mothers had made valiant, yet fruitless, attempts to push them into friendship. She could've lived the rest of her life without needing to see any member of the Turnbolt family again, but after all she'd been through, another piece of bad luck didn't even faze her.

Then again, it wasn't fair of Hannah to be critical of Mavis in exactly the same way she hated to be judged. Hannah hadn't been to the church in years, not since her eighteenth birthday, so for all she knew, Mavis had broken the hold that the church had over her, just as Hannah had.

"It's nice to see a friendly face. I had no idea you worked here," Hannah said, offering her hand for a handshake. "I work here now, too."

Mavis eyed Hannah's hand as if it were a snake. "I will not be associating with jezebels, so you'd best take that hand back."

So much for that fair chance. "And you'd best watch your attitude. Neither my baby nor I deserves your scorn."

"Scorn is the only thing a sinner like you deserves. Wait until the Coltons learn they've hired one of Satan's newest disciples."

Hannah wrapped a protective arm around her belly. "First of all, this baby *is* a Colton, thank you very much. And second, can you even hear yourself? Satan's newest disciple? Really?" She cringed inwardly, wishing she'd thought twice before engaging with someone who was so filled with hate. It wasn't as though she stood a chance of changing Mavis's mind.

Mavis's face broke out in a hard smile. "I guess I have a whole lot of news to share with our church, then. We'll be praying for the Coltons to cast you out of their lives before you sink your claws of sin any deeper into their family."

Oh, brother. "Sounds like a good plan, Mavis. Y'all just go ahead and get busy praying. In fact, with all that prayin' you need to do, I doubt you'll have time to work in a den of depravity like the Lucky C. What if our sinning ways brush off on you? If I were you, I'd quit right now."

"You'd love that, wouldn't you?"

"Honestly, I really would."

"The devil has no power over me." Her face screwed up as if she was going to sneeze, except that she didn't sneeze—she spit on Hannah's shoe.

Hannah was too shocked to do anything more than gasp as Mavis hurried away. Who went around spitting on other people's shoes? How was that even a thing that people did in the twenty-first century?

She dug through her purse in search of a tissue.

"The Lucky C is a den of depravity? Well, how about that. I had no idea," a drawling male voice said.

She glanced up to see a handsome man wearing a white Stetson pull a handkerchief from his jeans pocket. He looked to be about Brett's age, with a friendly smile and dancing blue eyes, one of which he used to wink at her right before he knelt and wiped off her shoe.

"Thank you," she said to his flannel-shirted back and hat.

He stood and pocketed the handkerchief again. "Pleasure's all mine." He stuck his hand out. "Name's Rafe Sinclair."

She shook his offered hand. "I'm Hannah Grayson."

"Pleasure to make your acquaintance. Now, I have to be honest here. I saw you tiptoeing around the big house, so I hope you don't mind if I inquire about what or who you're looking for. Maybe I can help you on your way."

"I was just having a look around. This is my first day at my new job here at the Lucky C and it's quite impressive."

He touched the brim of his hat. "A new job and you're expecting? My goodness, you're a busy bee. What kind of work were you hired for? Because I bet the ranch is gonna need a new laundress now that you've affronted Mavis."

Note to self—stay away from the laundry room, and Mavis. "I'm the new accountant."

A look of confusion flickered over his face, just for a moment, replaced anew by his smile. "How in the world is a pretty little thing like you going to handle the complexities of the accounting needs of the Lucky C?"

So much for her intuition that Rafe might be one of her friends at the ranch. She bristled inwardly at the derogatory implications dripping from his words, but fought to keep her outward demeanor cool. "Oh, I'm sure I'll manage just fine, but your concern is noted."

Noted and dismissed as useless drivel. A lot of men in ranch country shared Rafe's views, and he probably thought he'd done nothing wrong. She'd let her skills as an accountant prove him wrong and maybe open up his mind a little bit.

"Hannah?"

Brett's voice carried across the yard. She turned her back to Rafe and found Brett striding toward her. And dang it all if her heart didn't skip a beat at the sight of him. He was dressed in a light gray cotton T-shirt that was a shade too form-fitting, with the outline of his pectorals clearly defined and the sleeves pushed up above his biceps, tucked into snug Wranglers. His long legs ended in scuffed brown leather boots. With that look, and the ranch backdrop, he looked every inch the consummate cowboy. All he needed now was a cowboy hat, and she bet her bottom dollar he had one nearby. Thank goodness he wasn't wearing it now because turning into a puddle of hormonal lust wasn't the first impression she wanted to make with Brett's family.

"You didn't need to spring for a taxi. I was going to pick you up in a couple hours."

Clipped to his belt was what looked like a ranch radio, as though she'd caught him in the middle of his workday. Which she had, now that she thought about it. In her haste to prove herself self-sufficient, she hadn't considered that she'd be interrupting his duties at the ranch. "I didn't want you to have to, but it looks like I disrupted your day, anyway. I'm sorry about that."

He nodded past her, in greeting to Rafe, then leaned in close, his shoulder brushing hers, and got his lips close to her ears, whispering, "I told you I'd take care of you, and I know you're not used to that, but you have to give me a chance to try."

Behind the aroma of dirt and honest ranching work, she caught the scent of his soap or shaving cream, masculine and fresh. That was when her hormones decided it was their turn to take the wheel.

Wicked, red-hot need kicked up inside her. It hadn't been the first time since she'd hit her second trimester that lust had slapped her upside the head—or her nether regions, as it were—but this was the first time it'd happened while she was touching an honest-to-goodness man—a handsome one at that. One she knew from experience was an expert when it came to wringing pleasure from a woman's body.

A memory surfaced of his hands on her, pinning her wrists above her head, his mouth plundering hers with rough, wicked kisses. A hum of pleasure bubbled out of her before she knew what she was doing.

Brett eyed her curiously.

Mortified, she shook the image out of her mind. At least Rafe had wandered away, out of earshot. "And you have to give me a chance to prove that I'm not helpless."

Her gaze traced Brett's strong, clean-shaven jawline from his ear to red, luscious lips quirked into a teasing smile. "You don't have to prove anything to me, but for what it's worth, I believe that your general lack of help-lessness was one of the bullet points on your résumé, if memory serves."

She returned his smile. "Sounds like we have a lot to learn about working together since we're going to be parent partners."

"Parent partners. I like the sound of that."

In her periphery, she spied Rafe leaning against a beat-up white ranch truck, watching them. Beyond him, Mavis's face was visible in the doorway of a long, low-ceilinged building toward the stables. A few other work-ers had stopped what they were doing to watch, their gazes transfixed on Brett and Hannah. "There are a lot of people watching us."

"New arrivals always draw the workers' curiosity. Little do they knew that they're seeing the latest mem-ber of the Colton family."

"The baby's not going to be here for five more months."

His expression turned solemn. He rubbed a tendril of her hair between his fingertips. "I was talking about you. Doesn't matter what happens between you and me from this point on, because like you said, we're parent partners from here on out. Like it or not, we're bound for life. You're a permanent part of the Colton family now."

She'd never thought about it that way, but the idea wrapped around her like a quilt. She'd always longed to be a part of a big family, even if they took a while to warm up to her. She was going to hold out hope that they got over their misgivings and that everything would turn out all right.

"Speaking of your family, where is everyone?"

He nodded toward the house. "Edith, who you'll meet in a minute, had the idea that tomorrow night would be soon enough to meet everyone. She thought you might appreciate getting settled here first and she shooed everyone out the back door."

Hannah loved Edith already, whoever she was. "Yes, a night to settle in first would be heaven-sent. I'm looking forward to meeting her so I can thank her myself."

"I saw that you already met Rafe. He's an indispensable member of the Lucky C operation. Has been for a couple years now."

"What exactly is it that he does for the ranch?" *Besides insult women's intelligence and capability?*

"He's a jack-of-all-trades, but mostly, he helps run the day-to-day operations of the cattle-breeding program."

Then she probably wouldn't have much contact with him. "And I saw Mavis Turnbolt, too, before you found me. She and I go way back, but I didn't know she worked for your family as a maid."

"What a small world. I'm glad you got to see a familiar face."

"She's a member of my parents' church," she said drily.

"Ah. Tulsa really is a small world. I had no idea, but I guess I'd better make sure Mavis isn't let into the kitchen before meals so she doesn't spit in our food."

She couldn't help but smile at his support, as well as his spot-on prediction. "Gross, and I wouldn't put it past her to try."

The light in his face changed. He brushed his thumb across her cheek. "You are aware of the effect those dimples have on a man, right?"

Oh, this man was smooth. For all she knew, he'd used that same line on dozens of women. The trouble was, the more she fought against a smile, the wider it grew and the deeper her dimples probably got right along with it.

"I was not aware of that, actually." The only time her dimples were ever mentioned was by customers at her parents' store by lonely old grandfatherly and grandmotherly types that she didn't pay any mind to.

He cupped her cheek in his hand, his eyes growing dark. "No, I reckon you wouldn't be."

Brett's light touch sent a shiver skittering over her skin, evoking the memory of every delicious detail of their one wicked night together. From out of nowhere, an all-consuming hunger came over her, to be touched, cherished. Most likely, it was a product of her haywire pregnancy hormones as she recalled, or maybe it was just because she'd been really lonely lately. She pressed her cheek into his palm, her eyes closing and her lips parting.

At the realization that she was barely fighting the wild urge to turn her lips into his hand to taste his skin, she pulled away from his touch and gave herself a vigorous mental smack.

He swallowed hard and stuffed his hands in his pockets. "Seriously, though, if she gives you any hassle—if anyone here or in town gives you any hassle at all—you let me know and I'll handle it. Deal?"

She was tempted to reiterate that she wasn't helpless, but she could tell how important it was to him that he take on the role of her protector. Besides, she was warming to the idea of him in that role, too, as long as he didn't turn into a chauvinist about it like his employee Rafe. "Deal."

A crack of thunder pulled their attention to the gray clouds piling up in the sky beyond the smattering of barns and buildings to the west.

Brett tipped his head toward her suitcases. "Where's the rest of your stuff? Do we need to take a trip back into town today to get it all? I have time this afternoon and a big ol' truck you can fill."

"This is it," she said. "I've got a couple boxes of mementos and books at Lori's apartment, but I'm pretty low-maintenance when it comes to shoes and fashion, and after I got evicted from my apartment, I sold just about everything but the essentials."

He frowned at that, which rubbed her wrong. "Don't go reading into that too much or feeling sorry for me. I'm fine and I have everything I need. Material goods aren't important to me—they never were. It's no big deal."

His frowning lips twitched into a grudging smile. His eyes glowed, not with fire but affection. "Yes, ma'am. My mistake." He nodded at the house. "Let's get you indoors before today's afternoon shower hits."

Chapter 5

There was no other word to describe Brett's house besides *mansion*. Certainly, it was the largest and most elegantly appointed home that Hannah had ever been in, with a marble-floored grand entrance that extended up to a vaulted ceiling and had as its focal point a circular table in the center of the space boasting a massive floral arrangement that oozed the word *rich*.

The formal sitting room on the far side of the foyer was too stiff and stuffy to look lived in, with sparse furniture and a glass fireplace that seemed more for show than warmth. Every room and hall that she could see was decked out in marble and white decor, and the light palette should have brightened the place up, but there was a heavy weight to the overt grandiosity. As if a person could never get fully comfortable there or kick off her shoes and relax.

Then again, perhaps the weight and gravity in the house were side effects of the violence that had occurred there the month before and the heartbreaking reality that, even as Hannah stood in the home casting judgment on the place, Brett's mom was fighting for her life in the hospital. That had to be taking a toll on everyone who lived and worked there.

Two women waited at the far end of the foyer near the base of a grand staircase. The taller, slimmer of the two had silvery hair pulled into a tight bun and the shorter one looked to be about Hannah's age, with brown hair and eyes, an olive complexion and a curvy build.

The taller woman stepped forward with her hand extended in greeting and a bright smile lighting up her face and accentuating her abundant laugh lines. "You must be Hannah. I'm Edith, the Coltons' housekeeper."

From her firm, confident handshake to her perfect posture, Edith exuded efficiency and poise. Hannah bet she never missed a beat, but in the best, most genuine way.

Brett leaned in and gave Edith a kiss on the cheek in greeting. "You're a lot more than just a housekeeper."

She waved off the praise. "Oh, pish. The title suits me."

"Edith is in charge around here. Anything you need or any questions you have, she's the one to ask. And this," he said, nodding at the other woman, "is Maria, our talented chef. We were lucky to steal her away from the New York City restaurant scene a few years ago."

Maria's eyes glowed with warmth. "The luck was all

mine." She enveloped Hannah's offered hand in both of hers. Her hands were rough, calloused, and her nails trimmed short. "I was ready for a change from those long, late nights in New York kitchens, and since my parents live in Tulsa and they're getting older, it was the right move to come home to be near to them. Managing the Coltons' kitchen has been an honor."

Brett draped his arm across Maria's shoulders. "I'll have you know that I was only able to lure Hannah here by tempting her with the promise of your signature, small-batch cured bacon every morning."

Maria seemed delighted. "Consider it done."

Hannah gave him a chiding look. "I didn't agree to this arrangement because of bacon."

"So you're saying it was the real maple syrup and butter I plied you with that reeled you in?"

The preposterous idea tickled her funny bone, and before she knew what hit her, she was back to smiling like a lovesick fool. How did he do that? How did he make her so instantly comfortable and joyous? He had the gift of charm, for sure, but not with the artifice of a snake-oil salesman, as she'd originally compared him to. More like a gifted leader.

"You're going to give Maria and Edith the mistaken impression that all I care about is food."

Edith's eyes twinkled. "Well, you *are* pregnant, if you don't mind me mentioning. So a healthy preoccupation with food is perfectly permissible, you know."

"And if Edith says it's okay, then you're good to go. I learned that growing up," Brett said.

"You're going to love the dinner I'm making for you

tonight," Maria said. "And tomorrow night, the whole family will get to meet you. I'm planning a feast in celebration."

Hannah drew a fortifying breath at the idea of being the center of attention in a room full of Brett's whole family—the same people who were eager to run a background check on her. Then again, if she could confess to her parents that she was pregnant out of wedlock and resist their attempts to cajole the father's name from her, then she could handle meeting Brett's family all at once—her family, too, now.

There was just one problem—Brett's mother, the family matriarch, wouldn't be there. "Thank you. Both of you. But I wonder if perhaps now isn't the right time for a celebration, given that Brett's mother is in the hospital."

Edith didn't miss a beat. "The way I see it, the Coltons could use a little uplifting, and what better way to inspire hope in this family than by celebrating the news of a new Colton coming into this world?"

As Brett said, if Edith deemed it so, then there was no salient counterargument to be had.

"Then I look forward to it. Thank you both for making me feel so welcome."

"Our pleasure. We're going to let Brett show you to your bedroom suite. Brett, you let me know about tonight." Edith's smiling eyes darted between Hannah and Brett before both women walked away on silent feet.

Brett picked up Hannah's suitcases and they started up the stairs. After a particularly powerful crack of thunder, lightning flickered outside the window, casting long shadows of the grand stairway's ornate chandelier onto the walls as they climbed to the second floor.

"Edith and Maria are very nice," Hannah said.

"Most of the people here are. We consider it a job requirement," he added with a wink.

Hannah thought about Mavis Turnbolt. Maybe not all the employees were as nice as Brett seemed to think. He did seem to see the best in everyone, which was a quality of his she found endlessly attractive—yet another one on her growing list of them.

"What did Edith mean with her question about tonight? If she's wondering about your dad, because I know he lives here, too, then I don't mind meeting him tonight at dinner. I don't want him to dine alone."

"No, it's not that. My dad already made plans to eat at Jack's house tonight. Maria thought you might prefer to eat a low-key meal in the kitchen or your suite tonight." They crested the top of the stairs. Brett stopped and set her suitcases down. His hand, big and strong and sure, slid over her arm as his gaze met hers. "But if you're amenable to the idea, I'd like to have you all to myself in the dining room. A dinner date, if you will."

Oh. She felt heat rising on her cheeks, even as her lusty hormones started clamoring for attention again. "You really are a smooth operator, aren't you?"

"Is that a bad thing?"

She smoothed her hands over his chest, letting her fingers bump over the ridges of muscle beneath it, muscles she remembered quite well from their night together. *Mmm.* Her hormones definitely approved. "No, it's not a bad thing—as long as you use your powers for good and not evil."

He chuckled. "'With great power comes great responsibility'?"

"Exactly."

His smile turned contemplative. "Please say you'll have dinner with me tonight. I want to get to know you, Hannah. You're carrying my child—"

"Our child."

His focus dipped to her belly. "Yes, *our* child." His gaze turned distant, but only for the span of a few heartbeats. Then he cleared his throat. "So dinner seems like a good place to start to get to know each other better. Like, middle name, birthday, favorite dessert. You know, the important stuff."

"Bernice, October twenty-second and red-velvet cupcakes."

A smile lightened his features. With her suitcases in hand once more, he led her over thick burgundy carpet through a dimly lit hallway. "Cupcakes rather than cake?"

"Yes. Only cupcakes will do."

"I'll be sure to inform Maria."

The hallway ended with a floor-to-ceiling window, but this afternoon, with the sun gone behind a curtain of darkening clouds, the hall was dim. With the quiet and the shadows, Hannah's thoughts drifted once more to the tragedies that had befallen the family the month before. She scanned the doors they passed, wondering behind which one Abra's attack had occurred.

"Your mom, she was attacked in your parents' bedroom, right?"

Brett froze midstep. His face went pale.

Hannah regretted the question instantly. "I'm sorry I asked. I didn't mean—"

"No. It's a fair question. She and my father sleep in separate quarters. She was attacked in her suite, which is adjacent to his on the other end of this hall. Listen, Hannah, you're safe here at the ranch. On my word."

"The police think your mother's attacker is still on the loose." She cringed inwardly at the slip. She'd come by that information by eavesdropping and wasn't eager for Brett to find out.

Brett's lips flattened into a straight line. "You're right. Some of her jewelry that was stolen the night of the attack turned up in a Tulsa pawnshop this week so the police are investigating, but that would have to be one stupid criminal to come back here again. If it makes you feel any better, we're starting nightly patrols around the perimeter of our acreage to make sure everything's as it should be, starting with my brother Jack and my dad tonight—not because of what happened to my mother, but because we've had some fences tampered with recently. You're safe. I promise. Just do me a favor and don't go walking around after dark by yourself, okay?"

Another crack of thunder shook the house, followed by the sound of rain pelting the windows. Dread tightened Hannah's chest as she thought back to the conversation she'd overheard just minutes ago in the sitting room. What had she gotten herself into?

He took hold of both her shoulders. "Hey. There's nothing to worry about. You're safe. I wouldn't have asked you here if you weren't. We're just taking extra precautions."

"Okay. I can accept that answer."

"Good, because it's the truth."

She drew her shoulders up and rubbed her arms. "I just… I can sense the heaviness and heartbreak in this place. Despite Edith's optimism, I know it couldn't have been easy to spring the news of the baby on your family, with everything else you're all going through. I know it doesn't sound like it with my questions about your mom, but I'm glad I'm here. I'm going to do a great job as your bookkeeper."

His expression softened. "As if there was ever any doubt about that." They set off again along the hallway. He stopped next to an open door and ushered her in ahead of him. "Your suite."

Forget comparisons to her apartment—the suite was bigger than her parents' *house*. Like the rest of Brett's house, the sitting room of the suite and what she could see of the bedroom beyond it had no shortage of windows. Tall ones that showed off the uninhibited view of the Oklahoma landscape—rolling hills of grassland and scrub trees that had been turned to a quilt of deep greens and mustard yellows by the rain and dark gray clouds that served as a foil for the rich colors.

The rectangular sitting room was decked out in blue-and-gold shabby-chic decor, including royal blue, gold and white embroidered curtains framing every window and delicate whitewashed wooden furniture with artfully distressed flair. The whole suite looked as if it belonged in a magazine and was the most luxuriously appointed space Hannah had ever been in.

"This suite is incredible. I love it."

"My mother's handiwork. It's always struck me as ironic that she could decorate rooms to look so warm and inviting."

He didn't elaborate on the odd comment, but disappeared with her suitcase through the double doors that opened into a bedroom. She made to follow him to check out the next room when a mouthwatering aroma caught her attention. There was no mistaking the smell of chocolate chip cookies. Inhaling deeply, she followed the scent to a cozy sitting area near the balcony doors composed of a sofa and chairs clustered around a spindly-legged coffee table.

Eureka. On the table sat a tray loaded with cookies and a carafe of milk set in a small ice bucket. Edith and Maria's loving touch, no doubt. The chocolate chips on the cookies shimmered. Could it be that they were fresh from the oven?

She lifted one from the plate. It was warm to the touch. She took a decadent bite, barely stifling a moan of pleasure as the melty chocolate hit her tongue. She had the rest of the cookie gone in the next bite, then strolled to the bedroom in search of Brett, blissed out on the sugary, chocolaty goodness.

She found Brett arranging her suitcase on a luggage rack near the wall of windows in the bedroom and devoted a few moments to properly appreciate his backside as he leaned over. When he glanced over his shoulder at her, she wrenched her gaze away, feeling positively lascivious, though not at all remorseful about it. Her attention landed on the bed in the center of the room and she nearly choked on her last bite of cookie.

The bed was enormous.

"You okay?"

"I don't think I've ever seen a bed that big."

"Yeah, it's nice, huh?" He walked to her side at the foot of the bed, smiling at her. He tapped his lip. "You have something on your lower lip."

"Oops. I found chocolate chip cookies in the sitting room. I couldn't help myself from indulging in one already. And I'm glad I did because it was melt-in-your-mouth delicious."

She darted her tongue out and licked the bit of chocolate off.

His gaze lingered on her mouth until with a grunt, he wrenched his gaze away, not unlike she had when she'd been caught staring at his backside. What a pair they made, pretending not to be affected by each other. But there was a reason that the two of them had fallen into bed together that night four months ago, an attraction that had crackled between them from the first moment that their eyes linked.

He cleared his throat, his focus on the wall. "Uh, anyway, as I was saying. Guests who've stayed in this room have said the mattress is great, so you should be really comfortable here."

"How could I not be comfortable in a bed this size? I bet I could lie in the middle of it, spread-eagle, and neither my feet nor my hands would touch the edge."

Really, Hannah? Spread-eagle? Could you make any bigger a fool out of yourself?

He said nothing to that, nor did he look her way, but his lips went flat. With a sharp intake of breath, he spun on his heel and fast-walked out the bedroom door.

Way to go, champ. Huffing in frustration at herself, she gave him a minute of space before joining him in the sitting room once more.

He was at the windows, pushing the curtains all the way open. "As soon as the afternoon storm passes, it'll brighten up in here. There's a great view of the ranch from your balcony."

She seized on the topic change with gusto. "There already is a great view. Your ranch is beautiful. Where's your suite? What kind of view does it have?"

He tipped his head left. "Mine is right next to yours. You could knock on the wall behind your bed and I'd hear it in my sitting area."

So they were back to talking about her bed. Right. Okay. Maybe she wasn't the only one navigating a minefield of Freudian slips.

Shaking his head, he hooked his thumb toward the main suite door. "I'd better go. I'll come by your room tonight at seven to escort you down to dinner."

"Brett?" she called to his retreating form.

He paused halfway out the door.

"Thank you. For all of this. You're being really great for a person who found out his life just got permanently turned upside down."

His posture straightened. Trust and strength radiated from his eyes. "Your life did, too," he said. "We're in this together, Hannah. More than anything, that's what I want you to know. I'm not sure it's fully sunk in yet that I'm going to be a father or how my life is going to change, but it will and it's going to be fine. I'm going to do right by you and by the baby. I promise."

She loved that he got that, how they were in the same boat and that lamenting their life changes or having a negative attitude wouldn't do anybody any good, especially their child. Right then and there, she knew he was going to make a magnificent father. "I'm going to do right by you and the baby, too."

A warm, genuine smile tugged at his lips, the kind that made her knees go weak all over again. "Then it sounds like we've got the makings of a great partnership."

Hannah prowled her suite, looking in drawers and cabinets and under the bed, getting a feel for the place. After that, she unpacked, which took about two seconds, then prowled some more, restless. She couldn't stop thinking about Brett's room on the other side of the wall from her bed. She couldn't stop thinking about how he'd smelled and the feel of his body close to hers. She'd been at Lucky C for less than an hour and already she was stir-crazy and man-crazy all at the same time.

There was only one solution to an emergency situation like that. From her purse, she found her phone and hit the first speed-dial number for the one person who knew her inside and out and loved her unconditionally—her best friend.

"Hey there," Lori said. "Are you calling from your new digs?"

"New *temporary* digs."

Lori clicked her tongue in protest. "Maybe."

Hannah rolled her eyes.

"I can hear that eye roll," Lori said, bringing a smile to Hannah's face. "I didn't expect to hear from you so soon. Is everything going okay?"

"More than okay, but I need to do a *pros and cons.*" One thing she loved about Lori was how great a sounding board she was, and *pros and cons* with Lori was Hannah's favorite way of navigating difficult decisions.

"All right, let's do it. What's the topic this time?"

Hannah took a deep breath and locked gazes with her reflection in the vanity mirror. "Sleeping with Brett Colton."

"Whoa, whoa, whoa. Back up. You just moved in to his family's house this afternoon—and he's already coming on to you again? Damn. That man is as much of a horndog as we'd always heard."

"No, he hasn't come on to me. *I'm* the horndog. My hormones are so out of whack right now, I've got whiplash. I vacillate between wanting to hurl because of my morning sickness, resisting the urge to weep uncontrollably, wanting to shovel cookies into my piehole, and fantasizing about doing naughty, naked things with my baby daddy."

"Dang, sweetie. You're a hot mess."

"Tell me about it. I'm like a one-woman soap opera. For the foreseeable future, my bedroom suite shares a wall with Brett, and he's so charming—like, pantie-melting charming—and he arranged for us to have a private dinner tonight. A dinner date, he called it. And you should see what his butt looks like in the jeans he's wearing. I'm dying over here."

"Wait—you don't just have a bedroom, you have a *suite*? How rich are the Coltons?"

"I have no idea, but now that I'm their accountant, I wouldn't tell you even if I knew."

"That's no fun."

Hannah snapped her fingers. "Back to my problem."

"You mean your sex problem," Lori teased.

"Yes, Lori. Thank you. My sex problem." Geez, she hoped Brett wasn't listening on the other side of the door. Cringing at the idea, she walked into the bathroom and pushed the door mostly shut.

"Continue," Lori said.

Hannah lowered her voice. "Okay, so, I pretty much want to throw myself at him tonight at dinner. I mean, I'm already pregnant with his child, so what's the harm? And you know me, that's *so* not my personality."

"You're the good girl," Lori offered.

"Yes, exactly. I'm the good girl. Except now I'm the jezebel who got pregnant from a one-night stand, so maybe I should just own it and embrace my inner slut."

"First of all, take a breath, Hannah."

She braced her hand on the bathroom's marble countertop. "Trying."

"And second of all, I hate the word *slut*. That's your parents' shame culture talking through you, so knock it off."

That was another thing she loved about her bestie;

she told it like it was and didn't let Hannah get away with any defeatist self-talk. "Okay. You're right."

"Of course I am. Third of all—"

Despite herself, Hannah grinned. "There's no such term as 'third of all.'"

"In this case, there is. Third of all, what's up with the word *jezebel*? Where the heck did you come up with that ancient insult?"

Hannah allowed herself a sound of disgust, even though her run-in with Mavis would also make a juicy bit of gossip to share with her best friend. "Remind me to tell you that story some other time. For now, we need to focus on the pros and cons."

"Right. Okay. I'll start," Lori said. "Pro—he's hot."

"Con—he knows how hot he is."

Lori chuffed. "How is that a con?"

"Hello? Pantie-melting charm is not selective. It works on all panties."

Lori chuckled. "Sorry. That's funny. Plus, I got an awesome visual there." She cleared her throat. "All right, continue."

"He's a player, but because of this baby, we're bound together for life, which he reminded me of this afternoon."

Lori whistled and muttered some silly innuendo about bondage and Brett.

Hannah ignored her and pressed on. "So, there's no such thing as casual sex between us anymore. Our relationship will always be complicated, but having a fling with the baby daddy who also happens to be my boss and my housemate is the most complicated scenario I can imagine, especially when it wouldn't lead to anything more than a temporary affair."

"How do you know it wouldn't lead to anything more?"

Hannah gave the phone a skeptical sidelong glance, as if Lori could see it. "Hello? He's a player. He's *the* Brett Colton."

"I'm getting the picture now. You're worried about falling for him and him breaking your heart because he's not the type of guy who settles down with one woman."

Hannah wanted to resist the idea. Because it was crazy and stupid. Falling in love in a forever way with anyone in this huge, gonzo world carried a one-in-a-billion probability, much less doing so with the random guy she met in a nightclub who got her pregnant. She didn't even want to think about calculating those odds.

"Brett and I have spent exactly five hours in each other's company, total. I know next to nothing about him and he knows next to nothing about me. That's not a foundation for love."

"You're worried about falling for him and him breaking your heart," Lori repeated, more adamantly this time.

Hannah gave the phone the evil eye again. What the heck was a best friend good for if she wouldn't let you hide behind your denial? "Of course I'm worried about falling for him and him breaking my heart. Have you met the man?"

"Nope."

Suddenly claustrophobic, she stomped out of the

bathroom and straight to the balcony door. She was annoyed that Brett was so attractive and charming, and annoyed at herself for being a hot mess. But mostly, she was annoyed that she was light-years away from being financially independent so that she and Brett could tackle the issue of parenthood and their relationship on even footing. "We'll fix that soon because I want you to meet him. Let me get my bearings around here and get started in my new job first, and then I'll have you over, okay?"

"Can't wait. In the meantime, I have another *pro* and *con* for you," Lori said.

"I don't think I'm in the mood for that anymore."

Lori ignored her protest and forged ahead. "Pro— you should sleep with him because you've had a crappy few months and you deserve to blow off steam with a hot guy who's into you."

True, that. A bit of Hannah's bluster deflated. "And the con?"

"Don't take this the wrong way because you know I love you, but the con is that you're a neurotic math geek who overanalyzes everything and I know you're going to overanalyze this decision to the point that you might not be able to properly blow off steam and relax."

"That is true, too. So what am I supposed to do?"

"Have dinner with him tonight. Maybe after spending some time in each other's company doing something other than screwing, which is how you two have spent almost all the hours you've clocked together so far, you'll realize that your attraction to him isn't as potent as you thought it was."

Hannah considered herself to be an eternal optimist, but even she knew that the odds that having dinner with Brett would snuff out her lust for him were dire, indeed. The man had a gift for words and when he looked at Hannah, he really looked at her, in a way that was both sincere and maddeningly flirty. She seriously doubted that spending more time with him would quell her lust. Still, she said, "That is sound advice. Thank you."

"You're welcome. Call me tomorrow, okay? I want to hear how this turns out."

After they ended the call, Hannah stood at the glass French doors, looking out at the ranch and the vistas beyond. The land was beautiful, with the dark clouds and rain turning the grass a vibrant green and the fences surrounding the corrals and fields a brilliant shock of white. On a whim, she lifted her phone and took a picture.

From behind a line of single-wide trailers near the barn that were probably offices, something white caught her eye. She took a second look.

A young woman wearing a white dress was standing in the rain and watching a group of ranch workers guiding cattle through a series of chutes toward a large fenced-in area. The woman didn't hold an umbrella or move to shelter herself from the storm, so her dress was soaking wet and her brown hair was plastered to her cheeks. None of the workers seemed to notice the woman.

A flash of lighting zinged through the sky in the distance. A few moments later, a loud crack of thunder sounded and the rain turned into a deluge.

The woman didn't move. She didn't lift her hands or sidestep under the nearest roof eave.

Hannah zoomed her camera phone in on her and took another photograph. Now that she was looking through the zoom lens, she would swear that the woman was trembling, though the summer rainstorm was warm, the air humid. Through the lens, she could just barely make out something in the woman's left hand. She zoomed in as tight as the camera would allow, but couldn't make out what exactly the long, sticklike object dangling from her hand was. A baseball bat? A cane? *An ax?*

Yeah, right. Ridiculous, Hannah. She was letting the eerie feel of the mansion and the lightning and thunder send her imagination on a wild adventure. She shook her head to clear it, refusing to add hallucinating to her list of pregnant quirks.

Lori was right. She was overthinking everything instead of relaxing into the idea that maybe it would be okay to let down her guard around Brett and his family. Maybe bringing her to this heaven on earth at the Lucky C was God's way of letting her know that everything was going to be okay for her and her baby if she'd just open her heart to the possibilities He'd set before her.

She dropped onto the sofa and lifted another cookie from the plate. It wasn't warm anymore, and the chocolate wasn't melty, but it was almost as delicious as the first one she'd eaten. Unable to resist another look, she stood again and returned to the French doors, curious if the rain-loving mystery woman was still enjoying the foul weather. Hannah scanned every inch of the ranch that she could see, looking for the shock of white fabric against the browns and grays and greens, but the mystery woman was gone.

Chapter 6

Brett had never been a fan of the Big House's dining room, which sat at the back end of the ground floor and boasted a semicircle of glass French doors that opened to a veranda and overlooked the pool and the Coltons' pastoral domain beyond. The space reminded him too much of itchy formal wear he'd been forced to stuff himself into as a kid when his parents hosted dinner parties for other cattle-breeding bigwigs and state senators and the like.

The room itself had been decked out with tasteful, high-end decor. A smattering of white candles surrounded by bud vases of wildflowers graced the center of a massive, dark-stained wood table and the heavy burgundy drapes had been pulled back to reveal a darkening horizon, the lingering glow of the now-absent sun turning the prairie into a sea of indigo shadows.

Edith had set up two place settings at the corner of the table nearest the veranda. Brett had offered Hannah the chair with the best view in the room, and they'd dug into course after course of delectable plates from the kitchen. From a spinach salad with warm bacon dressing to seared shrimp canapés, Maria presented each of the first two courses as though they were entertaining the queen of England.

As Hannah sipped the sparkling apple cider that had been set up in an ice bucket next to the table and ate heartily of Maria's offerings, she seemed entranced by the view as much as Maria's culinary talent or Brett, which suited him just fine. He wanted her to grow to love the ranch as he did.

"I can't stop looking outside. Your ranch is incredible," she said.

Brett took a drink of his beer, his gaze fixated on a whole different kind of beautiful view—his luminous dinner companion. "Every time I think you're looking at me, your attention slips over my shoulder to the windows."

He touched his shoe to hers to let her know he was merely teasing her.

"I've been looking at you plenty. I've just been sneaky about it." She winked at that and Brett's heart did a heavy *ba-dum* in his chest. "But honestly, I grew up in a postage-stamp-sized house in town, where you'd look out the window and all you'd see was the peeling paint and dirty windows of the house next door. I can't imagine what it must have been like growing up here with the prairie as your playground."

He flashed a bright smile. "That was the best part. I was the fourth child, yet another boy in my father's quest for a girl, so I was on my own a lot, exploring the ranch, following my big brothers around." He almost added, *it was the perfect setting for children to grow up in, like it will be for our child.* But that might have been overkill for day number one of their arrangement.

"Just your father?"

"My mother's not exactly maternal. Pops wanted a big family and for reasons that I certainly don't understand, she obliged him, but in between pregnancies, she'd take off for parts unknown. Spas in Europe, cruises and all manner of escapes."

She set a hand on his forearm, her smile dimming, which was a shame. "No wonder you're so close to Edith."

To counter the conversation's turn for the serious, Brett smiled wider and sat up a little straighter. "Edith is going to spoil our baby rotten, just like she did my nephew, Seth. I can't wait to watch."

Maria buzzed in, a covered plate in each hand. "Your main course. Braised beef tenderloin from an award-winning steer right here at the Lucky C and accented with a Cabernet mushroom reduction."

Hannah patted her belly. "Speaking of being spoiled rotten, you're so talented, Maria. I can't believe the Coltons' luck to get to eat your cooking every day."

"Your luck, too, now." Dang it. There he went skirting the line of overkill again.

"You're very kind, both of you. I'm glad you're finding the meal pleasing." Then, as fast as Maria had breezed in, she was gone again, leaving Brett and Hannah to each other's company.

They dug into the beef, with Hannah making blissed-out moans that sent Brett's thoughts right into the gutter, not that it'd been out of the gutter since they'd stood in the driveway that afternoon and she'd turned her dimpled smile on him. Being with her in her bedroom suite had damn near killed him—long before she'd invited the visual of her lying spread-eagle on the bed.

He cleared his throat, desperate for a distraction. "What were we talking about before Maria came in?"

"You, growing up."

"Ah." And now that he was recalling it, their conversation had taken a turn for the somber, talking about his mother's depression-fueled negligence. He wasn't crazy about continuing that topic, but it was a little late to worry about that.

"What was it like growing up with three older brothers? I'm an only child, and I can't get enough of stories about what it's like being a sibling. What a glorious feeling that must have been to have playmates 24/7. My house was so quiet all the time."

Grateful that she'd spared them from delving into a painful topic, he sat forward, all smiles. "Ours definitely wasn't. Oh, the stories I could tell you…"

She laughed at that, the sound echoing in the vast room. "I bet you could. Were your brothers good to you? Or is it like a lot of stories you hear about, with big brothers tormenting little brothers?"

"If you asked them, they'd claim they were angels."

He spread his arms wide. "Shepherds who taught me the ways of the world and kept me safe from danger."

The sidelong gaze she gave him put those heart-stopping dimples of hers on full display. "But…"

"But they're all full of horse pucky because the truth is that there was a fair bit of torment involved. The way I usually put it is to say that they designated me the proverbial royal taster."

"Royal taster?"

"Yeah, you know like in medieval days, with kings and queens, how servants would have to taste the king's food first to make sure it wasn't poisoned? That's what I was for my brothers, except about more than food. 'See if there are leeches in that creek,' they'd say. 'Go find out if that's poison ivy or not. I can't remember what it looks like.' Or 'You go inside first and see how mad Dad is that we're two hours late for supper.'"

She chuckled. "Oh, no! And you fell for that?"

"Every time. I ate it up. I suppose the messes they got me into could've made me cynical, but I liked the attention. With every bit of trouble I got in, the more attention I got, both from my parents and my brothers, which just fueled my bad behavior. Call it 'fourth child syndrome.'"

"Did things change when Greta came around? Did she become the royal taster?"

"No way. That girl was treated like a princess from the moment my father found out he'd finally managed to sire a girl." He refilled her flute with sparkling cider. "But that didn't stop us from doing our brotherly duty of tormenting her every chance we got, despite the punishments we subjected ourselves to with our rowdiness."

"What did your punishments usually entail?"

"Switches were a popular choice with my mom, but my dad preferred the firm application of his palm to our backsides."

She rubbed her arm. "My father preferred a belt."

After meeting her father at the family's store the day before, he had a good idea why she seemed rattled at the memory. He touched her arm. "Just so we're clear, I don't believe in using those kinds of methods. There are more constructive ways to discipline a child than hurting them physically. I've learned a lot by watching my brother Jack with his son, Seth."

Her shoulders relaxed. "I'm glad we agree on that. I've been worried, wondering if our parenting styles and life philosophies will mesh. I know so little about you."

"That's why we're having this dinner." He covered her hand with his and squeezed. "And many more to come, I hope."

Then Maria was back again, clearing their plates. "I'll be back in a few minutes with dessert, hot from the oven. It'll be worth the wait."

Hannah's attention slid to the darkening ranch beyond the artfully lit pool and patio. "This has been wonderful tonight. I'm absolutely taken with the Lucky C."

"I'm glad to hear that. So am I, actually. And I have a vision for this place, for the future," he said. "The original reason I put that job ad in the classifieds."

"We're finally getting around to that, then. I was

wondering if you'd ever come clean with the truth about why you placed that job ad."

He felt a wince coming on and let it happen, poker face be damned, because he was ready to own up to his white lie. He shouldn't have been surprised that she'd known all along he was fudging the truth with his job offer, as smart as she was. He'd told only Jack and their dad about his vision, and neither had been exactly encouraging. But if he wanted Hannah's help, if he wanted her trust, then he had to trust her, too.

"Yes, I am ready to own up to it, because the truth is that I still need your help with it, if you're willing," he said.

"I'm willing."

"Hear me out first."

Maria hustled into the room, the scent of baked chocolate preceding her. In front of them, she set two bowls. "Brownies à la mode."

Brett didn't recall Hannah's orgasm face from their one-night stand, but he was willing to bet it looked a whole lot like the face she was making at that moment, looking down at her dessert. Of its own accord, his body stirred to life. Ignoring his physical response, he dug into his dessert.

"You gonna be able to listen to my plan for the ranch or would I be better off waiting until your browniegasm ends?"

"Brownie-gasm is right. I've had a lot of chocolategasms today, actually, between this and the cookies in my room. A girl could get used to that kind of twicedaily pleasure."

He was just starting to wrap his brain around the double entendre when she slapped both her hands over her face and groaned. "I didn't mean that. I mean, I did." She shook her head. "I mean, a girl *could* get used to—" She winced. "I'm going to shut up now. Please continue your story. Tell me your plans for the ranch's future while I sit here and die of embarrassment."

He bit the inside of his cheek, fighting the urge to tease her. Or kiss her. Maybe both.

He cleared his throat. "The majority of Lucky C's revenue comes from cattle breeding, but it isn't the lucrative industry it once was. The Lucky C needs to diversify if the business is going to stay strong for generations of Coltons to come." His attention darted to her belly for an instant. "The way I see it, the future of this ranch is in horse breeding and training."

"I don't know that much about either industry. What kind would you breed?"

"Cutting horses. My brother Daniel—well, half brother, technically—he's the resident horse whisperer of the family. He runs a horse-training program on our property, renting the land from us. The Lucky C also gets a cut of his profit, so we've been able to watch that profit double every year he's been in business.

"This year, the demand for his horses has exploded, and my gut's telling me that he's going to outgrow the arrangement very soon. He's already been approached by other horse-breeding ranches to come work for them. They're wooing him with blank checks to buy the DNA for any prizewinning stud he wants.

"Jack, my oldest brother, who runs the Lucky C,

gave me the green light to buy a highly rated stallion named Geronimo for Daniel to breed, with the Lucky C splitting the profits with him as a way of testing the waters for getting the Lucky C into the horse-breeding business, but that's not enough. If we want to keep Daniel and his profits at the Lucky C, then we're going to have to play ball, big-time. One stallion's not going to cut it. My plan is to set up a new arm of the Lucky C Corporation with Daniel and me as comanagers so we can finally give him the budget he needs to grow his breeding business. And I'd like your help in setting up that business plan to present to Jack and my dad."

She took his hand securely in hers. "Of course I can help with that. We'll knock their socks off."

"That's the plan."

They shared a smile, which brought Brett's mind right back around to imagining what it would feel like to kiss those lips. He slipped his hand out from under hers and picked up his fork again.

"Why isn't Daniel already a part of the Lucky C Corporation?" Hannah asked. "I can already tell how important the idea of family is to you, and Daniel's family, so why wouldn't your dad and brothers invite him to be a part of the family business?"

If she could already tell how important family was to Brett, then that was a very good sign, even though she was asking a minefield of a question. "It's complicated. My mother isn't Daniel's biggest fan, to put it mildly. She sees him as a constant reminder of my father's infidelity."

"Ouch."

"Yeah. But my dad's terrible choices aren't Daniel's fault. None of the rest of us would ever hold that against him, but he feels it all the same. Add to that the fact that Jack doesn't want to shift the ranch in a new business direction, especially a direction that's my idea. He sees cattle breeding as our brand and he wants to keep with the old ways."

"Why would Jack oppose an idea just because it's yours? Is that a sibling-rivalry thing?"

"No. That's not it. Until a few months ago, I wasn't worthy of Jack's trust." He found her hand under the table and gave it a squeeze. "Or yours, either, for that matter."

"Hard on yourself much?"

"With good reason. My father used to joke that the Colton family DNA ran out of ambition genes by the time I was born. All I got was the cowboying ones that revolved around whiskey, women and horses."

She eyed him skeptically. "I find that hard to believe. And that's terrible that your father made you feel that way."

"It was the truth, as hard as it is to come clean to you about that. Growing up in the shadow of four smart, successful, career-driven older brothers, I never felt like I could live up to the lofty bar they set. By the time I hit high school, I realized just how easy it was to skate by on my looks and family money, so I stopped trying. In no time flat, I became my own worst enemy, hard drinking and partying all the time, nearly flunking out of school, and taking so many stupid risks."

Her look of skepticism gave way to a slow nod. "That

I do remember. There were some girls from my high school who were sweet on you, even though you were in a school across town. Every Monday, it seemed, students whispered about the hell-raising you got into over the weekend."

Damn, this was rough. It made no common sense to be attempting to prove himself worthy of protecting and caring for Hannah and the baby by coming clean about what an entitled, shallow jerk he'd grown into, but there was no way around this guts-spilling to the mother of his child. "My hell-raising didn't stop at high school. I went to college, but dropped out. I just couldn't see past the moment-to-moment fun to the bigger picture of my life."

He paused, taking a long, slow swig of beer, fortifying himself to continue to the hardest, darkest, bleakest days of his life.

She threaded their fingers together. "I'm not judging you, just so you know. Nobody's perfect and it seems like you've been hard enough on yourself as it is. Too hard."

He really wasn't being too hard. Maybe not hard enough. "The weekend that you and I met in the club, I was in the middle of a bender. The next night, I was at a different club, coming on to a different girl—or, rather, three girls."

Her expression shuttered and her fingers went stiff, though she left them twined with his. But what had he expected? It was such an ugly truth. She'd meant nothing to him that night but a moment's pleasure—a terrible beginning for their child. All he could do now was keep telling her the story so she'd understand how much he'd changed, and why he couldn't seem to shake his reputation with his family.

He rubbed her knee. "Hear me out, okay? There's a happy ending to this story. I promise."

Her gaze rolled up to meet his. In her eyes, he saw stubbornness, the same look that had made him instantly smitten with her in the diner the morning before. "I appreciate you telling me all this, but I already know all about the kind of man you were. I knew it when we slept together, too. Just like I now know that's not who you are anymore."

Brett closed his eyes, overcome with a potent cocktail of relief and shame and affection for Hannah, his throat constricting painfully. He had to swallow before saying, "No, it's not."

Hannah partially stood and scooted her chair around the corner of the table, flush with his chair. She snuggled in tight against his side and took his hand again. Then she set her head on his shoulder. "Keep going with your story. I want to get to that happy ending you promised."

He kissed her hair and left his nose buried in it, it smelled so sweet and feminine. "That night, those three girls followed me back to the ranch for an after-party. I never should have gotten behind the wheel, I was so drunk out of my mind, but thank goodness I was alone because, just past the entrance to our property, I drove my truck off the road and flipped it. It rolled twice, or so the girls said. I have no memory after leaving the club. I barely have any memory of that weekend at all.

"The girls witnessed the whole accident. They left one person with me while the rest drove on to the Big House and got my dad. Dad called my brothers and an ambulance, and thankfully I was only bruised and banged up. No major injuries. The seat belt and airbags saved my life."

"Thank God for that," she said.

"It took me almost dying to realize that I was wasting my life. I wasn't contributing to my family's legacy or living by the code I'd been raised to follow. I was only hurting my family and myself."

"That was one heck of a strongly worded message that God sent you."

He pulled his arm out from between their bodies and wrapped it around her back, holding her close. "And effective."

They were quiet for a long time, staring at the shadows of the French doors on the wall in the moonlight and the flicker of the candles on the table. Hannah felt good in his arms. Good in a way that reminded him that he'd never really held a woman just for the sake of being close to her, for the sake of contact—and now that he had, he loved it. The heat of their bodies together, a woman's soft curves melting into him, Hannah's sweet scent, the feel of her breathing and moving and simply being. What a simple, yet vital, pleasure his previous lifestyle had prevented him from experiencing.

That cocktail of relief and humility and affection rippled through him again. He had to be the luckiest man alive to have been given a second chance at life. It wasn't everyone who could claim to be living proof that people could change for the better and turn their lives around by sheer determination.

Hannah's hand spread over his chest in a lazy exploration until her fingers took to worrying a button on his shirt. "I was always so envious of you and your life," she said in a dreamy, faraway voice. "You seemed so free and happy, while my parents were so strict. Growing up, I never felt like I wasn't suffocating to some degree or another. It took coming of age and moving out for me to finally catch my breath."

"Given that your parents are the type of people who would disown their only child over one mistake, then I can imagine that your life was no picnic growing up."

"No picnic, indeed. I wasn't allowed to go to any high school dances or mixers, or go on any dates in high school. According to my parents, I was always in danger of being snared by the devil's slippery slope of sin." She patted her belly. "I'm still reeling from the notion that, in the end, I proved my mother right about forbidden fruit leading to many jams."

He kissed her hair again, just because he could and she didn't seem to mind it. "I've never been referred to as forbidden fruit before. It has a certain ring to it." Then a horrible thought occurred to him and it took all his mental wrangling not to bolt upright and ruin their cuddly moment.

Carefully modulating his voice, he said, "Please tell me you weren't a virgin that night. I'd never forgive myself for tarnishing a memory that's supposed to be beautiful by being drunk and careless with you."

She gave a soft laugh. "No, so you can relax again. I

tarnished that memory all on my own, giving that gift away to a different boy who didn't deserve it when I was eighteen. I was so starved for experience when I got out from under my parents' thumb after I turned eighteen that I kinda went crazy. My friends called it my own personal Rumspringa, after the Amish tradition. True, I'd never had a bona fide one-night stand before I hooked up with you—or after that night, for that matter—but I don't regret it. I was due for some fun. That was the day I graduated from college."

"I didn't deserve your gift, either. For the record."

Her hand found his chest again. "I'm sorry you don't remember much about that night, because you were quite good, actually. You lived up to your reputation."

The performance review was so unexpected, he couldn't stop a surprised bark of laughter. "Good to know I did something right by you that night. Still, I'm sorry that I put you in this monumental jam."

The hand on his chest moved higher until it hit the skin of his neck. Chill bumps raced over his body at the contact as her fingers explored his neck and jaw and ear. "You didn't do anything *to* me." Her words came out as a purr, husky, seductive. "We got into this jam together. I was the one who suggested we take our conversation back to my place."

His hand slid from her shoulder down her ribs and lower still. He had no idea what the hell he was thinking, getting handsy with her when he'd sworn off sex until he got his life on track, but that logical place in his brain had gone radio silent. When she shifted her weight toward the leg nearest him, of its own accord his hand slipped even lower, cupping her backside.

He splayed his fingers over her curves and turned his face into hers, brushing his lips over her temple. "If you're calling what we did that night a conversation, then what do you call this right now?"

Her fingers deftly popped open the top button on his shirt. "This is your pantie-melting charm mixing with my dangerously out-of-control hormones."

A chuckle rumbled up from his chest. He'd never thought about pregnancy hormones as lusty, but then again, he'd never given much thought to pregnancy hormones at all. All he knew was, he wanted to kiss Hannah in a bad way and there was nothing or no one to stop him.

Hannah's fingers were talented in the button-popping department. She had half his shirt undone before Brett knew what hit him, probably because she was distracting him from logical reasoning by smoothing her parted lips along his jawline.

He tucked his chin in, his lips reaching for contact with hers, his hands itching to haul her up onto his lap. Brett had never wanted to kiss someone so desperately, but then his arm brushed her belly and he remembered who they were and why they were there. With a growl of frustration, he wrenched his face and hands away from her body. Though his body and heart protested, he pushed up to his feet and paced to the French doors, breathing hard.

"I'm a changed man from the one who hooked up with you in that club." He had a plan for his life now,

---

and it didn't involve taking advantage of the mother of his child on her first night at the ranch. He dropped his forehead to the window, relishing the sting of cold on his skin. "I didn't bring you to the ranch so I could seduce you. I asked you to stay here so I could take care of you and the baby, not take advantage of you."

He felt her eyes on his back. "That's a shame," she whispered, breathless.

He rolled his forehead along the glass, twisting to look over his shoulder at her. Her lips were parted and dewy, and even in the dim lighting, he could see the color staining her cheeks. With that good-girl conservative blouse she wore clashing wildly with her parted lips, dark eyes and mussed-up hair, she was a sight to behold. And he wanted her in a bad, bad way.

As he watched, she stood and sauntered toward him—a seductress intent on the object of her desire. In a flash of memory, he saw her the night they'd hooked up, that same wicked gleam in her eye. Clearly, she was not a woman who demurred, and damn, if that didn't just make him rock-hard and desperate to give her what she wanted.

He braced for impact, but she didn't touch him. She stood next to him and pressed her forehead and palms to the glass, her gaze searching the dark ranch grounds beyond the window.

"Are your dangerously out-of-control hormones going to keep testing my resolve for the rest of your pregnancy?" He'd meant it as a jest, to break the tension, but his voice was still thick with need.

"Probably. But if you're expecting an apology, you're going to be sorely disappointed."

He chuffed at that. What else could he do? One of these times, he had no doubt he'd cave and give Wicked Seductress Hannah what she wanted, but it wasn't going to be tonight. "Let's get out of here so Maria and the staff can do their thing cleaning up."

"Should we help with that?"

"On a normal night, sure. But I wanted this dinner to be special, and how's it going to feel like a proper date if we have to bus the table ourselves?"

They strolled through the foyer to the grand staircase. "How's it going to feel like a proper date if you don't kiss me good-night?" she said in quiet purr of a voice as they mounted the stairs.

Oh, man, she wasn't making this easy on him. Then again, she hadn't pretended that she was going to. "Your hormones again?"

A mischievous grin graced her lips. "No. That was all me."

He fought a grin, way too turned on by her good-girl/bad-girl dual personae. "Hannah, we talked about that. I don't think getting physically involved with each other is the best plan."

"It's not the worst plan, either."

In loaded silence, he walked her to her suite door, then kissed her lightly on the cheek. "Sweet dreams, Hannah. I'll see you in the morning."

Chapter 7

That night, not even Hannah's teeth-gnashing frustration at Brett for leaving her as an unsatisfied puddle of need at her bedroom door kept her awake for long. After a good stomp around her suite, cursing Brett's level-headed logic, she'd thrown herself onto the expensive, luxurious bed calling to her from the other room, figuring she could at least fume in comfort. But, being that it was her first time lying on a real bed in three months, she fell into a fast, deep slumber. She'd slept so soundly that she didn't wake until long after the sun had risen on Friday morning, despite that she'd never so much as taken off her shoes or crawled under the covers.

She had no idea what the day was going to bring or which of Brett's family members she'd be meeting, but, despite Brett's insistence that she wait to start work on

Monday, she hoped to convince him otherwise. So she took a nice shower, blow-dried her hair and dressed for the career in a pair of black slacks that fit under her belly and a long, fitted blue cotton dress shirt that stretched over her belly, showing it off. With a touch of cosmetics, she felt fit, pregnant and ready for her first day on the job—right up until her stomach lurched.

"Oh, boy." She braced her hands on the vanity and breathed. The pregnancy book said that she should be getting over her morning sickness any day now, but apparently her stomach didn't give a whit what the book said.

She took a sip of water, then blotted her now perspiring face with a tissue. So much for fit, pregnant and ready for her job. With her ghostly pallor and clammy sweat, she only matched one of those three descriptors anymore. Maybe once she got to work, she'd be too busy to think about her nausea.

She threw open the doors of her suite and marched through the hall to the stairs. The first scent she detected was bacon. That was a good start. Some nice salty bacon might do her stomach some good. She was nearly to the ground floor when she caught a whiff of coffee and—oh, heck, no—scrambled eggs.

She barely made it to the powder room on the first floor in time, and didn't manage to get the door closed or the fan on before the water she'd had to drink decided to come back up.

"Oh, dear. Morning sickness?"

Hannah didn't yet trust herself to raise her face from over the toilet, but she recognized Edith's kind voice.

"It's more about the food than the time of day, but yes. That's exactly it."

"Brett specifically requested bacon in this morning's meal because you like it, so I'm assuming that's not what made you queasy."

"Not the bacon. It was the eggs and coffee." She gagged again at the thought, then pressed a tissue over her nose and mouth.

A hand stroked her hair. "Poor dear. From now on, you can rest assured I won't be fixing eggs again. The Coltons do love their coffee, but I'll figure out a way to prepare it somewhere you won't be able to smell it."

Hannah sat back on her heels. "I'll get some crackers for my room to eat first thing in the morning so I'm not walking around with an empty stomach. That's helped in the past. There's no need to put you and the Coltons out like that by moving breakfast."

"Nonsense. We don't mind," Brett said, hovering in the doorway behind Edith. "Are you okay, Hannah?"

Hannah hid her face, wishing Brett wouldn't see her in such a pathetic state. Edith must have sensed her unease because she shooed Brett away.

Edith sidestepped, shielding Hannah from view. "She's just fine. Morning sickness is all. Perfectly normal. All we need is a few minutes of girl time and then I'll bring her out."

"Are you sure, Hannah? There isn't anything I can help with in here? A glass of water or something?"

Hannah watched Edith corral him out the door. "Bless your heart. We've got everything under control in here, but you know what you can do? Tell the others that you've all got about three minutes to finish your eggs and coffee, then we'll have the rest of breakfast on the porch. No eggs or coffee or else you'll have to answer to me."

"But—"

The door shut with a decisive *click*, leaving no time for Brett to question the order.

"He's so sweet," Hannah said, sounding as miserable as she felt.

"Yes, he is. Don't let word get around, but between you, me and the wallpaper, I've always had a particular soft spot for Brett."

It was official. Next to Brett, Edith was Hannah's favorite person on the ranch.

Edith retrieved a washcloth from the cabinet under the sink and wet it. "Usually, I set up a breakfast buffet in the kitchen so the Coltons and their employees can eat when they get the chance. The Lucky C is a working ranch, so most everyone is up before the sun." She pressed the washcloth to Hannah's forehead. "But this morning, Brett didn't want you dining alone, so he stuck around the house. And I've got to warn you, Big J and Jack, Brett's brother, have let their curiosity get the better of them. They're out there, too."

"I'm not fit to meet anybody right now."

"Nonsense. We'll have you fixed up in no time. And to avoid the bad smells, we'll move breakfast out to the porch."

"I don't want to put you and the Coltons out by changing their breakfast routine."

With a *tsk* of protest at Hannah's comment, she gathered Hannah's hair, then moved the washcloth to the back of her neck. "Brett told me yesterday that your comfort and needs are my first priorities. Not that I needed him to tell me that, because I'd already arrived at that conclusion on my own."

With Edith's aid, Hannah stood. She blew her nose, then brushed off her knees.

Edith smoothed Hannah's hair, then reached for a tissue. "For your eyes. Your mascara's running."

From seemingly out of thin air, Edith produced a compact of powder and a brush, then doted on Hannah's face and hair for another few minutes, making her feel thoroughly cared for. *Like a good mom*, she thought with a private smile. Like the kind of mom Hannah wanted to be. So full of love that her children would never doubt that they were the center of Hannah's universe, or that her love for them was unconditional.

"Thank you for all your kindness. I've been kind of lost lately."

"Then it's a good thing Brett found you and brought you home."

Home. Hannah had been at the Lucky C for less than a day, but she already knew that this home was nothing like the house she grew up in. Her baby was going to thrive here, and Hannah would, too.

"Brett told me you had a big part in raising him and his brothers and sister. I can see how you're like a mother to everyone around here. And I bet you're going to be a great honorary grandma for this baby." Realizing how dismissive that sounded about Brett's actual mother, she added, "No offense to Abra, of course."

Edith took to fussing over Hannah's outfit. "Oh, I don't think Abra would take offense. She was the first to admit to her delicate constitution and her inability to tolerate children."

The assessment of Abra had been given in a matter-of-fact tone that left no room for questions. After the hints that Brett had dropped about his strained relationship with his mother, it came as no surprise that his mother had neglected the family when he was growing up, or that Edith had filled that role for the Colton kids. In fact, she was certain that Edith got a lot of credit for Brett's turning out to be such a good man.

"As for me," Edith continued, "I never had children or a family of my own, and being a part of the Colton family has brought me so much happiness. I can't wait to meet your little bundle of joy. Being considered one of his grandmothers would be an honor, indeed."

Linked arm in arm, Edith and Hannah walked from the powder room, skirting the foyer in the direction of a short hall, with Hannah holding her breath.

"Another five steps and we'll be at the nearest exit. You've got this," Edith whispered.

Edith walked her to a service hall and through a door that opened onto the wraparound porch. Hannah gulped in a huge breath of fresh air, not minding the singular aromas of the ranch's livestock and dried grasses and dust. The scents reminded her of her parents' shop when she first unlocked the doors in the morning, when the scent of livestock feed and the lemony soap she used to mop the hardwood floors the night before hung heavy and concentrated in the stuffy room.

Good thing those didn't activate her morning sickness or she'd be plumb out of luck. She released her grip on Edith and straightened. Her stomach was still unsettled, but the nausea was manageable.

"Better?" Edith asked.

"Much. Thank you."

The two women walked along the porch to the front of the house where Brett sat with two men who looked strikingly like the ones she'd seen from the dining room the night before. Brett's father—whom she guessed was the man who looked as she imagined Brett would in thirty years—and his older brother Jack, who was maybe ten years Brett's senior, and had the same proud jaw and shape of his nose as Brett and his father.

Brett stood upon seeing them, looking concerned.

Hannah waved away his worry. "Just morning sickness."

"I'm glad that's all it is, but that still stinks." He offered her the chair next to his.

"Tell me about it. I'm sorry y'all had to move out here. I told Edith you didn't have to."

"Nonsense. Of course we did," the older man said in a booming, jovial voice. "I wouldn't dream of going against one of Edith's mandates." He held his hand out. "Name's Big J. Brett's dad."

She stretched her arm over the table and shook his hand. His smile was broad and genuine. She felt as if she already knew him, he looked so similar to Brett. And he was just as charming, too.

"I can see where Brett gets it," she said.

Big J puffed his chest out, hamming it up. "What, this striking and rugged silhouette?"

She chuckled. "No, the charm."

"Well, we've got a lot of that, too, don't we, son?"

"Yes, sir. For better or worse." As his dad chuckled, Brett gestured to the other gentleman. "And, Hannah, this is my brother Jack."

After Hannah shook his hand, Edith patted her shoulders. "I'll bring you bacon, toast and orange juice straight away."

"Thank you, Edith. You're a lifesaver."

The view from the porch stretched over the land in the same direction as the windows and balcony of Hannah's bedroom suite, facing the cluster of ranch buildings, feed sheds, corrals and stables that looked to be the heart of the ranch's business. Her gaze settled on two men working a forklift, moving bales of alfalfa.

She could feel Big J's and Jack's gazes on her, drawing conclusions, testing her motives. She wondered if it'd been either of them who'd referred to her as the "good-time girl of the week."

No, Hannah. That's a toxic way of thinking. That was her parents' vitriol oozing out. She had nothing to be ashamed of, and she shouldn't care what Brett's family thought about her. So far, everyone had been lovely, and even if they weren't, what did it matter? She and Brett were committed to coparenting this baby, so his family and the ranch's workers were just going to have to learn to live with her in their lives.

Thusly resolved, she shifted her gaze away from the view and smiled at Big J. "Again, I'm really sorry that y'all had to move because of me. The smell of coffee and eggs activates my morning sickness."

"We really didn't mind," Brett said.

"When my ex was pregnant with my Seth, she had terrible morning sickness at first, but it went away after a few months."

"I'm still waiting for that blessed day. The books say I should be over it any time now. Either way, I'm looking forward to getting to work after breakfast."

Brett draped an arm across the back of her chair. "Like I told you yesterday, you don't have to work today. You should just take it easy."

"I know, but I'd like to work. I've been really bored the past few months, not getting to use everything I learned in school."

Brett pursed his lips. "I'd rather you rest."

"So you're saying that the ranch doesn't need help with the books?"

"Careful there, Brett," came a drawl from beyond the porch. "Never get into a war of semantics with a woman." Rafe Sinclair's head popped into view, all smiles and greasy charm. He propped his elbows on the rails and his boot on the porch and winked at Hannah. "Especially one who's got a bat in the cave. Am I right, Jack?"

It got Hannah's defenses up to have Rafe interrupting breakfast, though she wasn't sure why. He wasn't exactly lecherous, but he rubbed her the wrong way, and not just because he was impeded by a sexist state of mind.

"A bat in the cave?" Jack said through a chuckle.

"That's a new one. How's it going, Rafe?" The two men shook like old friends.

Rafe turned his attention back to Hannah, tipping his hat. "Morning, Miz Grayson."

"You two have met?" Big J said.

Hannah couldn't bring herself to smile, per se. "Yesterday. He was a member of the welcoming committee."

Big J tipped back in his chair and chuckled. "Rafe here is smart enough to greet a pretty lady when she comes around, aren't you, Rafe?"

Rafe's gaze flickered over Hannah's body. "Yes, sir."

Brett's arm settled on Hannah's shoulders, not possessively, per se, but protective, as though Rafe put his defenses on alert, too.

"Unlike your 'bat cave' reference, Rafe, I prefer the term 'bun in the oven,'" Big J said with a wink to Hannah that was light-years different from the wink Rafe had sent her.

Edith set a plate of bacon, toast and fruit in front of Hannah. "I was a candy striper at a hospital before coming to work here, and one of the obstetricians who also worked there was from England. She called it being 'in the pudding club.'"

Hannah smiled, though she was still unsettled by Rafe's presence. "That's ridiculous."

Big J gave a hoot of a laugh. "Yeah, but I can see the merits of organizing a club of like-minded pudding lovers."

"How about 'pea in the pod'?" Brett said. "That's my favorite, except that our baby is way bigger than a pea already." It could have been Hannah's imagination, but

Brett had seemed to stress the words *our baby*. Another subtle warning to Rafe?

Whether it was or not, Rafe pushed off from the rail. "I'll let y'all get back to your breakfast." To Big J, he added, "I just swung by to see if you needed me today, boss."

Big J scratched his neck, considering. "I reckon I don't, but thanks all the same. Look here—our Hannah is a bona fide accountant now. This little lady's gonna have everything under control in a flash, aren't you, darlin'? Better than you or I could manage, I can tell already."

Rafe's eyebrows flickered and he gave a mild nod, probably still trying to assimilate the idea in his Neanderthal mind that a woman was capable of reading spreadsheets. "Congratulations again on your new job, Miz Grayson. And good luck. Don't let Big J boss you around too much." With a tip of his hat, he set off with a cowboy swagger along the dirt road.

With Rafe gone, Hannah dug into her breakfast with unapologetic zeal. As Edith had said the day before, she had a pregnancy pass to indulge in a temporary food obsession.

"What's your plan for today, Hannah?" Big J said. "Is Brett gonna give you the grand tour of this place or am I gonna get you set up in the office?"

"My vote's on *tour*. You deserve a little R & R," Brett said.

Hannah gave him a chiding smile. "The tour can wait until this weekend. I'm used to keeping busy and these past few months without work have been maddening.

Nothing but R & R. Besides, the reason I'm here at the Lucky C is to work, right?"

"Right," Brett said, his expression shuttered and his tone flat. "Exactly."

Brett and Big J flickered a look at each other that Hannah had no problem interpreting. Her accountant job wasn't the reason she was at the ranch, and everybody knew it, including Hannah. She was smart enough to be aware that her excellent qualifications as a CPA weren't the reason Brett hadn't offered her the job. Just like she was smart enough to know that housing wasn't a typical perk that came with most of the jobs at the Lucky C.

Brett might be determined to provide for her and the baby, but she was equally determined to earn her keep, quash rumors of her being a gold digger and help the Coltons out while she was at it. Before she could second-guess herself, she was turning to Brett's father. "Brett told me that you've been handling the ranch's finances, but I can help free up your time to be with your wife and your grandson. I'm truly grateful for this opportunity to put the accounting degree I broke the bank to get to good use."

Big J chuffed at that. "Opportunity? My son knocked you up."

"Pops, please," Brett growled.

Hannah set a hand on Mr. Colton's arm. "There were two of us there that night to share the responsibility, so don't be so hard on Brett."

"Or else what?" They were fighting words, save for

the twinkle in Big J's eyes and the benevolent way he patted her hand.

She decided to assume he was teasing her and run with it. "Or else I'm going to be forced to defend Brett's honor. And I don't think you want to be messing with the likes of me. I can be pretty ferocious, bat in my cave and all."

Everyone at the table chuckled at that, just as she'd hoped.

One of Big J's dinner-plate-sized hands closed over hers. He tipped back in his chair to meet Brett's gaze, his eyes dancing. "I like this one."

One side of Brett's lips kicked up in a lopsided smile that turned her legs to rubber every time. "Me, too."

Big J stood and tossed his napkin on the table. "And since the books at the ranch are my job—or, were—then I say, if you want to work, then let's go get to work." He offered Hannah his arm.

Hannah stood, grinning and so darned relieved to have been accepted by Brett's dad that she didn't care what happened the rest of the day. Even Jack seemed lighter and less judgy than when she'd first walked onto the porch. "I'd be delighted."

As the chorus of voices chatting downstairs grew louder with each Colton family member who arrived for dinner, Brett's nerves kicked up. Really, there was no good reason to be nervous about introducing Hannah to the rest of his family, not after her introduction to his dad and Jack had gone a lot better than he'd anticipated. In general, Jack was by far the most critical of Brett's choices, and he'd thought Jack would be the slowest person to warm to Hannah, but she'd made short work of winning both him and Dad over.

Even still, his stomach was full of butterflies when he knocked on the door of Hannah's bedroom suite. She opened it wearing a blue dress that accentuated her creamy skin and black hair and had him doing a double take, she looked so pretty.

"You look fantastic. I like that dress."

She patted the fancy braid in her hair self-consciously. "I swear, Maria and Edith are like a pair of fairy godmothers. Edith helped me with my hair and Maria brought me a huge bin of maternity clothes that'd belonged to her cousin."

He hadn't meant to touch her, not after their conversation the night before and the now-constant battle he was waging with himself to keep from kissing her, but before he could stop himself, he molded his hand to the curve of her waist and bussed her cheek. "I'm glad they're taking good care of you. I want to make sure you feel safe and happy here."

She ran her palms along the collar of his slate-gray dress shirt. "I'm sure you say that to all the accountants you hire."

She fluttered her eyelashes and her lips parted. He had no idea if she consciously meant to invite a kiss to those sweet lips or not, but the effect was the same. Just like that, the urge to take her face in his hands and kiss her until her toes curled returned with a vengeance. Truth be told, he'd thought of little else since their dinner the night before besides touching her, kissing her.

About finding out if the experience was as decadent as he recalled in his fuzzy memory of their one-night stand.

Drawing a sharp breath, he peeled away from her touch and walked to the balcony door, his back to her and his hands in his pants pockets. "Not every accountant, no. Just to the mothers of my children." He cringed. So much for that smooth charm of his that she kept pointing out. "That didn't come out right."

Her footsteps sounded in approach. "Maybe we're both a little anxious about dinner with your family."

Actually, he'd forgotten all about that when he'd had her in his arms. "That must be it, but there's no reason for you to be nervous. Because of course they're going to be taken with you, like my dad and Jack already are."

Then her hand was on his shoulder blade. He flinched and locked his knees, lest he spin around and take her in his arms once more. Actually, forget taking her in his arms. He wanted to seize hold of her hips and push her up against the wall, caging her between his arms as he plundered her mouth with his tongue and lips. She was so bold and so full of passion, he had a feeling she preferred her lovemaking with an edge of roughness, even if he could only give it to her like that just a little, because of the baby.

"Your dad's so sweet and funny," she said, cutting into his wayward thoughts. "I had a great time at the office with him today, learning the job."

Shaking off the vision in his imagination of the two of them locked together as he took her against the wall, he turned to face her, not sure how he'd stop himself from enacting his vision if she had that come-hither look on her face again. "I just hope my brothers can keep their inappropriate jokes to a minimum. Sometimes, when we all get together, things get a little rowdy."

She chuckled at that.

"What?"

"It makes me smile to imagine a rowdy, happy family get-together. My own family dinners were always such solemn affairs. My mom used to say we had to be quiet because it was easier to hear God that way. But I always had the sinking suspicion that their marriage was so unhappy that they preferred the quiet to having conversations with each other."

"Sounds like my parents' dysfunctional marriage."

"I don't want that for myself," she said. "That was a promise I made to myself a long time ago. Never to get trapped in a loveless marriage like them."

"Same with me. Life's too precious to spend it with the wrong person." He hesitated for a moment, then added, "I do have to warn you that my dad will probably bring it up tonight that you and I should get married."

Her smile turned impish. "He already asked me about it today."

Brett rolled his eyes. "Sorry about that."

"It's okay. You and I have a plan to be parenting partners, and it's none of anybody else's business how we go about that."

Smart, funny, bold, proud, sweet, sexy... Brett's head was swimming with adjectives to describe the inimitable Hannah Grayson. She was strong in a way that made him feel stronger, and so funny and generous of spirit that he didn't think he'd ever smiled so much in his life. *Get a grip, man.* She might be strong, but she was also vulnerable—pregnant and depending on him for a roof over her head, a job and support—and he was hell-bent on sticking to the role of her protector and partner, rather than her seducer.

He reached for her hand and tucked it in the crook of his elbow. "Let's get going. Edith isn't a fan of tardiness."

Chapter 8

The dining room had been transformed from a mood of soft, candlelit romance the previous night into a bright, festive party atmosphere, the lights turned up, the table decked out in teal, silver and black, from the tablecloth to place settings to the artistically scattered baubles and candles adorning the center.

From Hannah's hasty count as she and Brett entered, six members of the family were already present, including a little boy who had to be Brett's nephew, Seth, Jack and Big J.

"There she is, my new accounting wizard!" Big J's boisterous voice hushed all other conversations. "Hannah, get on over here so I can gush to my boys about what an asset you're going to be to our business."

Brett's head cocked to the side to send her a look full

of warmth and pride as he guided her to Big J and the circle of people around him.

Hannah blushed, of course, a ridiculous reflex to praise, and one she'd tried hard to shake. Clearly, she had some work to do on that front. But even she could admit that Big J was right. She *was* going to be an asset to their business because it'd taken her about two-point-one seconds in the office to figure out that the ranch's books were in disarray and that they were bleeding money every quarter due to a lack of tax planning. She had her work cut out for her, but that was fine. Nothing wrong with a little job security—even though the baby in her belly was probably all the job security she needed with the Coltons.

Brett let Big J go on and on about how he'd gotten Hannah up to speed before interrupting him in order to introduce Hannah around. Brett's brother Ryan, a Tulsa police detective, looked so much like Brett that she did a double take. They boasted a similar muscular yet slim build and shared the same brown hair, cut short, and vibrant green eyes. But where Brett's eyes sparkled with an unending well of charm, Ryan's were serious, contemplative.

Daniel, Brett's half-brother, shared a Colton essence in his facial features, but his hair was nearly as black as Hannah's and his skin was darker. He was quiet, distant even, and stood apart from the others. It wasn't until Brett gathered him in a hug and slapped his back that Daniel's brown eyes warmed.

The mood in the room shifted when they heard the sound of the front door closing.

Big J clapped his hands together and gave a whoop. "Got to be my princess!"

Sure enough, women's voices sounded, and then a young woman appeared. Hannah was hit with a surprise moment of déjà vu, Greta looked so familiar. And it wasn't just that Colton essence or her eyes that mirrored Brett's and the rest of the family. Hannah couldn't quite put her finger on what it was about her. Behind Greta stood a handsome young man that Hannah assumed was her fiancé.

Big J greeted them at the entrance to the room, beaming, his arms spread wide. "Greta, Mark. Now my night is complete." He hugged Greta, rocking a little. "I'm so glad you two made it."

Greta kissed his cheek. "Of course we did, Daddy. Sorry we're late. We stopped by the hospital to see Mom first. Eric was there. He sends his regrets."

"Ah, well, he's a busy man. So much responsibility. Any news on Abra? How did she look today?"

Greta moved farther into the room and hooked her purse over the back of a chair near the center of the table. Mark, whom Hannah assumed was her fiancé, trailed her, quiet, and looking thoroughly out of place. It wasn't lost on Hannah that Big J didn't greet his future son-in-law with more than a nod, and save for a handshake from Ryan, nobody else really did, either. Clearly, Greta was the star of the show.

"Eric had some good news. He said that Mom had an increase in brain activity today. That's a really good sign, he said. He said it increases the odds of her waking up from the coma and not having brain damage."

Big J raised his hands to heaven. "Thank goodness. We'll take all the good news we can get."

Greta's eyebrows knit together as her eyes scanned the room. "Speaking of good news." Her gaze landed on Hannah and she strode forward, her hand extended in greeting. "You must be Hannah. I'm Greta. Congratulations on the baby and on snagging Tulsa's most eligible bachelor."

Greta slugged Brett in the shoulder, and that's when it hit Hannah where she'd seen Greta before. The previous afternoon, the woman in the white dress standing in the rain near the ranch office. Except that Greta and Mark had just come into town tonight, so Hannah had to be mistaken. There were a lot of workers at the ranch, so surely some of them would have a slight resemblance to Greta from that distance and in such foul weather. She shook off the thought, though made a note to check the photograph on her phone the first chance she got.

Maria and Edith chose that moment to walk in, each pushing a tray loaded with platters of food. "Go ahead and take your seats, everyone," Edith said. "Dinner is served."

Big J assumed the seat at the head of the table and tucked the silver napkin into his shirt collar. When Maria set a plate of salad in front of him, he picked up a piece of lettuce and let it flutter back to the table. "This isn't all we get, right? I know you've had me on a diet lately, but a man can't survive on lettuce alone."

Maria patted his shoulder. "I made your favorite tonight, so be patient and eat your vegetables."

"I swear, between you, Edith and Abra, it's like I've

got three wives henpeckin' me all the time. I don't know how them polygamous fellers with all those wives stay sane."

Brett showed Hannah to a pair of seats across from Greta and next to Daniel, leaning in as he pulled her seat out. "Pops is in rare form tonight. He loves having the whole family around."

Hannah gave a quiet giggle. She loved how gregarious Big J was.

Edith and Maria served the remainder of the salads and were on their way out when Big J called to them. "Edith, Maria, pour yourself some champagne. I have a couple toasts to make and since you two are part of our family, you might as well stick around."

Once Maria and Edith had full flutes in hand, Big J held up his. "First, I'd like to make a toast to the Coltons. We've had a rough summer so far, but I know in my heart that Abra is going to pull through and be back at this table soon. And what better news for her to wake up to than the discovery that not only is she about to be a grandmother again, but she'll soon be having a new daughter-in-law, too, if Brett cowboys up and marries—"

Brett squirmed. "Pops, please."

"Sorry," he said, though his cat-eating-a-canary grin didn't look the least bit sorry. "As I was saying, the Colton clan is about to be two more strong. Hannah, welcome to the family. And we can't wait to meet Baby Colton come this November. Cheers."

They clinked glasses. Hannah was filled with so much affection for this family, who'd embraced her wholeheartedly. It was everything she'd never had in her life but always wanted. Her eyes clouded with unshed tears of happiness and she leaned a little closer to Brett as she sipped her sparkling cider.

"Don't put those glasses down yet," Big J warned. "I have a second toast to make, this one to my lovely daughter, Greta, and her fiancé, Mark. Your engagement party didn't go as planned, but I know your mother would want you to carry on with the wedding. Nothing is more important in this world than love. And—"

"Actually, Dad, let me stop you there," Greta said.

Big J snorted and lowered his glass. "Can't a man toast his family without getting interrupted these days?"

Greta set her hand over Mark's. "We have a tough announcement to make, something we've given a lot of thought. We've decided to postpone wedding preparations until Mom is awake and better. She's been so excited about the wedding and helping me plan it that I can't imagine forging ahead without her."

The room was quiet. That had to be so hard, thinking about getting married while her mother lay in a coma. Hannah didn't blame her one bit, but Big J's face fell.

"I don't think that's what your mother would want," he said.

"I do," Greta said gently. "And maybe knowing that I'm waiting for her will inspire her to wake up."

Brett was the next to speak. "We understand, sis. And I'm sorry for both of you that what's supposed to be the happiest day of your lives has become anything but."

Greta threaded her fingers with Mark's. "It *will* be the happiest day of our lives, because we're going to wait until Mom is with us again. All that matters to us now is her waking up and making a full recovery."

Hannah offered Greta a smile. "She will wake up. I'm sure of it. There's so much love in this family, how could she not want to rush back into your lives as quickly as possible?"

She felt Brett stiffen. Yes, he'd told her the night before that his mother hadn't been there for him growing up, but that didn't mean she couldn't change. After all, Brett's near-death experience had opened his eyes to what was important in life. Perhaps her brush with death would do the same.

Greta dabbed her eyes with her napkin. "Thank you, Hannah. And that's enough sadness for tonight. I want to hear more about you and Brett. How did you two meet? Dad didn't say over the phone. I didn't even know you were dating someone, bro."

Brett rubbed the back of his neck. "Yeah, about that. I take the full blame for—"

"We met at Avid, a nightclub in downtown Tulsa," Hannah said, cutting him off and sparing him from trying to dance around her reputation, as he'd seemed poised to do. "I'd just graduated from college and wanted to blow off steam and celebrate getting my degree. I wasn't looking for anything more than a single night of fun and neither was Brett, so it was good that we found each other there. I know that's not a pretty story, or sweet, but it's real. As Big J said in his toast, you're our baby's family, so we have nothing to hide."

A chill settled over the table. Brett's backbone was ramrod straight. His hand tapped the hilt of his steak knife against the table as his narrowed gaze roved over each person there, as though daring them to say something disrespectful. They didn't, but then again, they didn't have to. The unmistakable disappointment in their expressions as they returned Brett's stare got their message across loud and clear.

Hannah held her head high and kept a smile painted on her face. She was so dang tired of being judged that she'd lost all her tolerance for it. True, all the disappointment tonight was wholly directed at Brett, but even still, watching Brett's family regard him with that same negativity that she'd suffered at the hands of her parents and their church friends—albeit to a much lesser degree—made her spitting mad. She and Brett hadn't done anything wrong. Searching for a human connection in this crazy, harsh world, even a temporary one, was not a sin. Sex between two consenting adults was not a sin.

She covered Brett's hand with hers, stilling the knife tapping. "This baby is going to be the happiest mistake ever. I have no regrets." And, feeling as brazen and strong as a mother bear, she looked every one of Brett's family members in the eye, smiling her challenge to them to be happy right along with her.

Brett gave her a sidelong glance. She wouldn't have thought it possible, but his backbone grew even taller. His chest even puffed a little, if she wasn't mistaken. "Neither do I," he said with a tinge of wonderment, as though he was arriving at that conclusion as he said the words.

Tracy's smile broadened. "As Brett reminded us a

couple days ago, every baby is a blessing. We're so excited for you two."

"Then one more toast," Big J said. "If you'll keep your traps shut without interrupting me, I'll keep it short." He raised his flute. "To happy mistakes."

Brett's posture relaxed. He brought Hannah's hand to his lips and kissed it, then took up his glass in his other hand. "To happy mistakes and new beginnings."

The *clomp* of footsteps mounting the stairs that led up to the office told Hannah that her evening with Brett was over, which was a shame. They'd been poring over a draft of the horse-breeding proposal for hours, and Hannah had enjoyed every moment of it.

She and Brett worked great as a team, bouncing ideas off each other and molding his vision for the ranch into a fleshed-out business proposal. There was no way his dad and Jack could look at the projected figures that she and Brett had come up with, as well as the concrete business plan they'd articulated, and tell him no. She was sure of it.

When the door opened, they looked up from where they were sitting on either side of the desk, even though they both knew full well who would be standing there. Sure enough, Daniel tipped his hat in greeting to Hannah, then turned his attention to Brett. "Ready? I got the horses saddled."

Hannah tapped her pen, frustrated. "I wish you two didn't have to ride patrol tonight. The ranch has been quiet for the entire week I've been here."

Brett stood and replaced his hat on his head. "Maybe that's because the patrol is working."

Hannah followed them to the door. "Stay safe, okay?"

"No worries there. Like you said, the ranch has been quiet."

Sleekie, the black barn cat who'd taken a shine to her, appeared almost instantly, demanding to be petted with a series of loud meows. Hannah knelt to stroke her.

"Even still," she called to Brett and Daniel as they walked away. "Daniel, look out for him."

Daniel glanced at her over his shoulder as they walked toward the two saddled horses near the stable. "Always." And for a man of few words as he seemed to be, that was as much promise as she could hope for.

She remained at the office door, letting out an appreciative hum as she watched Brett swing into the saddle. "That is one fine specimen of a man, Sleekie."

But all Sleekie did was wind around Hannah's legs, purring.

Hannah scooped the cat up and stood, her attention on Brett and Daniel as they cantered along a dirt road headed west, into the setting sun. Despite having to bid Brett goodbye and her worry about him staying safe, evenings were her favorite time on the ranch. After near-daily afternoon rainstorms, the world seemed to hush in reverence to the setting sun amid the lingering storm clouds. The prairie glowed warm with oranges and purples and deep, dark greens. The ranch itself turned peaceful and sleepy. Even the cows and other livestock seemed to understand the coming of night.

After Brett and Daniel disappeared from view, she

lingered on the front steps of the office, absentmind-
edly petting Sleekie and watching the sunset over the
piece of land she was growing attached to. The moment
the sun dipped below the horizon, she closed her eyes
and said a prayer for Brett, for their baby, and to thank
God for providing such a good life for her. She hadn't
understood why He'd taken her life on such a difficult
path, but she was starting to see the plan for her at the
Lucky C with the Coltons and she definitely approved.

When Sleekie started to squirm, she set the cat down
and returned to the office. Flipping all the lights on, she
got back to business. After setting aside Brett's horse-
breeding proposal, she opened the spreadsheet for the
Lucky C. The numbers weren't adding up the way she
would've hoped. Every month for the past year, the
ranch's account was coming up short by several thousand dollars.

The errors were probably a result of Big J's hap-
hazard style, compounded by his occasional forgetful-
ness Brett had mentioned to her on the sly. Whatever
the cause, the result was the same. She had her work
cut out for her. Tonight's plan involved cross-checking
deposit receipts with the hand-printed ledgers and the
computerized spreadsheets that Big J had created, then
inputting the real numbers in the brand-new spreadsheet
that she'd created earlier that week.

Sleekie leaped onto the desk and sat herself down
right on top of the open ledger.

Hannah scratched her behind the ears before moving
her to the side. "Well, Sleekie, since you don't have fingers, how about you cross your paws that I'm right about

these shortages being typos? Otherwise that means someone's stealing money from the Coltons and we can't have that, can we? Not after everything they've been through."

The mere thought of someone stealing money from the Coltons made Hannah spitting mad. She really hoped she was able to find the nearly twenty thousand dollars that looked to be missing.

Sleekie gave a meow, then tipped on her side and got down to her own business of giving herself a bath, unconcerned with the missing money.

Not ten minutes later, Hannah cursed under her breath and shot to her feet, angry and shocked at what she'd found. She picked up the check stub that she'd cross-referenced with a bank statement and gave the two a second look. In her hands she held the first clue about what had happened to the money. "Sleekie, it's not a typo."

Footsteps sounded, coming up the steps. Sleekie dived off the desk, but Hannah didn't have time to do more than wedge the check and the bank statement into the open ledger she'd been working with and flip it closed before the door opened.

Rafe seemed as surprised to see her as she was to see him.

"Oh," he said, backing up a step. He removed his hat and pressed it to his chest. "Evening, Miz Grayson. I didn't expect you to be here so late."

"Then what are you doing here?" Too late, she realized how rude that had come out. "Sorry. You startled me and that came out wrong. I mean, how can I help you tonight?"

He moved farther into the room. "My apologies for giving you a start. I saw the light and thought it'd been left on accidentally. Thought I'd do my part for the environment and the Coltons' electric bill and come turn it off."

He propped one hip on her desk, his broad grin revealing a row of straight white teeth. "But come to find out, it's just purdy little Hannah making herself useful."

It struck her then that she'd once teased Brett that he was as slippery as a snake-oil salesman. She hadn't met Rafe Sinclair yet. With one eye on him, she reached a hand to the keyboard. One hit of a button and the computer monitor went into sleep mode.

"Yep. It's just me, trying to get these books figured out." She tried out a smile, but she had trouble making it happen. She'd seen the man nearly every day since arriving at the ranch, and so far he hadn't been guilty of anything except misogyny, but still, Rafe made her uncomfortable. He didn't seem to understand the concept of personal space and his gazes at her lingered a little too long and were a little too studious.

He picked up the ledger she'd closed. "I've got a good mind for numbers and I'd be happy to help you. In fact, I can see it now, the two of us working together, me helping you make heads and tails of this complicated business so you can get back to your evening and relax, maybe sneak some of Maria's strawberry jam, like you do."

Since when had he seen her eating jam? She only did that in her suite. Then again, she was so addicted to the stuff that there was a chance she'd had a spoonful at breakfast on the porch without remembering it. "That's sweet of you to offer to help, but I've got a good handle on my job." She eased her hands around the ledger and gave a tug, but Rafe's grip held firm.

"Doesn't mean you couldn't use a man's help."

Oh, brother. "Sorry to break it to you, but that's exactly what that diploma on the wall behind me means."

His attention slid past her to the wall. She took his momentary distraction as an opportunity and tugged on the ledger again, harder this time. He released it with a low chuckle.

"So it does, Miz Hannah."

She didn't want to remain in Rafe's company for a second longer. Men who felt entitled to come on to women no matter how uncomfortable they became and who paid no mind to personal boundaries made her skin crawl. There'd been men like that in the Congregation of the Second Coming, men like that at her college campus library, and there would always be men like that the world over. But that didn't mean she had to suffer in their company.

She slipped around the side of the desk, affording him a wide berth, strode to the door and opened it. "I'm afraid I have to ask you to leave so I can keep working. Thank you for understanding."

After a long pause, he stood and replaced his hat on his head. "Forgive me for interrupting your work. Have a safe night, Miz Hannah." When he reached the door, he gave the handle a jiggle. "And be sure to lock this door behind me so the bogeyman can't get in."

What a slimeball, shrouding his threats in disingenuous charm and implications, giving her no concrete grievances to share with Brett, should she choose, except for the way he creeped her out.

She certainly did lock the door behind her and pulled the curtains closed, but she couldn't concentrate on her work anymore. Rafe had gotten in her head. She locked the ledgers, bank statements and other evidence into the desk's largest drawer. On a gut instinct, she backed up the ranch's accounting files to a portable drive and pocketed it. Then she added a password to the computer's launch page before logging out—a version of her due date using random capital letters—just in case.

The whole time, she couldn't shake the sensation that someone was watching her. Of course, that was just her imagination being ridiculous, because the curtains were closed.

"Must be that bogeyman Rafe mentioned. Huh, Sleekie?" But the comment she'd meant as sarcastic, as a means to point out how silly she was being getting so freaked out, hovered in the stillness.

She hadn't seen Sleekie since Rafe's visit, so the smart cat must have hightailed it out of the room. To make sure she didn't accidentally lock the cat in overnight, she checked every nook and cranny of the office, under chairs and tables and behind the curtains.

She had one hand on the doorknob when she thought twice about leaving the ledgers and other possible evidence behind. Yes, she'd locked them up, but her gut was talking again and this time it was telling her to take it all with her back to her room for safekeeping.

After stuffing the loose papers and files into a manila envelope, she stepped outside, locked the office and set off across the grounds to the Big House. She still couldn't shake the notion that there were eyes on her, and her pulse pounded faster with every step she took. Thankfully, she was spared from walking in total darkness by floodlights gracing the eaves of the stables, the feed shed and just about every other building on the grounds. Her path was lit and out in the open and just about as safe as could be. There were no bogeymen, no ghosts, and no one was going to get her on this short walk home in the middle of the Coltons' property.

Chapter 9

On the porch of the Big House, Hannah glanced over her shoulder in the direction that she'd felt someone's eyes on her throughout the evening. Movement, a splash of white, caught her eye near the bunkhouse. The skin on her neck prickled. She stood still, watching the night, but saw nothing else. It had to have been a curtain blowing in the breeze because someone left a window open. Had to be.

She flung the main door of the Big House open a little too hard. It banged against the wall, the sound echoing in the silence within. She didn't draw a full breath again until she'd locked the front door and flipped on every light operated from the switch panel in the foyer.

"Hello, Edith? Are you still around?"

Nothing. As usual, Edith had retired for the night

with the setting sun. Maria must have left already, too. Knowing that Edith and Big J were somewhere in the house should have proven a comfort to Hannah, but her unease only ratcheted up. So silly. She was freaking herself out for no reason.

She made it up the stairs in record time. Subdued lighting glowed throughout the hall from wall sconces. The floor-to-ceiling window at the end of the hall was nothing more than a black rectangle, showing the darkness of the ranch's land. Brett and his brother were out there in the night, patrolling to keep her safe. She had nothing to worry about, tucked away inside a perfectly secure home.

Her attention pulled toward the hallway that led to Abra's suite. The crime scene.

Stop thinking about it, Hannah. For real.

She hugged the envelope to her chest and scuttled to her room. As usual, Edith and Maria had left a light on for her inside.

She opened the door and at the first glimpse of movement, yelped and stumbled back. Someone was in her room. She pressed herself to the hallway wall on weak knees, breathing and wondering what the heck she should do next.

Maria appeared in the doorway. "Oh, my God, Hannah. I'm so sorry I scared you."

Hannah sagged against the wall and let her hand holding the envelope flop to her side. "It's just you." She let out a peal of nervous laughter. "Oh, God. My heart."

"Are you okay?" Maria asked.

"I think so."

Maria disappeared into the room again, then reappeared holding a glass of water. "I knew you were working hard and I thought you might like a late-night snack when you got home. I'm sorry I scared you."

Hannah accepted the water and drank deeply from it, feeling her heart beat in her throat as she swallowed. "Truthfully, I was already spooked before I opened the door. Got myself all worked up over something I thought I saw on the walk back here. Of course, it was nothing."

"Was it the ghost? A woman?"

Hannah clutched the glass and gaped at Maria. "You've seen her, too?" she whispered.

Maria nodded. She wrapped an arm around Hannah and led her into a chair in the suite's sitting area. "So have some of the ranch workers. I think she might be the woman whose baby's bones were found at the Coltons' family cemetery last month." She made the sign of the cross on her chest.

Hannah's head was spinning. "Excuse me?"

"You didn't know?"

"Uh, no."

"Jack found them in the family cemetery, like I said. They don't know who the bones belong to or where they came from, but the police think they were planted there. Ryan said that they didn't look like they'd been there long. Soon after they were discovered, we started seeing the ghost. I think the mother still walks the prairie, looking for her baby."

"That's horrible." Not just because a baby had died, which was unbearably sad in its own right, but that someone had disrespected the bones by moving them. And if they'd planted some poor, sweet baby's bones at the Lucky C on purpose for the sake of scaring the family or confusing the investigation against Abra's attacker, then that was a despicable excuse for a human being.

Hannah shook her head, pushing away the thought that someone could stoop to such depravity. Though she was aghast about the bones, and frustrated on the Coltons' behalf, she didn't believe in ghosts. Did she? Then again, she sure had believed in the possibility a few minutes earlier. She thought about the photograph she'd taken on her phone. Ready to share the photograph with Maria, she looked around for her purse, but realized almost immediately that she'd forgotten it in the office.

"I hope I didn't frighten you all over again," Maria said. "I can't imagine anything else bad happening at the Lucky C. Not with so many people patrolling the grounds and the police investigating the crimes against the family. I'm sure the worst is behind us all."

"I'm sure you're right," she said instead. Hopefully Maria didn't hear the lie in Hannah's words. She clutched the envelope tightly to her chest—the possible proof that not all the worst was behind the Coltons. She hated the idea of breaking it to Brett that his family may have yet another crime to weather.

After Maria left, Hannah locked the suite door, then prowled the rooms, looking for the perfect hiding place for the folder of evidence. Before she'd found one, she saw a Bible she didn't recognize lying open on the vanity.

Even from a distance, she could see a circle of red

marker ink on one page. Baffled, she moved in for a closer look. What she discovered had her huffing in disbelief. Guess her first semilogical explanation that Maria had left it behind had been wrong.

"Mavis, you crazy girl."

The Bible was open to Deuteronomy, the circled verse commanding the righteous to stone unmarried fornicators as a way of purging evil—one of the most popular passages misappropriated by the Congregation of the Second Coming.

Shaking her head at Mavis's nerve, she slid the folder of evidence between the vanity and the wall, out of sight. Then she flipped the pages of the Bible to her favorite psalm about forgiveness. *Let's see you try to twist that verse into something hurtful, Mavis.*

Smiling now, she rummaged through the desk for a pen and circled the verse over and over again until she's created a thick blue frame for the exalted words. Just because her parents' cult could twist the word of God for their own agenda didn't make them right or true. Forget creeps like Rafe and religious fanatics like Mavis; Hannah was above them all. She knew in her heart who she was and what she stood for.

And what she stood for right now was indulging in the late-night snacks that Maria had left for her. Tonight's choices were a plate of fruit, nuts and crackers, as well as a bottle of sparkling apple cider. God bless Maria. She flounced onto the sofa and popped a nut in her mouth.

Inevitably, her thoughts shifted to Brett. He might have rejected her every advance and refused to consider the possibility of them as a couple, but he'd made all this possible for her—the comfy bedroom, the great job, the pampering from Maria and Edith, and, most importantly, the sense of security he'd brought to her life. No matter how jumbled up her feelings were for him, or how unconventional their arrangement, she knew she could count on him, no matter what, even if she hadn't felt very secure on the ranch itself that night. She glanced at the curtained windows, hoping his night had been more peaceful than hers.

The ranch was quiet and the night air was balmy and pleasant, neither of which explained Outlaw's restlessness one bit.

Brett and Daniel sat astride their horses on the far reaches of the ranch's epicenter, keeping one eye on the backcountry and the other on their homestead. The Big House glowed like a beacon in the distance, while the bunkhouse and barns stood like a line of matchsticks. Windows were lit and clusters of men sat outside smoking and shooting the breeze. One ranch hand whom Brett didn't recognize in the dim light strummed a guitar. Every now and then, he caught a chord on the breeze.

When Outlaw whinnied and stamped the ground for the hundredth time, Daniel tipped his head towards Brett's horse. "My horses have been on edge lately, too. Their appetites are low and they're nipping at each other. Something's in the air."

"We're feeling it at our end of the ranch with the

workers. A few of them swear they've seen a ghost in the field. A woman."

"What do you think?" Daniel asked.

Brett swung his attention away from the homestead and toward the darkness. "Like you said, something's in the air. All I know is that it sure wasn't a ghost who put my mother in the hospital or tampered with our fences."

"Not to mention the bones in the cemetery last month."

"Man, that was terrible. Disturbing." Even now, the memory of those bones haunted Brett's mind in Technicolor detail. "What I don't get is why the perpetrator would still be skulking around the ranch. And the hospital, if we believe that druggie who tried to sell Mother's locket to a pawnshop."

Daniel's gaze went distant. "Secrets."

"I don't follow."

Daniel shrugged. "Maybe the perp accidentally left something behind around here. Or he didn't find what he was looking for in Abra's room. There would be lots of reasons to come back, which is why you and I are killing a perfectly good night sitting out here in the dark."

Damn, Brett prayed that neither of those motives held true, because if that were the case, then no one on the ranch was safe. "I hope you're wrong. But I still don't get what you meant by *secrets*."

"The ranch is too far off the beaten path for a small-time crook to risk, so I don't think jewelry was the main point of the break-in. Not for the relatively low-value items that were stolen, and not given that photo albums were also taken. So if money wasn't the motivation, then that means secrets are involved."

Yeah, right. "That's a nice theory and all, except for one thing. My mother doesn't have any secrets. She's a depressed, bitter socialite." Saying the words dredged up all the frustration and pain of their combative relationship. He would forever regret his last words to her before her attack, and when—he refused to think of it as an *if*—she woke, he'd be the first in line at her bedside to tell her that he forgave her and ask for her forgiveness in return, but that didn't mean he was obligated to transform her into a saint in his mind.

Daniel gave him a look. "Everybody and every place has secrets, bro." He spurred his mount into motion, headed away from the homestead to the fence line in the distance.

Brett gave a long look at Daniel's back, at the shoulders that were unmistakably Colton DNA. Daniel's mother had been Brett's father's mistress—his father's secret. Maybe Daniel was onto something with his theory.

Brett urged Outlaw to catch up, his mind chewing over the possibility that his mother could have brought the attack on herself through keeping a secret of her own. No way. Not Abra Colton. If she'd gotten herself in hot water, she would've come racing to Brett's dad for help.

As fast as Daniel had taken off, he brought his horse to a stop. Brett instructed Outlaw to do the same.

Daniel brought his rifle up, aiming it to his right. "Did you see that?"

Brett scanned the countryside in the direction that Daniel's rifle was pointed, but saw only tall grasses and scrub trees in the last lingering indigo glow of daylight. "No. What?"

Daniel nodded to his right. "Three o'clock. I saw movement."

"Coyote?"

"Not sure. Probably, but it looked bigger to me."

They stood still and quiet. Brett strained his eyes. Then he saw it, a glimpse of movement more than two football fields away. With the gait and the shape, it had to be the head or back of a large animal or a small man, its form black against the night and moving quickly away from them on top of a small rise.

Brett took up his rifle and whispered, "Come on. Let's see what, or who, we've found."

They proceeded forward with caution, letting their horses pick their way quiet and steady over the land. Brett's senses were on high alert now. He heard every crunch of grass under the horses' hooves, every rustle of leaves in the breeze. He was keenly aware of his own loud, fast heartbeat and the twitchy urge of his trigger finger where he held it straight against his .22.

How long had it been since he'd shot a gun? Several months, at least. It was one of those skills that never left a man completely, but he sure hoped he wouldn't need to pull the trigger tonight.

They were nearly to the top of the rise where they'd seen the movement when a flare of light burst to life on the far side of the rise and reflected off the clouds. Brett and Daniel stopped their horses and exchanged a nervous glance. Brett adjusted his shotgun against his shoulder, his eyes locked on the glow coming from the other side of the hill.

That's when he saw it—a flicker that could only be one thing.

"Fire," Brett said, urging Outlaw back into motion.

With a curse, Daniel sped to join him. They raced over the hill. The hunting shed they sometimes used when there was evidence in the area of bobcats, coyotes or mountain lions was fully engulfed in flames.

"I'll radio for help," Daniel said. "You keep looking and I'll catch up with you. We've got to catch whoever did this and I'm guessing they're not going to hang around to watch us put the fire out."

Brett and Outlaw took off into the prairie, cutting a wide path around the burning building. He kept his head on a swivel, straining for a glimpse of movement in the darkness, but the light of the fire hindered his night vision. It took a long time for his eyes to adjust enough to see anything but the silhouettes of trees, boulders and the horizon.

Then, he saw it again. Movement. At first glimpse of something making haste across the prairie a good fifty yards to his left, Brett sucked in a breath in shock. He slowed Outlaw while his eyes got a read on the motion again. Something or someone was definitely out there with him, something as big as a person, rustling the underbrush and running on foot fast away from him. Contrary to Maria's imagination, this was no prairie ghost, so it'd only be a matter of seconds before Outlaw caught up to him. Or it.

Gun at the ready, he nudged Outlaw's flank.

Then, somewhere nearby, a gunshot fired.

Chapter 10

The darkness was disorienting, but the gunshot seemed to have come from the direction of the outbuilding. Out on the prairie, there were few places a man and horse could hide that would shield them from gunfire. Brett briefly considered pulling his flashlight from his saddlebag because the dark was so frustrating in its limitations, but that would do little more than blind him to the world beyond the limited scope of the beam. Listening for sounds of movement was still his best choice.

He held his breath, held Outlaw perfectly still, and opened his ears. Nothing but the hollow, droning whistle of wind across the grass and the faint crackle of burning wood in the distance. To his right, a twig snapped, followed by a rustling sound. Brett swung his attention and rifle in that direction.

"Freeze! Or I'm going to blow your head off," he bellowed.

He would never shoot without first having a visual on his target, but maybe his threat would inspire the trespasser to speak up. More rustling sounded, getting farther away. Brett gave a slight tug of pressure to Outlaw's rein, commanding him forward a few steps.

A howl cut through the breeze. Outlaw stiffened and stopped moving, his ears tall. Brett couldn't make sense of the sound, higher pitched than a dog's wail or the keening of tornado sirens. It was the kind of sound that crawled under your skin and came back out in nightmares, or when your mind was in the twilight zone between sleep and waking.

Brett kept up his visual scan of the surrounding prairie, but saw nothing.

Then the sound cut off as though someone had hit Stop on a stereo, though it echoed in Brett's ears for several moments longer until it was eclipsed by the sounds of Brett's pounding heart and his panting breaths.

The next gust of wind carried with it the noxious odor of burning wood laced with chemicals. The fire.

He pulled his phone from his pocket and called Daniel. "Did you hear that sound? That howl?"

"Huh? No, but I thought I heard a gunshot. Are you okay?"

"Fine. I heard the shot, too, but I lost the trail. Whoever set that fire and shot at us is long gone," Brett said.

"A crew's on their way from the ranch, bringing the water tank."

"Police? Fire department?"

"I haven't called them yet. I figured we'd see what we've got first. They might just get in the way of our investigation."

Ryan would be ticked off beyond belief if they didn't clue him in, but he agreed with Daniel's plan to wait and see. He gave a wiggle of the rein with his right hand, turning Outlaw in the direction of the fire. "I'm headed back your way."

"Keep your eyes open and your gun ready."

Brett gave one last look over his shoulder. "Copy that."

At the site of the fire, Daniel, along with Rafe, Jack and at least a half dozen ranch workers had already doused the flames with water from the tanker truck, which idled nearby, its headlights illuminating the scene. The men stood around the burned-out shell of the hunting blind, hands on hips, pointing and talking.

Brett dismounted a fair distance away, hoping to spare Outlaw from breathing the most concentrated levels of residual smoke and fumes. He walked toward the men, his gaze still scanning the horizon for movement, though he felt in his bones that the perpetrator had vanished.

Ash and carbon scattered in the breeze, kicking around Brett's boots as he walked. A particularly large piece of ash tumbled across the ground in his direction. Brett bent forward and plucked it up. He knew the moment his fingers touched it that it wasn't ash, but a photograph. He angled it into the light from the tanker's headlights.

It was from a Christmas card from years and years

ago. He, his brothers and sister, and his parents posed in front of a beige studio backdrop, all dressed in Sunday finery. Every set of their eyes had been gouged out.

The parking lot of the Tulsa police precinct that Ryan worked in was packed. Brett found a spot on the street, then texted Ryan about his arrival as he trekked to the main entrance. The lobby was mostly full. Behind the front desk, uniformed and plainclothes officers carried on with their busy morning, most anchored to their desks with their fingers busy at keyboards.

A bony woman with frizzy gray hair and a variety of tattered bags and purses slung over her right shoulder stood at the front desk, demanding answers about why her next-door neighbor hadn't yet been arrested for spying on her, despite the numerous police reports that the woman had filed. The receptionist had patient eyes and a serious expression, as though she earnestly valued every opinion and complaint lobbed at her throughout her shift.

A jingle of keys preceded Ryan's arrival in the lobby. He was dressed in beige slacks and a blue dress shirt unbuttoned at the collar. He'd rolled the sleeves up over his forearms and had affixed his badge to his brown leather belt, right next to his holstered firearm. Nobody exuded effortless confidence like his brother Ryan.

"Thanks for meeting with me," Brett said, standing.

"I've been at my desk this morning, drowning in paperwork, so I appreciate the break." The frizzy-haired woman at the front desk slapped her palm on the counter, her voice turning shrill. Ryan eyed her for a beat, then turned his attention back to Brett. "Let's go to my office. I just made a fresh pot of coffee."

He followed Ryan through the maze of hallways. The mention of coffee conjured a vision of Hannah in Brett's mind and brought a smile to his lips as he recalled her first morning at the ranch. She'd tried hard to tough it out that morning at breakfast, but he wasn't sure he'd ever seen anyone so green around the gills. Thankfully, her morning sickness seemed to be fading. Even still, she'd rallied like a trouper every morning, insisting on getting right to work—highlighting a one-two punch of moxie and self-deprecating charm that had—

He shook his head. There he went again, damn it all. Daydreaming like a smitten schoolboy. It was high-time he knocked that nonsense off because his wayward thoughts were making it harder and harder to think clearly when it came to protecting the woman and child in his charge. Now, more than ever, he needed to stay focused on what mattered most—keeping them safe.

Ryan stopped at his office door and ushered Brett in. "Don't try to tell me that smile is because I'm offering you coffee."

"Nah. Just thinkin'."

Ryan gave him a poke in the ribs as he passed. "About your baby mama, I bet."

"Lucky guess."

"No way. That was me using my advanced detective skills. How are the two of you doing?" He pushed the door to his office closed with his shoe, then made a beeline to the coffeepot on the table in the corner.

Brett took a seat in front of the desk. "She's already

proved to be a major asset to the business, and she's helping me come up with a horse-breeding proposal to present to Jack and Pops, which is invaluable."

Filling two mugs with coffee, Ryan frowned. "That's a cop-out answer."

"How do you figure that?"

He handed Brett a mug. "What I asked was, how are you two getting along? I mean, you'd only met her twice before she moved in with you, right? So, how's it going? Do you like her?"

"Don't you ever get tired of interrogating people?"

Ryan assumed his seat behind the desk. "Nope."

Brett sipped his coffee. "Well, she won over the whole house within the first five minutes of them laying eyes on her, just like I knew she would, and she's been charming the socks off everyone ever since. And at least once a day, she gets this look in her eyes like she wants me to kiss her, and every single time, I come about this close to caving. And there's nothing sayin' I'd be able to stop with just a kiss. So I'm pretty miserable."

Ryan snorted. "How would making out with her be a bad thing?"

"Because I'm ninety-nine percent sure that would've been the wrong move. Her pregnancy hormones tend to make her rather…passionate, you might say. But there's no getting around the fact that she's in a vulnerable position. No matter what Little Brett is telling me to do, sleeping with her is not the right move. She and the baby are my responsibility and I'm not going to muck all that up by overstepping my boundaries."

Ryan raised his mug in a salute. "Mature."

"Precisely. Thank you." That was exactly what he was determined to be—no matter how kissable she looked or how ardently she tried to seduce him. "Thankfully, most of our evenings together are cut short by my patrol shifts."

"That's a helluva thing, that fire last night. I'm glad you and Daniel called me in. I can't figure out why anyone would be motivated to start a fire all the way out in the back fields."

"The fire marshal had just arrived at the ranch before I left to come here."

"Good," Ryan said. "He should have some answers for us soon about the cause and origin point. But I'm fairly certain that you haven't come all the way here for advice on your love life or to talk any more about the fire, since we just saw each other a few short hours ago." He threaded his hands together behind his head and leaned back in his chair. "So, to what do I owe this visit?"

"I might have some insight as to the motivation of our arsonist." Brett slid the defaced Christmas photo across the desk. He'd taken the precaution of sealing it in a plastic ziplock bag, hanging his hope on the chance that the police would be able to salvage fingerprints or DNA from it. "I found this at the scene of the fire, but I haven't shared it with anyone yet. I wanted to talk with you first."

Ryan left the photograph on his desk and stared at it for a long time, his expression inscrutable. Then he scrubbed a hand over his mouth. He picked the bag up and held it close to his face while he took a slow drink of coffee.

"I'm pretty sure that's from one of the photo albums stolen from Mom's room," Brett said into the stretching silence. "And it's defaced in the same way as Greta's photograph in the stolen locket the police found outside the hospital."

Ryan set the photograph on the desk again and leveled a somber look at Brett. "Well, holy hell. If there was any doubt before, there won't be now. This makes it personal."

"My thoughts exactly. This confirms our suspicion that the hit man who went after Tracy last month wasn't Mom's attacker and that her attack wasn't a random robbery gone bad. Whoever it was, they knew where her room was, where she kept her jewelry and her photo albums, and—" he speared a finger onto the desk near the photograph "—they cared enough to deface our family memories. Multiple times."

"And they set that building on fire knowing you'd find it, along with the photograph. It was a plant. Just like the locket."

Brett nodded. "I hate the way this is shaping up."

"Me, too. Who knew where you and Daniel were patrolling last night?" Ryan asked.

"No one. We decided which direction we'd go after he came to the office to get me. But anyone who was at the ranch could've seen which direction we left in."

"That's what I'm afraid of."

"What?"

Ryan rolled his gaze up from the photograph to pin

Brett with a grave look. "That whoever's behind all this damage and Abra's attack works at the ranch."

A chill crawled under Brett's skin. How could he keep Hannah safe if the danger was right under their noses, invisible in plain sight? "Like I said, I hate the direction this is going."

"You said you didn't show this photograph to anyone else? Not even Daniel or Hannah?"

"No one. Not Daniel, and definitely not Hannah. I don't want her to worry unnecessarily."

Ryan nodded. "Let's keep it that way for now, until I've had a chance to think this through. If whoever's doing this lives and works at the ranch, then the fewer people who're aware of the evidence, the better. Someone wants to hurt our family. Not just Mom, but all of us."

Brett was too agitated to sit. He pushed up from the chair and paced to the door, staring blankly through the glass into the hall. "Why would someone do all this? What do they have against our family?"

Daniel's theory about secrets popped into Brett's head. But secrets about whom? And what?

"No idea what the motive is," Ryan said. "None of it makes sense yet, but it's going to very soon because I'm not going to rest until it does."

"I just moved the mother of my child onto the ranch. I told her I would take care of her and the baby and keep them safe, but how can I do that if Mom's attacker is right under our noses?" He pivoted and pinned Ryan with a stare. "I have a family to protect now, damn it."

Ryan pressed his hands into the desk and stood.

"We're going to get this guy. I promise you that." He took the bag holding the defaced photograph in hand. "Follow me."

He strode out of his office and down the hall. Brett followed. They stopped in front of a partially open office door. Ryan gave a little wave through the glass, then entered. Brett hovered in the hall, reading the name plate next to the door. Detective Susan Howard—Forensic Investigator.

Detective Howard was sitting behind her desk, working on her computer. She didn't look older than thirty, with blond hair pulled into a tight bun and a no-nonsense air about her that oozed competence and intelligence.

When she noticed Ryan, she rose. "Ryan. Hi. It's nice to see you." She rushed to stack files on her desk and toss some trash in the wastebasket. "I, um, wasn't expecting to see you today."

Once upon a time, Brett had fancied himself an expert on women, so he felt confident in his assessment that the good detective was flustered to see Ryan in her office. She also looked like the kind of woman Brett would've hit on in a heartbeat before his car accident, with a fit, curvy body that would make any man with a pulse do a double take, right up until he realized that she was armed and could probably kick his butt to Mexico, should she get it in her mind to.

"Hey. Yeah, sorry to bother you," Ryan said. "I need a favor."

She came around the side of her desk and propped a hip on the corner of it. "Everything okay?"

"Not sure. More trouble at my family's ranch."

She strummed her fingers on the desk. "You should let me help you more often, Ryan. It's my job. Just because you and I didn't—"

"Have you met my brother Brett yet? Brett, this is Detective Howard, our forensics investigator." Ryan practically dragged Brett into the room by the arm.

A flash of surprise crossed the detective's face, as though she'd assumed until that point that she and Ryan were alone. "Oh. Hello."

Brett held his hand out in greeting. "Pleased to meet you, Detective."

"I'm sorry for all your family's gone through lately." All business now, she folded her arms in front of her, tapping her fingertip against her elbow. "What's this favor that you need?"

Ryan held the photograph up. "A rush job on fingerprints."

She took the bag from him and perused the photo. "This is your family?"

"It is. Hard to tell with the eyes scratched out, I know."

She twisted to reach for a pair of reading glasses on the desk. Then, as Ryan had, she held the photograph up close to her face and studied it in silence. "Where did you find it? In a fire?"

"How'd you guess?"

"I see bits of ash." Her eyes tracked from one end of the photograph to the other as though she were reading a book. "Am I going to find a police report about this fire?"

Ryan's posture went stiff. "No. Not yet. It happened last night. But the fire marshal was sent to investigate today, so the report's coming."

She walked to a cabinet, unlocked the combination lock, then set the photograph inside and relocked it. "I've got another rush job to finish right now for that murder case that came in last week, but I'll process the photograph for you tonight."

"Thank you. You're a lifesaver. If I'm not here at the office, then text me the results."

She tossed a notepad at him. "You'll have to give me your number again, because it's not in my phone anymore."

Brett detected the slightest hint of a sharp edge to her tone and took a step back, deciding he might be better off waiting in the hall while Ryan finished up.

Ryan jotted on the pad and handed it back to her, then shifted his weight, looking uncomfortable. He hooked his thumb toward the door. "Thank you. We should go. But, uh, thanks again."

Back in Ryan's office, Brett had planned on heading out to let Ryan get back to work, but then Ryan topped off Brett's coffee cup, so Brett took a seat to enjoy it.

Ryan sat next to Brett and sipped from his own cup. "Hey, by the way, I like her."

"Who? Detective Howard?"

A bit of coffee sloshed over the rim of Ryan's mug when he jolted. "Huh? No, I mean. Susie's great, and I...uh. I was talking about Hannah. Earlier, we got sidetracked talking about the fire, so I didn't have a chance to tell you that. At the family meeting last week, you told us to wait until we met Hannah before casting judgment and you were right. She's pretty great."

The vindication felt good. He'd learned to endure their disappointment, but Hannah deserved better. "Thank you for saying so. You're right. She's incredible." He felt a stupid smile coming on and let it shape his lips without a fight. "She's got Dad wrapped around her little finger and he's loving it. Edith and Maria, Hannah's started calling those two her fairy godmothers because all they do is fuss over her, like the rest of us are chopped liver. I can't imagine what it's going to be like when the baby comes. We're all going to be invisible to Edith and Maria."

"You don't look like you mind that so much."

Brett shook his head. "It's been a heck of a year for me. It seemed like everything that could go wrong did, except I'm excited about the baby—now that I've had time to adjust to the idea—and I like Hannah. A lot. Too much."

Ryan's lips twitched into a grin. "For what it's worth, I think you're going to be a great father."

"Thank you. Seriously. It's nice to inspire confidence for a change."

But as Brett finished is coffee and stood, the truth came back to him about why he was at the police precinct that morning.

"You look like you're plotting a murder. What's going on inside your brain now?" Ryan said.

"It doesn't matter how great of a father you think I'm going to be, or how blown away everyone is by Hannah. Because the fact remains that someone has it out for us and our ranch. Someone violent and ruthless, with inscrutable motives that are anyone's guess. How do we catch a guy like that? With patrols and fingerprinting and constantly playing defense? That's the best we can do to keep our family safe?"

Ryan squeezed his shoulder. "Like I told you, we'll get this guy. I've got officers on the scene of the fire gathering evidence. With all the rain we've had lately, whoever did this had to have left tracks on the ground, coming and going. And the fire marshal is doing his thing, too. If he can pinpoint the accelerant the perp used, then maybe we have our first lead."

Brett breathed through his frustration until he'd collected himself. "You should know that I'm going to do everything in my power to catch this guy myself."

Ryan's eyes narrowed. "Within the purview of the law, is what you meant, right? You're not going to go vigilante on me, are you?"

Brett leveled a hard look at his brother. "I'm going to do whatever it takes to keep the mother of my child safe, so if you're worried about my methods, then I suggest you and the law find this bastard before I do."

Chapter 11

Hannah woke from another restless night's sleep. The baby's flutters of movement had morphed into full-blown soccer matches in her belly, and he or she was quite fond of midnight game times—just in time for her to hear Brett arrive in his room after the nearly nightly patrols around the grounds that he continued to volunteer for.

She couldn't decide if the ranch was really in that much danger or if he was trying to avoid her. Maybe he just loved riding around the ranch in the dark, for all she knew. Either way, the effect was the same: she was rarely ever alone with him anymore. But once she heard him enter his room after midnight each night, she couldn't go back to sleep because she was too busy listening.

It was torture on her overactive libido to hear his shower water start, and to imagine him stripping down, his muscles sore from a long night of riding. So many times, she'd knelt in her bed facing the wall, her fist up and ready to knock…right up until she thought better of it. Ever since their near-kiss that first night, he'd been polite and attentive, but emotionally distant. That was probably for the better because the more she'd gotten to know him, the more those same fears that Lori had guessed during their *pros and cons* game that first day at the ranch came rushing back to her in full force.

Not fears about Brett's indiscriminate pantie-melting charm, because she knew better now that he was no longer a partying womanizer. She had complete trust in him and in his assertion that his priorities and attitude had permanently changed from the man she'd hooked up with in the club. True, her physical attraction to him was even more potent than the night they'd slept together, but beyond that, she genuinely *liked* him. And that, in a nutshell, was her fear. It would be so easy for her fall for Brett Colton—and fall hard and fast in a forever kind of way.

His bedroom was silent this morning, which probably meant he'd caught only a few hours' sleep before rising to tackle the daily ranch chores. She pressed her palm to the wall, sending him a silent greeting, then emerged from her bedroom to find a tray holding a fresh biscuit, jam and a carafe of milk. Edith's doing. Ever since Hannah's first morning at the Lucky C and the terrible morning sickness she'd experienced, Edith had gone out of her way to make sure Hannah was comfortable and nausea-free.

No more eggs, ever, and coffee was now prepared on the front porch, which had turned out to be a welcome improvement for the ranch workers and Coltons, Edith had told her, because they no longer had to take off their boots to refill their mugs. And every morning, Hannah woke to find a tray of stomach-settling food in her sitting room. Whether it was from Edith and Maria's ministrations, or because her morning sickness was finally subsiding as the pregnancy books professed, Hannah was feeling stronger and less sick with every passing morning. She could proudly say she hadn't thrown up in a whole week, since her second day at the ranch.

As she nibbled the biscuit, she looked out over the ranch and watched the men and women work—cattle being moved, big machines moving alfalfa and feed. She gave a little gasp of surprise when Brett appeared in her field of view. Dressed in a black cowboy hat, a camo-green T-shirt and jeans, he strode over the grounds talking into a radio, a clipboard in his other hand and Rafe walking by his side, consulting his own clipboard.

She stood at the balcony door, eating jam right out of the jar, her eyes on Brett, studying, yearning. Probably, he was right that they should leave well enough alone. Sex and romance would overcomplicate their relationship, damage it, even, because relationship statistics weren't on their side. The odds of them starting a romantic relationship that was lasting were minuscule. Who did that? Who met at a club, had wicked animal sex, didn't bother exchanging phone numbers, got pregnant, and then ended up falling in love? That was crazy talk.

With her mind on Brett and their future, she emerged from her suite in search of breakfast. The door to Greta's suite was open. She'd been staying at the ranch on weekends, to give her dad moral support. When Hannah passed her door, she saw Greta standing in the sitting room of her suite, holding a paper, a hand over her mouth and a worried expression weighing in her eyes.

Hannah paused midstep. "Greta? You okay?"

With a gasp, Greta jumped, her hands flying up and the envelope fluttering to the ground along with what looked like a newspaper clipping.

Hannah rushed forward to pick up the fallen papers. "Sorry. I didn't mean to startle you."

Greta swooped down and snatched up the papers before Hannah could. "It's okay. I just… I got something in the mail that rattled me."

Hannah angled her face to look at the newspaper clipping Greta held. It was a copy of Greta and Mark's engagement announcement. The photograph was circled in a red pen and a large red *X* crossed out Greta's face. Her eyes were gouged out.

"What the…" Hannah said.

Greta pressed the clipping to her chest, hiding it from view. "I'm sure it's nothing."

"This isn't nothing, Greta. Are there any indications of who sent it?"

Greta walked to the sofa and sank onto it. "Probably one of Mark's ex-girlfriends. He has a lot of them."

Hannah wasn't sure where to start—at the pain dripping from Greta's admission that Mark had a lot of ex-girlfriends, or the fact that one of them might be crazy enough to send an anonymous threatening letter to Greta, despite how much she and the Coltons had gone through in the past month.

Hannah assumed a seat next to Greta. "Whoever did this, why would they send it here and not your apartment or Mark's apartment?"

She gestured to a tall chest of drawers near the door where it looked like a stack of mail sat. "I still get a fair amount of mail here. Edith collects it and puts it in here for when I pass through. The postmark is the downtown Tulsa post office."

"You should show Ryan. If someone has it out for you, then it's best to start an official paper trail now."

Instead of heeding Hannah's advice, she crumpled the newspaper clipping up and tossed it in the wastepaper bin by the bed. "Like I said. It's probably just a jealous ex-girlfriend."

"Do you really believe that? I don't think there are as many crazy ex-girlfriends floating around this world as television shows and movies make there out to be."

At that moment, Mavis chose to walk by, a laundry basket on her hip. Could she have done this? After planting that Bible in Hannah's room, she wouldn't put it past Mavis to do something like this to Greta if she got it in her head that Greta was a sinner, too. The thought of it made Hannah spitting mad.

"Maybe not, but who else could it be?" Greta said. "Regardless, something this minor isn't worth worrying my brothers or dad over. They have enough on their minds."

After a deep breath, Greta gave a whole body shake, as if sloughing off her worry.

"You should at least talk to Mark," Hannah said.

Greta winced. "Maybe. But until I decide what to do, don't tell anyone, okay?"

Hannah gathered her in a hug. They hadn't spent much time together or been able to bond since Hannah came to live at the ranch, but Greta was clearly rattled and a hug seemed like the perfect gesture to let her know she wasn't alone. "If you want to talk more, I'm here. Even if it's just about Mark and his exes. I mean, I can relate. Look at the man in my life right now. Brett and I aren't even romantically involved and I still don't want to know how many exes he has."

A halfhearted smile spread on Greta's face. "That's an easy answer—zero. He never dated anyone long enough to consider them exes."

Hannah chuckled. "Comforting. Thank you. I feel so much better now about the odds of convincing him to give a relationship with me a try." Hannah's face instantly heated. "I didn't mean that. I mean, I did. I do, because he's amazing, but—"

Greta braced her arms on Hannah's shoulders. "Your secret's safe with me. And here's some advice—give Brett some time. The accident he was in four months ago really scared him. He hasn't been the same since. I know my dad and brothers are hard on him, but he's trying his best to turn his life around. He's a good man."

"I agree. A very good man. Thank you."

They shared a smile.

"No, thank *you* for poking your head in here," Greta said. "We should go out together sometime. Maybe you'd like to go shopping one day? We could look at baby clothes, and maybe register for your baby shower."

Hannah leaned back and stared at the ceiling. "Oh, goodness, I haven't given any thought to that at all."

"I'd love to plan one for you. It'd help take my mind off my worries about Mom and postponing my wedding. Please say you'll let me."

Hannah hugged her again, because she looked as if she needed as many hugs as she could get. Hannah couldn't imagine how difficult the past month had been on Greta. For as distant and strained as Brett's relationship was with their mother, she and Greta had clearly been close.

"I'd love for you to do that. And I'd love to go shopping with you. Just name the day and time."

Greta sniffed. "Thank you for giving me something to look forward to."

After another round of hugs, Hannah gave an excuse of being hungry for breakfast, then stomped down the grand staircase, through the formal living room, through the servants' wing and down the stairs to the basement where the laundry room was located.

"Mavis Turnbolt, are you down here?"

She was greeted with nothing but silence, save for the hums and rattles of the running washer and dryer from the laundry room tucked under the stairs. She poked her head around every corner of the basement, but found no one. Back up the stairs and through the house she went, room by room, angry and determined not to let Mavis get away with any more passive-aggressive threats.

Before today, Hannah hadn't yet ventured into the wing of the house where Big J's and Abra's suites were, nor had she seen the crime scene yet, but that was exactly where she found Mavis—in the sitting room of Abra's suite, threading a gauzy, pale fabric through a long white curtain rod and muttering to herself. Bible verses from the sounds of it.

Abra's suite was awash in sand, cream and silver tones that could have graced a suite at a luxury resort in a desert oasis, from the simple, tight-looped pale rugs that looked as though they'd never been walked on to the elegant chaise lounge and potted palm tree near where Mavis was working.

Hannah surveyed the room, marveling at its beauty though it had been the scene of such a violent act a mere few weeks earlier. The family must have taken great pains to restore the room quickly, with the hope that Abra would return to it soon.

Thinking about everything the Coltons had suffered and that Mavis had poured salt into their wounds with her egregious behavior got Hannah's back up all over again. She barreled into the room, guns blazing. "Turn around and face me, Mavis."

Mavis gave a squeak and whirled around, the curtain rod in hand as though defending herself. "You frightened me," she seethed.

"It's time for you to own up to your own sins, Miss High-and-Mighty. I know it was you who sent that newspaper clipping to Greta."

She kicked at the curtain fabric pooling on the floor over her shoes. "Excuse me?"

Hannah strode closer. "Don't play innocent. You know exactly what I mean."

"I don't, but you'd best keep your distance from me. I don't suffer unrepentant whores well."

Oh, the nerve of this one. Hannah jerked the curtain rod out of her hand. "Is that another threat? What are you going to do, attack me?"

The moment the words left her mouth, a chill came over Hannah. Brett's mother was viciously attacked and left for dead within the very room in which Hannah stood. The carpet was a light cream color and looked brand-new, as though it'd been replaced since the attack. Probably because it'd had Abra's blood on it.

Mavis certainly didn't seem to mind being in Abra's room. Could it be that Mavis was far more sinister than circling Bible verses that threatened death and mailing defaced engagement photographs? Was she capable of assaulting Abra? Hannah wasn't afraid of facing off against Mavis, even physically, but she also had a baby to think about.

Confronting a possible attempted murderer wouldn't be the safest plan, but the more she considered it, the less likely it seemed that Mavis was capable of such an overt act as physically attacking one of her employers. The Congregation of the Second Coming preferred threats and passive judgment. They preferred to leave the actual punishment to God.

"You'd better explain what business you have coming after me. Right now."

Hannah tossed the curtain rod behind her. "The business I'm talking about is the mutilated engagement announcement you sent to Greta. Was that some sort of sick and twisted threat or condemnation of her 'sinful ways'? Well, congratulations, you only succeeded in making yourself look like a petty, vindictive fool."

She speared a finger at Hannah. "I didn't send nothing to Greta, and you'd better stop spreading lies. You had better stop harassing me or I'll—"

"Or you'll what? Leave another Bible for me in my room with more circled verses implying I should be stoned to death for my sins?"

Mavis huffed, indignant, then hoisted a plastic laundry basket onto her hips. "The thought crossed my mind. Heathens need all the divine help they can get. Especially one of Satan's disciples who's carrying a bastard in her womb."

With that, Mavis brushed past Hannah, bumping her belly hard with the laundry basket.

Hannah leaped back, her arms around her belly, protective. Though she knew better than to let herself be drawn in to Mavis's vitriol, the last shreds of Hannah's control snapped at the rough treatment. Nobody physically trespassed against her growing baby and got away with it. She stormed after Mavis, seeing red.

"Don't use that term in this house. And while you're at it, don't you ever speak of my baby again."

Mavis sniggered and pushed out a side entrance of the house, onto the wraparound porch. "And why not? This house is a den of sin. Do you think it's an accident

that so much tragedy has befallen this place? God pun-
ishes sin, and you'd best not forget it."

Hannah raised her open hand, ready to slap Mavis
before she thought better of it. Instead she curled her
fingers into a fist at her side. "Not my God," she said
through clenched teeth.

Mavis whirled to face Hannah, an ugly sneer on her
lips. "My point exactly. Maybe your parents ought to
follow through with their plan to hire an exorcist to rid
you of that demon you're hosting."

Of all the things. An exorcist? They wouldn't dare.
The final threads of her composure snapped. She
marched off the porch, hot on Mavis's heels. "Why
would you accept income from a place that's a den of
sin? What are you doing here, anyway?"

"I thought it was my duty to evangelize here, to get
you all to see that sin and the Devil are not the way, but
I'm done with that. There's no helping you or this cursed
family and I'm not giving any more of the Coltons'
dirty money to the church." She untied her apron and
threw it on the ground. "When you're ready to repent,
you know where to find salvation."

Big J strode up as Mavis stomped away. "What was
that about?"

"Mavis Turnbolt just quit."

"Hmph. Never did like that sourpuss." He swiped
the discarded apron from the ground and put it over his
neck. "Well, now that you're doing the ranch's books, I
suppose I'm in search of a new job around here. I think
I'm going to need a bigger apron, though."

Despite herself, Hannah smiled; he looked so silly

and the thought of a big old burly cowboy like him fussing over the laundry was so outrageous. "I don't think you'd last a day. Better leave the laundry to me and Edith while you undertake the task of finding someone new. Just don't hire anybody else from my parents' cult, like Mavis is."

They strolled together toward the office, Big J still with that silly apron on. "Your parents belong to a cult?"

"I used to call it a church, but I know better now. I struck out on my own the day I turned eighteen, without any real knowledge of how the world worked. I got a job at a drugstore and then another at a diner, just to make ends meet. My parents weren't pleased by my life choices, but when my father was forced to retire from working the feed store that he and my mother own, due to his arthritis, I sucked up my pride and took over management of the store. I figured when my mother retired, too, I'd buy it from them and I went to college so I could learn how to be a good business owner and manage the store's finances properly."

"And then you got pregnant."

They'd stopped in front of the steps that led to the office. "Yes. Everything changed."

He set a hand on her shoulder, then leaned in and kissed her cheek. "For the better. Because now we have you here."

She untwisted the apron string around Big J's neck. "Agreed. One hundred percent. I love it here."

And though she'd originally planned to move away as soon as she got her first paycheck, she couldn't imagine leaving now.

"Has my son asked you to marry him yet?"

Big J had asked her that same question a few times already. Brett had said his father was increasingly forgetful, but this was the first evidence Hannah had seen of it. "No. And I'm glad he hasn't because I'd turn him down. The only reason I would ever marry is for love."

And even though she was half in love with the man already, it wasn't enough to build a marriage on. Especially not when he didn't return her feelings.

"Ah. Well, he's got time to persuade you before the baby gets here. Say, is it a boy or a girl? I can't remember if Brett told me."

Another red flag went up in her mind. "We talked about that last night at dinner. We're not sure if it's a boy or a girl yet. We'll find out later this month at the ultrasound appointment."

"That's right. We did talk about it. Riding patrol last night with Brett dulled my mind, I'm afraid."

Hannah made a mental note to talk to Brett about his father. Perhaps letting Big J go out on patrol was too taxing a job. She was definitely going to caution Edith against letting him get anywhere near the laundry chores. "It's okay. It was a long night for me, too, worrying about you all out there in the dark."

"You don't need to worry about us. We'd welcome the chance to meet up with the attacker on our land again. Teach them about the consequences of doing harm to the Colton family."

His words chilled Hannah. What if they did confront the attacker? What would they do? Certainly not vigilante justice. She had to hope.

He gestured toward the office. "How's the job going? You making do all right? Do you have any questions?"

"I'm loving my new job. Thank you. The books are complicated, but I'm getting my system in place one step at a time." She debated mentioning to him about the discrepancy, then decided to wait until she'd talked to Brett.

He patted her hand. "You're a good girl. I think I'm going to go grab some coffee. You want any?"

She couldn't decide if he was merely having a bad morning, or if his memory lapses were something his children needed to worry about. She hated to add to Brett's burden, not when so much else was as stake around the ranch. "No, thanks."

"Say, I'm headed to the hospital this afternoon. What would you say about joining me? I know Abra's not conscious, but I'd like to think she can hear us. Meeting you, hearing about the baby, it might give her more of a reason to wake up and come back to us."

If Big J thought it would help Abra wake up, and would give her a reason to keep fighting to stay alive, then it was the least Hannah could do.

"I'd be honored."

Chapter 12

The thin, frail woman in the ICU bed didn't look a thing like Brett, nor Eric, who'd walked Big J and Hannah to Abra's room, nor any of her other children, really. Not only that, but she didn't *look* like she was capable of giving birth to five children, she was so bony and fragile-looking beneath the purple-and-cream-colored quilt covering her bed. Her skin was as translucent as tissue paper and her dark brown hair was going gray at the roots.

The room itself was peaceful. Little loving touches were all over, including the quilt, which looked home-made, innumerable cards and a large vase of flowers that adorned the table near the window. Hannah hung back with Eric at the door as Big J assumed the seat near Abra's head and took her hand.

"Honey, you've got a special visitor today and we've got something big to tell you. You're going to be so happy, just like we all are. We found out that Brett's going to be a father. The mother of his child is here to meet you. Hannah is her name. You're going to love her as much as we all do, I can guarantee it."

At Big J's urging, Hannah pulled a seat around to the other side of the bed and took Abra's hand. It was warm and full of life, yet smooth, as though she'd never worked a day of manual labor, despite living on a ranch for several decades. "Hello, Abra. It's so wonderful to meet you. I wish it was under different circumstances, but I want you to know that you're going to be a grandma again, in about eighteen weeks."

"We just want you to wake up, honey. The family isn't the same without you. Greta's putting her wedding plans on hold, waiting for her momma to help her out again." His voice caught on the last word. He brought a handkerchief out from his pocket and swabbed his eyes. "And we can't be disappointing Greta, not after all the trouble I went through to get us that baby girl."

Hannah cringed inwardly. No wonder Brett felt like a perpetual disappointment to his parents, with his dad talking about him as though he was nothing but a hindrance to them in their quest to have a daughter.

"What's going on here?"

Eric was gone and in his place at the door stood Brett, his eyes glinting with irritation.

Hannah's heart sank. He must have heard his father's unfortunate choice of words. Though she wished she could wrap her arms around him and soothe his torment, he didn't welcome her touch, and she'd do well to remember that.

She stood, feeling her own sudden surge of defensiveness.

"Your dad asked me to come with him, to tell your mom about the baby."

Her explanation did nothing to diffuse his defensiveness. If anything, his scowl intensified as he held his father's gaze. "I already have. I came and told her the day I found out."

Big J stroked a hand over Abra's hair. "Oh, well, now, that's even better. We've got to keep reminding her of all she has to live for until she wakes up. What are you doing in town, Brett? It's a surprise to see you here."

"I was in town getting a contract notarized for Geronimo's sale, and I thought, since I was already nearby, I'd stop by the hospital. Could I talk to you in the hall, please, Hannah?"

"Sure. Of course."

With a stiff stride, she followed him down the hall. He looked like she felt, his shoulders and back tight, radiating frustration. He couldn't possibly be that upset with her for coming to see his mother, could he?

As soon as they were out of earshot from his mother's room, she said to his back, "My coming here means a lot to your dad," she said. "There was no way I was going to tell him no when he asked." When he kept walking she snagged his arm. "Don't be upset with me. Please."

Brett spun to face her. "I'm not angry with you. I just…" He shook his head, his gaze on the floor. "I can't believe my dad keeps saying stuff like that. You'd think, after all these years, they'd stop thinking about me and my brothers as 'everything they went through' in order to have a girl. That's so screwed up. Just once, I'd like to hear my dad say he's happy to have me as his son. Just once."

Well, that explained that. She stroked a hand over his hair. "He does love you. I can see it in his eyes, and in the way he's showing me such kindness. He loves you and your brothers, but I know what you mean. I cringed when he said that, too."

He glanced up at her. "They have the most miserable marriage. I've never understood it. He loves her so much, and he would've never divorced her, yet he had at least one affair. Who knows how many? It's like the two of them are doomed to be locked in an eternally dysfunctional bond."

He sighed, his shoulders slumping. "I hate how angry I am at her. The last words we spoke before she was attacked were said in anger. I don't know how to forgive her for the years she neglected us all, as though we meant nothing to her. After she had Jack, my dad wanted a girl, and for whatever twisted reason that I don't understand, because she loathed being a mother, she kept popping out babies for him, trying for that little princess. Eric, then Ryan, and you can imagine how distraught they both were when they had me. I've been a disappointment since the day I came out of her womb and they've never let me forget it."

"Why didn't you move away from the ranch, or at least to another house on the property?"

"My mother was gone more than she was home. She

only came home from her travels abroad in Europe because of Greta's engagement party because she had to keep up appearances. I lived at the Big House so my dad wouldn't be alone. And the less noble part of me—the me before my car accident—felt like my parents owed me, that I was entitled to this huge house and a chef and a housekeeper and a laundress."

Hannah nodded. She could see how he'd feel that way, especially before his life-changing accident. "Whoever attacked your mom chose the perfect time because she was rarely ever home. The attacker knew about the engagement party."

"The police thought about that, too. The only problem is that everybody knew about it. It was in the newspapers and local society pages. My mom made sure to splash it everywhere that her little girl, her precious only daughter, was getting married."

"I've only known Greta for a little while, but I bet she didn't appreciate being put up on a pedestal like that."

A bit of the fight drained out of him. "Got that right. But she and Mother were still close, anyway, especially as Greta got older."

She touched his hand. "You're still full of a lot of resentment. That's a heavy burden to be carrying in your heart."

He cocked his head and looked at her for a long time. "I've forgiven both my parents. My dad, especially, a long time ago, but my mother, too. You would think that choosing to forgive someone would take away the anger, but it doesn't. Not completely. I'm not sure I can ever let go of it all. I just hope my mother wakes up so she and I can keep working toward finding peace with each other. This can't be how it ends between us."

She wrapped her arms around him and squeezed, burying her face in his chest. "She will wake up, Brett. We just have to keep praying."

She knew exactly what he meant about the difference between forgiveness and acceptance, because she was struggling in the same way with her parents. If one of her parents were grievously injured and she had to live with the possibility that they might never reconcile, she'd be just as torn up as Brett was.

His dropped his face and nuzzled the top of her head. "I'm sorry I snapped at you earlier. Seeing her here, hearing my dad go on about Greta, leaves me feeling so raw. I just want to be a better parent than my parents were to me."

Standing in a shadowy corner of the hallway, locked in an embrace with the man who'd shared his deepest, rawest feelings and fears with her, she'd never felt closer to another person before. "You will be. And I'm going to be right by your side, trying my best, too. We're a team, you and me."

After a long, quiet moment of connection, of breathing and being in each other's arms, Brett lifted his face and kissed Hannah's cheek. His hand stroked her hair. "I hope this comes out the way I intend it to in my head, but forgive me if it doesn't. I can't believe how lucky I am that when I made the biggest mistake of my life and knocked up a random girl I hooked up with in a club, that it turned out to be you. I mean, of all the women in the world, I can't imagine going through all this with anybody else. It blows my mind, how lucky a man that makes me. We are going to give this baby such an incredible life."

Her eyes crowded with tears that slipped down her cheek and soaked into the fabric of Brett's shirt. "It's the same for me, you know. I had no idea that the man I picked up at a club because he had a killer smile and a tight butt would turn out to be my own personal hero."

"Hero?"

She smoothed her nose along his jaw. "You swooped in and rescued me exactly when I needed it most."

He *tsk*ed, his puff of breath tickling her ear. "It doesn't count as rescuing for a man to take care of the mother of his child, as he's supposed to do, anyway."

"It felt like rescuing, all the same."

She angled her face up to kiss his cheek, but as her lips touched his skin, he turned and captured her mouth with a tender kiss. Her whole body lit up with sensation. She wound her arms around his neck and kissed him back, reverently, trying to let him know without words that he really was her hero.

This kiss was different from their kisses during their first encounter. Those had been reckless and sloppy—a means to satisfying a wholly selfish pleasure. That first kiss hadn't carried any of the connection they'd now forged. She wasn't kissing a hot guy from the nightclub. She was kissing the father of her child.

His hands came up to cradle her face. With a hum of approval, she swept her tongue over his closed lips, wanting more. His body went rigid, and then, as if something had snapped inside him, he pressed her to the wall with a growl, his kiss turning wicked, need-ful. When she opened her mouth for him, he took it, plundering her with his tongue. Her body came alive with a hunger so potent, so desperate, that it was all she could do to cling to him and let him take from her what he demanded.

As abruptly as he'd initiated the kiss, he stopped it. Still cradling her head, he kept his face close, breathing hard through parted lips as he met her searching gaze. "We can't do this. I can't do this."

"Of course we can."

He dropped his hands and peeled away from her.

She pressed her palms to the wall behind her, find-ing her footing and relearning how to breathe.

He propped a forearm on the wall opposite her, his head bent, and let out a sigh that seemed to well up from the deepest, darkest depths of his soul. "I shouldn't have done that. I'm sorry. It's just that I'm finding you harder and harder to resist."

Her heart gave a painful squeeze. She wished he hadn't apologized for doing what they both wanted. "That's a good thing."

His gaze shot up to lock with hers. Gone was the raw need and open heart he'd shared with her only a few moments ago, and it its place was a mask that might as well have been made of iron. "No, it really isn't. Tell me how starting a physical relationship helps us, long term, as coparents? We're in such a good place right now, why would we risk ruining everything?"

"Sometimes risk is worth it."

"Okay, yes, but not in this case. Because what if

things don't work out between us, which is practically a statistical inevitability, and you leave the ranch? Then what happens when the baby's born—I get weekend visitation rights? You already made up your mind to move out as soon as you have the money to afford it. At least if we stay friends, I have a better chance of convincing you to live at Lucky C permanently. We can be a family. It might be unconventional, but it's the best-case scenario to allow me to be a full-time father to my child."

She hated that he was right about so many points, but she couldn't shake the idea that this was a time to think with their hearts, not their brains. "Your whole life, your family's made you feel like you're not good enough, and you let that seep into your thinking and your self-worth. You know how I know that? Because the same happened to me, growing up, and then with this pregnancy. I've never been holy enough or repentant enough. I've never lived up to others' standards."

"You're more than enough, Hannah."

"You're more than enough for me, too. These past few weeks, I've come to care about you. A lot. The more time I spend around you, the more I want to spend. You make me laugh. You make me feel cherished. You make me feel like I'm where I'm supposed to be. I'm not leaving the ranch, Brett. I'm here for good."

The iron mask remained steadfastly in place. "That's easy for you to say today, but how about in a year or two? What happens if we don't work out romantically, and in a couple years down the road you want to start dating again? Are you still going to live with me then? Think about it, Hannah."

She touched his chest, but she may as well have been touching a statue. "I don't want to be afraid to try."

He sidestepped out of reach. "It's not about fear. It's about doing the right thing, the smart thing. Doesn't matter what your hormones or my hormones are telling us to do, I have a responsibility to you and the baby and I'm not going to go mucking it up by taking advantage of you when you're in a vulnerable state. That's something the old Brett would've done, but I'm not that loser anymore."

And with that, he strode away, down the hall, past the open door to his mother's room, and disappeared from view.

The way Hannah saw it, there were only two possible reasons that Brett was killing himself to protect the ranch by patrolling the ranch's eleven thousand acres at all hours of the day and night except for the time he spent mounting security cameras and motion-sensor lights on every building, and changing locks on all the doors of the Big House. Either he wasn't being honest with her and the others about what had happened the night of the hunting blind fire in the backcountry or he was desperate to avoid Hannah.

In the days since their kiss at the hospital, she'd barely seen him except for glimpses of him stolen from her balcony. He was strung out and on edge all the time. She longed to reach out to him, to soothe his worries and get to the heart of what was bothering him, but getting him alone had proved impossible. Even if she could, she wasn't sure she'd try to kiss him again, he was so dead-set on the two of them not getting involved romantically.

Rather than succumb to sleep only to have the baby wake her with its midnight soccer practice, she'd taken to staying up late and using the time to sift through the previous year's bank statements, checks and ledgers, doing as much as she could without the benefit of the computer spreadsheets she'd created. If only she hadn't sold her laptop to pay her student loan, she might be able to avoid the ranch office altogether, thereby avoiding the threat of Rafe stopping by to leer at her under the auspices of offering help.

As midnight neared, her eyes started to burn. She removed her reading glasses and rubbed her eyes. She hadn't finished going through the entire previous year's finances, but she'd gone through another two months' worth of data and had discovered another two thousand dollars to be missing, which put the total close to twenty thousand dollars and change.

She hadn't talked to Brett about the accounting discrepancies because she still wasn't sure if there really was something illegal happening or if she was overthinking the situation. After all, of the two possible scenarios—embezzlement or bad math and typos courtesy of Big J's lack of formal business training—it didn't take a genius to figure out which would, statistically, be the more likely truth. Until she had unequivocal proof of wrongdoing, she refused to burden Brett with her suspicions.

She was gathering the papers into the manila envelope when the baby started in with a thump-thump-flutter rhythm against her ribs. She rubbed the top of her growing baby bump as she hauled herself up from the floor using the sofa arm as support. "A bit early, isn't it, little one?"

She tucked the envelope in the hiding spot behind the vanity, debating how to kill time until the baby simmered down and she dared to attempt sleep. She had a hand on the television remote control when she spotted her phone. Tonight was Lori's night to close at the café.

Can you talk? she texted.

As she waited for a reply, she grabbed the jam jar and a spoon from the tray on the coffee table. Tonight's late-night snack had been a lemon-poppy-seed scone. The scone was long gone but the jar of Maria's homemade strawberry jam was still half full. Her eyes rolled back in her head as the first bite hit her tongue.

Her phone chimed. Sure. I just got home. Call me.

Lori picked up on the first ring. "What are you still doing awake?" she said.

Hannah swallowed another bite of jam and paced to the balcony door, looking out at the night. "Can't sleep. Baby's a midnight acrobat."

"How fun, though, right? To feel it move."

The ranch was quiet, though one of the motion-sensor lights on the barn had turned on. "I do love it."

"So then why don't you sound happier? Is everything okay with your baby daddy?"

How could she explain it to Lori? Her relationship with Brett was so complicated. "He's a great guy. Really great."

"What about that pantie-melting charm you were so worried about?"

"He really is charming, but he's not a player anymore. He's so committed to his family and to being a father. Almost to a fault. He's taking great care of me."

"And by taking care of you, you mean he's bringing you to screaming orgasms every night, right?"

"No. Not that. Not yet."

"His call or yours?"

"His."

Lori groaned. "Don't tell me he's an overthinker like you."

Of all the attributes she was discovering that she and Brett shared, she'd hadn't considered that one, but Lori had a point. "Little bit, yeah. But I've only been here a few weeks. There's time."

"Yes, except that you're a walking, breathing ball of lusty hormones who clearly has a mad crush on your baby daddy. Who happens to sleep *one wall away from you*."

Hannah swirled the spoon in her mouth, her lips kicking up in a smile. "There is that."

"Could you knock on the wall right now and wake him up? Or better yet, burst into his room wearing nothing but sexy lingerie?"

"I don't actually own any sexy lingerie, but I couldn't do that, anyway, because he's out."

"Uh-oh."

"Not like that. Some vandal's been tampering with the fences around the ranch, so he and some of the other men on the ranch have been conducting nightly patrols of the grounds."

"Oh, wow. That's not good. First his mother was attacked during a robbery the month before and now this. Hannah, sweetie, are you safe there?"

Wasn't that the million-dollar question? "I think so. Brett keeps telling me I am."

"I hear a *but*."

"But I don't know. Sometimes I get the weirdest vibes that someone's watching me."

"Creepy."

"Yeah, I know. I think I'm just psyching myself out because…" She debated the merits of sharing the accounting discrepancies with Lori, then decided against it. No need for her to worry.

"Because what?"

Hannah pressed her hand to the window, thinking fast for a reason that would satisfy Lori's curiosity. "A few of the workers swear they've seen ghosts on the prairie."

Lori snorted. "Remember, you're an overthinker. Of course you're psyching yourself out. You're staying in a new home where someone's been attacked and people are talking about ghost sightings. I'd be wigged out, too."

"That's my thought." She mindlessly scooped another spoonful of jam. It wasn't until she'd put the spoon in her mouth that she realized there hadn't been any jam on it. The jar was empty. Disgusted with her lack of self-control, she dropped the spoon into the jar and set it back on the tray.

"But if you ever start to feel unsafe for real, you know we've always got room for you here."

Hannah had briefly considered moving off the ranch

until the culprit had been caught, but she'd dismissed the idea almost immediately, knowing that Brett would consider that a personal failure of his to be her and the baby's provider. Moving away would damage their fledgling partnership. Besides, she didn't yet own a car and had no idea how she'd get to and from the ranch every day to work if she moved back in with Lori.

"Thank you," Hannah said. "I'll keep that in mind, but every day I'm more sure I belong here."

"Okay, well, my offer stands."

"I love you, sweetie."

"Love you, too. Now start planning how you're going to seduce this new, gentlemanly Brett Colton before he steals your heart completely."

He already has. "I'll give it some more thought. And thanks for the sexual pep talk, as usual."

"That's what I'm here for."

When their call ended, Hannah navigated the touch screen of her phone to her photographs and checked out the shot she'd taken of the mystery woman. Really, it could be anyone. The daughter of one of the ranch workers, a girlfriend, one of the maids who worked for Jack. Anyone. But it looked an awful lot like Greta. Same length and color of hair, a similar build and same shape of her face.

If there had been a strange woman lurking about in broad daylight, then Hannah wouldn't have been the only person to spot her. *Others have spotted her. They think she's a ghost.*

With a shiver, Hannah dropped her phone back to the table where it was charging and walked to the balcony.

After belting the robe she wore, she flung the French doors open and stepped outside. There were no ghosts in sight tonight, no lurking young women or would-be robbers. Just the balmy July night. The sky was cloudy, the half moon shrouded and casting only a faint gray glow over the roofs of the ranch buildings and the tips of the wild grasses.

The longer she stood outside, taking deep breaths, the stillness and peace of the ranch seeped into her bones. Then, in the distance, she spied movement, all shadows and darkness silhouetted in the moonlight. A tingle of fear crept up her spine.

That had to be Brett and Daniel coming home from patrol, didn't it? But what if it wasn't? What would she do if that was the perpetrator? She backed into a shadow on the balcony, hiding in plain sight from whoever it was who was approaching the ranch.

Then the clouds moved from in front of the moon and she saw that the movement was two horses, with men on them. That had to be Brett and Daniel. She strained her eyes, watching. When the riders crested a short rise, she made out their identities clearly. Her heart gave a flutter. She stepped from the shadows again and walked to the balcony railing.

It wasn't long after Hannah stepped to the rail that Daniel noticed her. He said something to Brett and gestured with his head. Brett's face shot up. His gaze locked onto Hannah. She raised a hand in a wave that he didn't return.

Daniel said something else to him, then tugged the reins of his horse and took off in a gallop toward the stable. Brett continued on a direct path to her. He cut such a fine figure on the horse, a rifle slung across his back on a strap.

The closer he got, the more she realized that he wasn't happy to see her. She kept a smile on her face and affection warming her features, but he looked worn to the bone, with dark circles under his eyes and a permanent frown on his lips.

He pulled his horse to a stop below her balcony, his gaze roving her body before settling on her face.

"Hi," she called, letting her hair cascade around her like she was some princess in a tower, greeting the knight who'd come to rescue her. "Long night?"

He shook his head and looked away. His lips parted, then closed again, as though he couldn't find the words to reply. "You shouldn't be out here."

She ignored his sour mood, clinging to her princess fantasy out of sheer stubbornness.

His horse sidestepped restlessly. He shifted the reins and made a clicking sound with his lips, bringing the horse back to standing still. "Your horse isn't nearly as tired as you are."

The next time he looked at Hannah, he wore a slight smile, his gaze still tired, but warmer. "This is Outlaw. And he's definitely as tired as I am. He's ready to get back to the stable, get cleaned up and go to sleep. A lot like me."

"Then go ahead and get Outlaw tucked in bed," she said. "I just wanted to say hello."

"You shouldn't be outside this late," he repeated.

She crossed her arms and swung a hip out in mock

defiance. "Who's going to get to me all the way up here?"

She hadn't meant to say that as a challenge, but the moment the words fell from her lips, she got the craziest vision of him swinging off his horse and scaling the wall to reach her.

Frustration flashed across his face. "I don't know and that's what I'm afraid of."

His words and his concern were a reminder of why he and the others patrolled the property every night, and it wasn't because they enjoyed the sleepless nights. She wrapped her robe more tightly around her. He looked so beat down, and was working so darn hard to make sure everyone in his care was safe. It should be her climbing down the wall to reach him and be a balm for his troubles.

Her concern must have shown on her face because his expression softened. "Go on inside, Hannah. Get some rest. I didn't mean to make you worry."

He was right that she was worried, but more about him than anything else at the moment. This huge house, these thick walls, and the aura of family and love made her feel safer than she ever had before. Yes, Abra had been attacked in that same house only a month earlier, but whoever had done so had to be long gone.

He didn't wait for her reply before nudging his horse into motion again. Defying his command, she watched his proud, strong back move in the saddle until he reached the stable.

It only took her a moment of deliberation for her to decide what her next move was. She stopped by the bathroom in her suite, brushed her teeth and her hair, then stole from her room on quiet feet.

She really wasn't a fan of the dark house. It was eerie as all get-out, probably because she didn't yet feel 100 percent at home there. She didn't know the sounds or what every shadow meant. But she blocked the creepiness from her mind, flipped lights on as she moved from room to room, until she got to the kitchen.

Of all the spaces in the house, she loved the kitchen most of all. With its earth-tone color palette and cluttered counters and good smells and worn wood table in the corner, it felt like love. Like a big hug from Maria and Edith.

Grooming and settling his horse in for the night would take time, so she made herself a cup of tea and waited, imagining her child in this kitchen. She could see Maria and Edith doting on him or her, sneaking them tastes of the sweets they were making, chiding him for eating jam straight out of the jar like his mama. Such a comforting vision. Maybe Hannah would be there, too, doting and laughing and loving.

More than anything, she wanted to give her and Brett a chance at something real. Even if he wasn't ready to entertain the idea right now, they had all the time in the world. All she needed was a hefty dose of patience, of which she was in short supply at the moment.

When she heard the door open in the mudroom that sat between the kitchen and the back porch steps, she stood, her tea forgotten. Though she wanted to rush to him and throw her arms around his neck, she waited by the table until he'd come in the house and locked the door behind him.

When he saw her, one side of his lips kicked up in a tired smile. "I should've guessed a stubborn woman like you wouldn't take my advice and get some rest."

"Did you eat dinner?" she asked.

The last time they'd shared a meal was the night of the hunting blind fire. She loved dining with Big J, Edith and Maria, and sometimes Jack, Tracy and little Seth, but she missed Brett's conversation. She missed his smiles and levity.

"No. Not hungry."

To be fair, he didn't look hungry. He looked exhausted. But there was no better cure for that than some TLC. She poured him a glass of water as he emptied a flashlight, keys and a pocketknife from his pockets onto the counter.

Then she stepped close and held the glass out to him. "You're not taking care of yourself."

His lips pressed together, pulling into a straight line. "I'm managing fine, but thank you for caring." Still, he took the offered glass and drained it in a few gulps.

Anticipation and nerves made her heart pound as she inched closer. She slid an arm around his middle, her hand smoothing over the soft, worn flannel of his shirt. He gripped the empty glass hard, his knuckles going white. Then she set her cheek on his shoulder.

"You're a good man, Brett Colton."

With an incredulous huff, he averted his gaze.

Affection bloomed in her heart. She lifted the glass from his hand, though it took some coaxing to get his grip to ease, and set it on the counter. Then she cradled his cheek in her palm, her thumb scraping over thick stubble. Before she could overthink it, she angled her face up and let her nose brush along his jaw.

He wrenched his face away. "Woman, you're going to be the death of me," he growled.

Undeterred, she took his hand and pressed it to the curve of her flesh where her hip met her backside. "But what a way to go."

His fingers tightened over her flesh, gripping her with purpose. Even through the layers of fabric from her robe and nightgown, she felt his warmth, his strength. It was all she could do not to moan at the pleasure of finally—*finally, damn it*—feeling his hand on her body. Their kiss in the hospital hallway felt like a lifetime ago.

Chancing another bold move, she brought her hands to his shirt collar and slid the top button through the hole, releasing it. She moved to the next button.

"Hannah, please. We've been over this." His hand left her backside and clamped around her wrist, stilling her progress, but her mind crowded with memories of their one-night stand.

He'd cuffed his hands around her wrists that night, too. He'd pinned them over her head, positioned her against the wall in her living room and ripped her underwear off. He'd actually ripped them away from her body as though the idea of having her had turned him into a madman. She'd loved every second of it.

She allowed herself a quiet pant of arousal through her open mouth. The flesh between her thighs turned sensitive and tingly. She squeezed her inner muscles, wallowing in the tender, needy feeling the action evoked.

In one abrupt motion, he released her wrist and backed away from her, as though he'd noticed her reaction. He prowled to the sink and braced his hands against the counter. His jaw was tight, his eyes hard as he gazed on the darkness beyond the window.

"Would it be so bad for me to take care of you for once? Since you're doing such a good job taking care of me?"

"We're having a child together. We can't afford to be careless with our relationship." His words were clipped, his tone little more than a growl.

And there they were again, back to that same circular argument they seemed doomed to have for all of eternity. Careless or not, she was determined to be the kind of person who took chances—and there was nothing she wanted more than to take a chance on her and Brett. "We can't just ignore what we want from each other indefinitely."

"I'm not willing to jeopardize everything because I want you in my bed."

Heat and need raged through her body with the force of a wildfire. There was no way she was giving up this midnight seduction after that admission. *You're going down, cowboy. You just don't know it yet.*

With her eyes on his back and the stiff set of his shoulders, she untied the belt of her robe. It fell open, cool air swirling over her body, tightening her nipples.

"So you think this is just going to go away on its

own?" She shrugged the robe off her shoulders. The silken fabric licked at her legs as it pooled on the floor.

His grip on the counter turned his knuckles white. His jaw, his gaze, everything about him was stone. "This?"

As if he hadn't just admitted that he wanted her. As if the air around them didn't crackle with lust, with the urgent hunger to get their hands on each other, to connect on the most intimate level a man and woman could—hearts, bodies and minds.

"The need, Brett." Her whisper came out strained, as though the desire implicit in her words were a visceral thing, jagged and coarse. "The need."

Her body quivered with the craving to press her nude body against his back and wrap her hands around his waist, feeling that hard, male body beneath her palms. It would be so easy to wrap her arms around his waist and unlatch his belt, then set her fingers to work on the button and zipper of his jeans. It would be so easy to show him exactly what she meant in a few short moves.

Instead, she stayed the course of her seduction and pulled her nightdress over her head, then added it to the pile on the floor. Cool air swirled around her breasts. But either Brett hadn't heard the rustle of her clothes being shed or he was choosing to ignore it because he didn't flinch, nor turn his focus from the window.

Though every molecule in her body was straining for contact, she pivoted on the ball of her foot. She stepped over the pile of clothes, leaving them on the floor for him to trip on, and walked with silent, measured steps toward the hall that led to the stairs.

She didn't speak until she was in the hall, far enough away that if he turned, he'd see flesh, but only a glimpse before she vanished around the corner. "Good night, Brett. Sweet dreams."

She felt him watching her mount the stairs and added a little sway to her hips. His footsteps stopped at the base of the staircase, but she forced herself to keep her face pointed straight ahead, and forced her legs to keep moving. *Come on, cowboy. Follow me...*

Chapter 13

Hannah held her breath as she turned the doorknob to her suite, straining to hear the sound of his footsteps, but the house was silent. Was he really going to let her walk away? Was he really so determined to keep her at arm's length that her naked body didn't provoke him to action? How depressing.

She cast a final look down the hallway, but all she saw was darkness. Fine, then. Okay. Maybe her seduction technique hadn't been as effective as she'd thought. There was plenty of time to prove to him that their relationship was worth taking a chance on. Her heart giving a painful squeeze, she stepped into her room and closed the door behind her.

At a loss for what to do next, she stood for a moment in the middle of the room in the darkness, then walked to the nearest window, her attention on the moon. Pressing her palm to the cool glass, she allowed her mind to go blank, to think of nothing but how vast the world was and how breathtaking the moon looked shining down on all of creation.

The suite door flew open and banged against the wall. With a gasp of surprise, she spun around. Brett's silhouette filled the threshold. In his hand, he gripped the bunched-up wad of her clothes. "Do you have any idea how crazy you're making me?"

"What?" she breathed.

He kicked the door closed again, then prowled in her direction, tossing her clothes on a chair as he moved. "Do you have any idea how badly I want you right now? How badly I've been wanting you since that first night you came to the ranch?"

"I…"

And then he was before her, his face a savage cut of shadows and moonlight. "I've been working so hard to resist you, but while I was fighting to stay strong and trying to put our baby's needs before my own, you were stripping off your clothes behind my back."

He crowded against her, pressing her against the glass door, his eyes dark and volatile. She shivered at the first contact of the cold against her warm skin, but all thoughts of discomfort vanished at the feel of his jean-clad erection pressing into her belly.

One of his hands came up to cup her neck. The other gripped her hip. "You're making it so damn hard for me to do the right thing."

She opened her mouth to protest, but his lips descended over hers, hot and demanding. His hands gripped her hips, locking her body against his. She threaded her fingers into his hair. The rush of getting what she'd been longing for made her knees weak. She opened her mouth for him, mating her tongue with his.

While his mouth plundered hers, his hand slid over her backside, then down to her thigh. He cupped the back of her knee and jerked her leg up against his hip. The metal latch of his belt poked into her, rough and unforgiving against the stretched, tender skin of her belly. She reached her hands between them and un-latched the belt, the sides of her hands rubbing against the impressive erection that even twenty weeks later was still emblazoned in her mind. Her body's center pulsed at the memory.

She pushed the buckle off to the side, then closed her fingers around the button of his jeans. A flick of her fingers and a tug of the zipper made his pants gape open, his erection pressing against dark cotton. She curled her fingers around it.

He broke off the kiss, growling out as his hands closed around her wrists and pinned her hands against the glass near her shoulders, such a similar movement to that first time that she cried out with satisfaction.

Breathing hard through flared nostrils, he gazed down at her. "You need to know something first."

She remembered this with perfect clarity, too—the way he took control in the bedroom, rough but not too rough, brazenly confident right to the edge of smug-ness. The perfect mix of wicked and kind. She strug-gled against his hold on her wrists just for the pleasure of him tightening his grip. He pinned her lower body with his hips and slid her hands higher against the glass until her body was stretched out and utterly at his mercy.

She heard the surprise in his throaty growl when he said, "You like that, don't you?"

The question proved that he hadn't been exaggerating when he'd admitted to not remembering much about their one-night stand, because that night she'd proved to him over and over again how much she got off on his proclivity for dominance, for making a woman submit to his will. For her answer tonight, she strained her neck to brush her lips against his, though she could barely make contact and he made no move to get closer.

Before she could catch her breath, he took her mouth in an aggressive kiss, his tongue a hard, wet instrument of his mastery. This time, when he wrenched his face away, breaking the kiss, he was breathing as hard as she was.

"If we do this, then you'd better be ready for me to fight for you." His voice was low and harsh, as though he was speaking through clenched teeth. "Because I'm warning you right now, Hannah, that I don't take my responsibility to you lightly. And despite the carelessness of the first time we slept together, I don't take this lightly, either. Not anymore."

"Neither do I."

He nodded. "I want you and the baby here at the ranch with me and I'm going to fight for that, even if sleeping together proves to be one complication too many. You get in bed with me tonight, then I'm expecting you to fight for us, too. Do you understand? Can you accept those terms?"

His words wrapped around her, carrying with them the unmistakable weight of his fear and his determination, and so much honor that it made her heart burst with love. She met his hard gaze. "This is me fighting for us, and I plan to keep fighting. You know how stubborn I am."

This time when he kissed her, his aggression was laced with tenderness. "I love the sound of that." He brought her arms around his neck, then moved his hands over her back. "There's one more thing we need to discuss first," he said.

She tipped her head back, battling a sudden rush of frustration. "I'm going to self-combust pretty soon if we keep talking. This pregnant lady needs some action, cowboy."

His lips twitched, as though he was battling a smile. His hand moved between her thighs to cup her mound. "You mean, this kind of action?"

She whimpered. Bracing a hand on the back of his neck, she spread her legs wider. "That's a good start."

One of his fingers pushed between her folds. "You're so wet for me, and so on edge." His finger made a lazy swirl around her most sensitive flesh, rendering her limbs weak and trembling. She squeezed her eyes closed and rode out the sensation. "Do you need to come right now so you can relax and enjoy everything else I'm going to do to you?"

Without waiting for a reply, he added a second finger and pushed them inside her.

Her fingernails dug into his neck. All she could manage was another whimper.

"I'm gonna take that as a yes."

He braced an arm around her waist as his right hand worked a relentless pattern of thrusts and swirls that shattered any last vestiges of her composure. She threw her head back, arching, rocking her body in time with his movements.

"That's it. Take what you need."

But she was incapable of taking anything. All she could do was cling to him and feel and reach for the relief he offered against the near-painful pressure building inside her.

He bathed her neck and shoulders with kisses and nips of his teeth. When she was panting and desperate and so, so close, he sucked her earlobe, then said in a gravely whisper, "I want every inch of you."

Her whole body rippled with pleasure at the idea. And she thought she'd been ready to combust before. Her body turned into molten heat.

"Yes," she said between labored breaths.

She rose onto tiptoes, the balls of her feet pushing, pressed her back against the wall, her shoulders rising. Everything she was, inside and outside, lifting and tensing and building. Here it came, closer, closer…

Her mouth opened with the beginning of a whimper that died in her throat when he slipped a third finger inside her. Clamping his other hand on her hip, he pulled her down and thrust his fingers up with a force that tipped her right over the edge.

He stabilized her body between his own and the wall,

his teeth grazing her neck, as she lost herself to the release and succumbed to pulse after pulse of ecstasy.

When she'd recovered her wits, he removed his fingers from her body. His lips lingered on her shoulder, kissing and soothing. "That better?" he murmured.

She threaded her fingers into his hair and held him tight. "You have no idea how badly I needed that."

Raising his head, he gave her a wolfish smile. "Oh, I had a pretty good idea." His hand cupped her breast, toying with her nipple. She hooked a hand around the back of his neck and pulled his face to hers, kissing him hard and wet, stroking her tongue against his in his mouth.

Tired of having her access to his skin hindered by his clothes when he had full access to her body, she made short work of his shirt buttons and pushed the shirt off his shoulders. He let her work the rest of his clothes off as he explored her body with his hands and lips.

"Anything we can't do, with you being pregnant? I don't know much about that stuff."

"Me, neither. We're both new at this. I think we can do whatever we want, as long as you don't put much pressure on my belly."

"Got it. I'll be gentle."

"Not too gentle, I hope. I might be pregnant, but I'm not breakable."

He wrapped his hand around her leg and jerked it up against his thigh, his lips near hers. "Have I been treating you like you're breakable?"

"No. Just making sure."

His free hand cupped her breast, plumping her nipple as his mouth descended over it. He sucked her good and hard, getting his teeth involved until she cried out. "Who would've thought that my sweet little Hannah likes it a little rough?" he crooned against her skin.

Holding back a teasing comment about his terrible memory of their one-night stand, knowing he might take it wrong and feel guilty, she took hold of his erection and gave him a long, slow tug that twisted his mouth into a crooked scowl. "Sweet little Hannah needs this. Now."

He took her by the wrist and pulled her behind him to the sofa. When they arrived, he guided her in front of him, facing the sofa. "Climb up. On your knees."

She obeyed his command, kneeling on the cushions. He pressed his hand between her shoulder blades, pushing her gently down until her chest rested on the sofa back.

His next touch was his lips against her spine, kissing a path down.

"You ready for me?" His words were thick and raspy. He might have complete command over her body and her pleasure, but she could tell he was hanging on to that careful control by only a tenuous thread.

"Yes," she whispered. "Take me, please, Brett."

But rather than what she expected, his lips found her body's center. Tender from her first orgasm, she cried out at the first touch of his tongue to her swollen flesh. He was relentless in his pursuit of her pleasure, working her body with his mouth and tongue until she was trembling and sweaty. Her chest had sunk down into the cushions and her hips reached for the ceiling, obscene and shameless, giving him unfettered access to her body.

When at last she felt first tremors signaling the inevitability of another release, he ceased his ministrations.

"Brett, I need…" she gasped.

He surged into her with a groan. His hand smoothed up her sweat-slick back, then took hold of her shoulder. He lifted her torso until it'd cleared the cushions and her hands were braced on the sofa back, then his hand closed around her neck. He brought her body up close, her face near his.

Her arms flew back and grasped at his head and his hair as her body exploded in a fierce, swift shock wave of bliss. His thrusts had grown harder, creating an aftershock of energy that rippled through her flesh every time their bodies collided. He turned her face sideways, then kissed her, as sloppy and wet and wicked as he had during their one-night stand.

The hand on her neck shifted to her breast. His other hand moved from her hip around to her front. He tucked his arm between her hip bone and her belly, hooking his hand around to her pleasure center. At the first touch of his fingertip, her cry filled the room.

He nipped her ear. "You're going to come again."

"I can't."

He pinched her nipple between his finger and thumb and tugged. "Yes, you can."

His touch was as insistent as his words.

"Give it to me, baby. Give me one more release from your hot body. Come on."

His teeth bit down on her shoulder, a lightning bolt

of the perfect storm he'd created within her. Ignition. Lost to the sweet agony of Brett's total command over her body, she threw her head back and shattered again. He crooned his approval as he buckled forward, spending himself inside her with a roar of release.

Chapter 14

Brett woke disoriented by the brightness of the room. Ranchers' schedules meant a lifetime of waking in the dark. He had, in fact, woken around 5:00 a.m., but had forced himself to stay in bed, not wanting Hannah to wake up alone and wonder why he'd left. Guess he'd drifted back off, because now her room was as bright as the middle of the day. His eyes, behind his eyelids, ached from the light.

He peeled one eye open. The sun was shining through the open windows. Sleeping next to Hannah had felt like heaven. He'd been so tired lately. He hadn't realized how on edge he'd been—about the ranch, about Hannah. But somehow, knowing that she was going to stay at the ranch, that she was going to fight for a future with him, lifted a huge rock from his chest. He was more determined than ever to make the ranch a safe place for her and their child.

"Good morning," she croaked.

"Did I wake you?"

"No. Our little guy—or girl—did. Baby's crazy active right now. I think he's learning how to play soccer." She took his hand and set it over her belly. "He or she has no respect for its mama's need for sleep. So rude."

He heard the love in her every word and snuggled back into the pillow, no longer in a hurry to get to work.

It wasn't long before something thumped against his palm. He couldn't speak, it was such a miracle. He buried his face in Hannah's hair, gritting his teeth against a wave of emotion. That was his child in there. His healthy, growing child that he'd get to meet in only a few months.

What a thin line he was walking, sleeping with her, risking losing full-time fatherhood if he and Hannah's relationship crashed and burned. Last night, that risk had paled in comparison to his blinding need to claim Hannah's body, but with the light of day and the feel of his child moving beneath his palm came a clarity of perspective about everything he stood to lose.

"When's that ultrasound appointment?" he croaked. She'd wanted to wait until her Lucky C health insurance kicked in at the turn of the month, but Brett had been insistent that they spare no cost.

"On Friday."

"I can't wait. Is it too soon to talk about names?"

She drew a circle over the back of his hand where it still sat on her belly. "I'd figured we'd wait until we found out the sex of the baby, but there's nothing stopping us from throwing some names around. I was thinking, if it's a boy, we should consider naming him John after your dad. If you're open to that idea."

Brett rolled to his back. "Oooh, doggie. My dad would be the proudest grandpa in all Oklahoma. I don't think his feet would ever touch the ground again."

"Then that settles it. John Colton it is, if it's a boy. But I have no ideas if it's a girl."

Brett hadn't spent a single second considering names before this moment, but the perfect one popped into his head. It was time to fight for what he wanted instead of being paralyzed by fear. It was time to have faith in himself and in Hannah, just as he was asking her to have faith in him. "Faith."

"Why Faith?"

He took her hand and threaded their fingers together. "Because that's what you had to have in me to come to this ranch like you did. And to keep the baby, in the first place."

She rolled over to face him, which was no easy task given the size of her belly, and kissed him. "I love that idea. Faith Colton. It has a ring to it."

They lay in contented silence. Brett's mind spun out in all different directions. About his future with Hannah and his legacy with the ranch, about the crimes that had been happening lately, about which room they'd transform into the nursery if he could convince her to stay by his side to raise their child at the ranch. After a while, he realized Hannah's breathing had evened out. Her eyes were closed.

As much as he hated to leave her, he really did need to get to work. Jack was probably impatiently waiting to ream him for sleeping in.

When he eased out of the bed, her eyes fluttered open. "Are you going?"

"Gotta work. You go back to sleep."

"If the baby will let me, then I'm going to try. I'm sleepy this morning."

He nuzzled her cheek. "Gee, I can't imagine why."

They hadn't fallen asleep until the wee hours of morning, and even though he didn't know much about pregnant women, he figured they needed as much sleep as they could get. She hummed and snuggled more deeply into the pillow. He smoothed a hand over her hair, then tiptoed from the bedroom in search of his pants and underwear. He'd gotten his boxers on when the suite's main door opened.

Brett didn't have time to do more than put on his underwear and hold his jeans up in front of him.

"Oh!" Edith stood in the doorway holding a tray of food, her face beet red.

"Oh is right." After a moment's hesitation while he processed Edith's presence in the room and his state of undress, he decided he didn't care. He was relatively decent and she was like a mom to him. "Come on in. Sorry to embarrass you like that."

He pulled his pants on, then walked to the bedroom door and eased it closed.

Edith set the tray on the coffee table. "She gets queasy in the morning. Biscuits and tea help," she said in a quiet voice.

He nodded. "Then thank you. I'm late for work, but I didn't want her to wake up alone and wonder why I'd left without…" He shook his head, letting his voice trail off. And the *why* didn't explain why he was talking about it to Edith.

"A wise call, if you're interested in this wrinkled old lady's opinion."

He poured himself a glass of water from the pitcher atop a table near the door. "You're too young to be calling yourself an old lady. I don't see a single wrinkle on your pretty face."

She swatted away his comment, but blushed all the same. "Jack stopped through about an hour ago asking after you. I called your room, and when you didn't answer, I suggested to him that you'd probably gone off to the backcountry early. You've been doing that a lot lately."

"I've had a lot on my mind."

"I imagine you have." She nodded toward the bedroom door, her hands clasped behind her back. "Are you going to marry her?"

He choked on the water he was sipping. After a coughing fit, he said, "You sound like my dad."

"Well, are you?"

He swirled the water in his glass, considering his best, most diplomatic response. "It's come up on and off since the day I found out she was pregnant. She and I have discussed it at length and neither of us want to end up in a loveless marriage like our parents have. Hers, too."

Edith crossed her arms over her chest. "All right, that's a good plan. So are you going to marry her?"

Brett gave a quiet chuckle. "I wish it was that simple, but first I've got to get her to fall in love with me."

"And what about you?"

He set the water down and grinned at her because that was an easy question to answer. Hannah was smart and resourceful and sweet. She got him in a fundamental way and when she looked at him, she saw his best self, the man he'd worked so hard to become. She got along with his family and she had the most remarkable way of laughing with her whole face, eyes and cheeks and lips, that socked him in the heart every time. He loved talking with her, he loved working with her and he loved sex with her.

"The truth? I'm already gone."

Ready for another long evening of patrol, Brett bounded downstairs to grab a quick dinner with his dad and Hannah before heading out. It'd been a good week. The sale of Geronimo had gone through and the horse was settling down and getting used to his new digs at Daniel's stable, which made Daniel and Jack happy. And Hannah's morning sickness had subsided completely, which was one worry off his mind. Best of all, after he got home near midnight every night, instead of dragging his butt into a cold, lonely bed, he got to snuggle in close to Hannah.

Adding to his peace of mind, there hadn't been any more crimes or suspicious incidents around the ranch since the fire the week before. Sure, the police didn't have any new leads, but he'd take the respite from trouble as the gift that it was.

When he reached the dining room, he found his dad there, but not Hannah. Pops looked old tonight. And lonely. Not that Brett's mom had been good company for him, but she'd been somebody, and her absence had a palpable effect on the feel of the house. Even Hannah had felt it her first day there. And for a man who'd fathered and raised six kids, it had to have been difficult on his dad to watch them grow up and leave to start their own lives, all but Brett.

Brett absolutely could not wait to fill the house with the cries and laughter of a baby. The thought of it almost made him laugh, the thought filled him with so much joy.

He rubbed his dad's shoulder as he passed, then dropped into the chair next to him. "Hey, Pops. How are you tonight?"

"Oh, fair to middling."

Brett nodded at the untouched place setting and empty chair where Hannah usually sat. "Where is she?"

"Who, Abra? I don't know where that woman goes when she disappears."

Alarm bells sounded in Brett's mind. If his dad was confused about where Abra was, then they needed to get him evaluated by a doctor pronto because he was far worse off than they all believed.

He studied Dad's face, looking for signs of his usually sharp wit, proof that he was merely making some kind of inappropriate joke. But all he saw was the faraway look in Dad's eyes, his slightly slack-jawed mouth and the tremors in his hands. With all that had happened recently, the transformation from the robust, charming man to a senior battling dementia gave Brett a sinking feeling in his stomach. It was all he could do not to grab Dad in a bear hug.

"Mom's still at the hospital," he corrected, taking care to keep his tone patient and free of the worry that now plagued him. "I meant Hannah. Have you seen her?"

He gripped his thighs, bracing himself for Dad not to remember who Hannah was, but to his great relief, Dad's eyes sharpened and he seemed to fully inhabit his body again. "Huh? No. Not since this morning when I checked in at the office and she had her nose in the books. She's a go-getter, that one. You should think about marrying her."

He patted Dad's arm, his heart sinking all over again because his dad had given him that same advice almost daily since Hannah had arrived at the ranch. The only difference now was Brett's response. "I am, Pops. Trust me on that."

A clatter of silverware and dishes preceded Edith's arrival in the room. She slid a tray onto the table. "Good evening, Brett."

Brett bussed her cheek. "Good evening to you, too. Where's Maria?"

"She asked for a night off to be with her parents, which I was more than happy to oblige. How's that new horse of yours?"

"Looking good. Now we just need to give Daniel some time and space to breed Geronimo, and I think

Colton's Cowboy Code

we're going to have the start of a great new direction for the ranch."

She served Dad a plate of lasagna. "Jack on board with you yet?"

"Not yet." With all the turmoil around the ranch, he'd decided to put off showing Jack the business plan that he and Hannah had created until things settled down. "But even Jack was as excited as a kid on Christmas when Geronimo walked down the trailer ramp."

Dad chuckled. "Attaboy. You'll bring your brother around soon enough."

Edith set a plate of lasagna in front of Brett. "Is Hannah still at the office?"

"That's what we think," Brett said. "She probably lost track of time."

"Shall I call her?" Edith asked.

"Nah, I'll run over and get her." He loved catching her in the act of working. That look on her face of singular concentration, her reading glasses perched on the tip of her nose. Maybe he'd get to steal a kiss or two while he had her alone. "Don't wait on dinner for us. We might be a while."

Edith's eyes twinkled with delight. Geez. Hannah must've been rubbing off on him, that was such an obvious Freudian slip. "I meant because she might be in the middle of something. She's been working magic with the ranch's books and I'm not going to pull her away until she's at a good stopping point. Not that we'd be late for dinner because I plan on holding her up."

"Mmm-hmm," Edith said.

"If that's the case, then you're not as smart as I thought," Pops said.

Shaking his head and grinning like a fool, Brett swatted the air behind him as he left, dismissing the teasing.

"Hold on," Edith said. "I'll make you a tray. You two can eat dinner in private at the office. You're riding patrol tonight with Ryan, correct? I thought I heard Jack say something to that effect this morning."

"I am, but Hannah and I'll come back here for dinner. I don't want Pops to eat alone."

Dad craned his head around to glare at Brett. "Pshaw. I'm not some decrepit old geezer. I can entertain myself. Maybe there's a game on TV."

Edith winked at Brett. "I'll keep him company."

A few minutes later, loaded with plates of lasagna and red velvet cupcakes, he made his way along the dirt path to the office, anticipation speeding him along. He hadn't seen Hannah all day, and though they'd texted each other a few times, he couldn't wait to be near her again.

Evening was descending on the ranch. It was bound to be a beautiful night, weather-wise. The sunset turned the whole sky orange and purple. The colors and clouds reflected off the office windows as Brett mounted the stairs to the office. He turned and watched the dark orange sun appear below a fluffy purple cloud above an expanse of deep green rolling hills as far as the eye could see. Brett defied any man to find a more breathtaking view than the Lucky C at sunset.

He was nearly to the office when Ryan drove up in

his unmarked police car. Damn. Guess he'd have to make his visit to Hannah faster than he'd wanted to.

"You're early!" Brett called.

Ryan unfolded from the car and a grabbed a jacket from the backseat. "Been a while since I've been on a horse. Thought I'd brush up on my skills before we get going."

Like the rest of the Colton kids, Ryan had learned how to ride before he'd learned to walk, which meant he'd arrived at the ranch early for some other reason that he wasn't keen on broadcasting. Something having to do with the investigation, Brett guessed. They'd have plenty of time that night to discuss the investigation. But for the next half hour or so, Ryan was on his own because Hannah was the only thing Brett wanted to think about.

Brett held the tray of food aloft. "I'm going to go eat dinner with Hannah in the office. I'm sure there's plenty of lasagna in the house if you're hungry."

"I'm good. Take your time. Like I said, I've got some rust to brush off the old brain when it comes to riding."

Sure he did. Hopefully, when they were out on the range, Ryan would come clean about his true reason for poking around the ranch.

Brett pushed open the unlatched office door, but Hannah had the radio on, tuned to a country station, and she didn't seem to hear him. She was sitting at the desk just as he'd imagined, with those glasses on her nose, her lips silently mouthing the numbers she was reading, and her hair wound around a pencil to form a disheveled bun on her head. He leaned his weight against the door frame and drank her in.

"I take it back," he murmured.

She startled just a little, dropping her pencil as her face shot up. When she realized it was only him, she smiled in a way that hit him straight in the heart. "Take what back?"

"There is such a thing that's prettier than an Oklahoma sunset."

Her expression turned demure at the compliment. "You've got to stop that."

He made some room on the desk, then set the tray down. "Why?"

She removed her reading glasses, looking bashful. "Because I don't know what to do with it."

He leaned over the desk and cupped her cheek in his hand. "I'd take a smile in response in the future, but right now, I'm going to go crazy if I can't kiss you."

He leaned across the desk and angled his lips over hers. He kept it tender and light and full of love. When the kiss ended, he stroked his thumb along her cheekbone. "That's what I've been looking forward to all day."

Hannah rose from her chair and licked her lips, her eyes appraising his belt buckle. "Really? Because that's not what I've been looking forward to."

Her gaze was hungry, as if he hadn't wrung several epic orgasms from her body the night before.

He eyed the room. There was a lock on the door, curtains on the windows and plenty of options on where to get comfortable while he satisfied her. Besides, what kind of decent provider would he be if he didn't give his woman what she needed? "You want to eat first, while it's hot."

She walked around the desk and hooked her hand down the front of his pants. "Unless that's a euphemism, then no."

He laughed out loud at that. "Let me lock the door."

"I'll close the curtains."

They came together again in the middle of the room, their kisses desperate. This was going to have to be a quickie because Ryan was waiting, but with the way she was ripping at his clothes right now, she wasn't interested in taking her time.

He smoothed a hand over her breasts. "You are so sexy."

"I was just thinking the same about you."

He cleared off the desk, stacking files and papers onto chairs, returning pens to their holder.

"You know," he said as he removed the last of the items from the desktop. "I was born a cowboy. Never been much into staying indoors or being fenced in, and office work, that's my idea of hell, but tonight, I'm suddenly inspired to perform some desk work."

He wrapped his arms around her. His hands grabbing hold of her backside, he lifted her onto the desk.

"Is that so?" she purred, onto his game. "You're going to put in a little overtime on the job?"

He stripped her shirt off over her head, then laid her back like an offering on an altar. "You see, I have a very demanding boss with a lot of desperate needs that are my duty to address."

The leggings she wore pulled off easily. He added them to the chair where he'd tossed her shirt. It'd been too dark last night for him to see much of her body, but tonight he drank his fill of her in the full light of the office. Beyond lust and the urgency to brand her body with his touch, the sight of her belly swollen with his child brought forth a surge of possessiveness and ego. He was a modern guy, but damn, it brought out the inner caveman in him to see his beautiful, brilliant Hannah pregnant with his child.

"What a burden, to be so needed," she said. "Maybe she's just trying to help you live up to your full potential on the job."

With a wry huff of laughter at her words, he brought her ankle to his mouth. He dragged his lips and tongue along her leg, reveling in the scent and taste of her skin and the way her breath hitched when he reached her inner thigh.

If his true potential as her man was to screw her brains out whenever need took a hold of her, then that was one element of his job description that he was fully on board with now. He pulled the nearest chair toward the desk, right between her legs, and propped her feet on the chair arms. With his arms wrapped around her hips, he scooted her backside to the edge. She squirmed and whimpered at the first gentle swipe of his tongue.

"You drive me crazy, Brett."

He slid his hand up her side until he found her hand and twined his fingers with hers. "You ain't seen nothin' yet."

Then he put his lips and tongue to work, feasting on

her wet, hot flesh until her cries bounced off the office walls and her thighs tightened around his head.

When her release had subsided, she sat and stroked her hands over his hair. Her cheeks were flushed and she wore a languid smile. "My turn now. You want to get up on the desk or stay in the chair?"

He swiped his thumb over his mouth, then kissed her. "I'm going to take a rain check on that until tonight, after patrol. Knowing I get to come home to you is going to keep me going tonight while we're on the range."

He helped her off the desk and back into her clothes. In his periphery, he caught sight of the tray of food. "I'm afraid dinner's cold. Sorry."

She straightened her shirt. "Worth it and then some."

"Agreed."

He slid the tray back onto her desk, then reached for the papers he'd cleared from it. Now that he wasn't distracted by lusty thoughts, he realized that the paperwork she'd been poring over had been the previous year's ledgers as well as a stack of check stubs and invoices. "What're you doing with these invoices? They're dated last November."

She eased the stack of papers from his hands. "It's nothing."

She set the stack off to the side on the far end of the desk as though she didn't want him looking too closely at them.

"You're not acting like it's nothing. Is everything all right?"

"Yes." She worried her lower lip and sank into her

desk chair. "No, actually. I wasn't going to say anything to you until I was sure there's an issue, but the truth is that I can't get the monthly balances right, not for any month in the past year."

He pulled his face in surprise. His dad was a great businessman with a head for numbers. Then again… "My dad's mind is going. Could he have done the math wrong?"

"That was my hunch, too. At first look, the numbers that were incorrect looked like easy mistakes, numbers transposed and things like that. Except that the weekly totals are off by about the same amount every time. Five hundred dollars, give or take some change. So far the account seems to be short about twenty-three thousand dollars."

Brett cursed. "That's a lot of money to go unnoticed."

"It is. I wasn't going to say anything to you until I was sure, but I think somebody's skimming money from the Lucky C."

Brett walked to the window and flipped the curtain open, looking outside. He wished he didn't have to go on patrol that night. His instincts were telling him that something bad was brewing, and Ryan's ambiguous reasons for being on the ranch early weren't helping him feel secure about leaving Hannah alone.

"That's a serious allegation."

"Which is why I hadn't said anything to you yet." She touched his shoulder. "Don't worry yet and don't mention the discrepancies to anyone, okay? Let me triple-check my math first. There's no need in upsetting your dad and brothers unnecessarily."

Before anything else happened, he needed to talk to Ryan. They'd stick close to the homestead tonight, but there was no way he was leaving her alone and vulnerable in the office. "I have to go. Ryan's waiting on me. But I'd feel better if you were safe and sound inside with Dad and Edith."

"That's fine with me. I'm not crazy about the idea of working here after dark, either. Rafe stops by the office sometimes, especially if you're not around, and every time he does, he makes me feel a little uncomfortable. Okay, a lot uncomfortable."

Okay, that was a name he hadn't expected to hear tonight. "Wait. Rafe comes by the office to see you?"

"Almost every time I'm alone."

"For what purpose?"

Hannah shrugged. "I'm not sure. He's flirty and... I don't know. I get a weird vibe from him, but it's nothing to worry about, especially right now. I'm going to pack up and get to the Big House."

He rubbed his temple, his head spinning with all these new revelations. "How long has that been happening?"

"Since the afternoon I arrived, but it's just a gut feeling. He hasn't done anything, really. Just hangs around too much, stands too close, looks at me a little too intensely, and he's always slipping sexist remarks into the conversation. He's a bit of an ass, honestly. I'm not a fan."

"You should have told me."

She wrapped her arms around him again. "You've

had enough on your mind, and there really isn't anything specific to tell."

"Hannah, you can tell me anything. Especially if a man is making you feel uncomfortable."

"You really are my hero, you know that?"

He kissed her head. "I'm trying. How about you let me walk you home?"

"Not necessary. I'll finish eating and get my stuff together so I can work in my room. I promise to be in the Big House by dark."

He tipped her chin up and gave her a lingering kiss. "Good. Thank you. That'll be a load off my mind. You and I can talk more tomorrow about the discrepancies with the books. I'll help you get to the bottom of it. And I'll be paying Rafe a visit, too. You won't have to worry about him anymore."

"Thank you." She walked him to the door. "Stay safe out there. I couldn't bear it if something happened to you."

"I will. Same goes with you, okay?"

A rumble of thunder caught him off guard as he stepped outside. He'd forgotten about the weatherman's prediction of a storm that night. Wouldn't be the first time he and Outlaw had been out in weather. He pulled the brim of his hat lower, his eyes scanning the ranch grounds for any sign of Rafe. Not seeing any, he looked toward the bunkhouse. The light in Rafe's corner bedroom was on.

He had half a mind to go give the man a dressing-down right then and there—and half a mind to fire his sorry ass—but Ryan was waiting. After one last look, he turned away from the bunkhouses and headed across the grounds to the stable where Ryan sat astride his horse, waiting for him and wearing a teasing grin.

"When I told you to take your time, I didn't mean I wanted to stand here counting the cattle while you got your rocks off. I guess you decided to help your baby mama work through her pregnancy hormones after all."

Brett bit the inside of his cheek against a smile. "We were that subtle, huh?"

"Oh, yeah, real subtle, what with the way you slammed all the windows shut and closed the curtains at lightning speed. I think I actually saw the trailer rocking."

"Hannah and I are happy. Get over it."

Ryan shook his head, his smile firmly in place. "Get Outlaw saddled so we can get out of here."

"Something's up with you. Can you talk about it here or should we wait?"

Ryan's smile fell. He glanced back and forth as though checking to make sure no one was in earshot, then dismounted and got close to Bret. "You know that rush job we asked Susie to do? She found a set of prints, but she wasn't able to identify who they belonged to. They don't match any of the prints we have on record from the Lucky C. And believe me, we printed everyone after Abra's attack."

"Then why were you here early?"

Ryan gave another look around, then stepped closer. "The accelerant that the fire marshal determined was used in the fire was an ammonium nitrate compound common in the same agricultural fertilizer the Lucky C uses."

Brett's ribs gave a squeeze as all the pieces fit together. "You were here early to take samples. Even though the prints don't match, you still think someone got the accelerant here at the ranch. Is that part of the message they're sending us?"

"I don't know about the message, but it sure looks like it's shaping up that way. The samples I took are off the record. Susie's going to see if there's any truth to our hunch before we show our cards. Just about every ranch and farm in Tulsa uses some similar combination of the same agricultural products, so it's a long shot. Especially with that unidentified fingerprint. The important part is that the clues are stacking up. It won't be long now."

Brett looked toward the office. Inside it sat his whole world, his new family. "It better not be. I'm getting itchy for some justice to be served so we can get on with our lives."

"Come on. Let's get out of here. I'd like to take a look at the hunting blind again before this rain hits."

The hunting blind was out in the backcountry much farther than Brett had wanted to travel that night, given the warnings that his instincts were niggling him about, but they were starting early and he couldn't think of a solid reason to refuse Ryan's request. With a nudge to Outlaw's flanks, they got their patrol under way, riding straight into the gathering clouds.

Chapter 15

As the last glow of daylight succumbed to the encroaching storm clouds, Hannah walked to the Big House, carrying the food tray with the manila envelope of possible embezzling evidence tucked under her arm. She was nearly there when Big J burst out the main door and practically flew down the porch steps.

Hannah quickened her stride and met him in the driveway. "Big J, are you okay?"

"Hannah, there you are," He was pale and anxious, his sweater misbuttoned, as though he'd thrown it on in haste. "I just got a call from the hospital. Abra's taken a turn for the worse."

"Oh, no. Let me set this stuff down and then I'll drive you."

"That's okay. Jack's meeting me here. He's going to drive me to the hospital."

"I'll go with you."

"Actually, Edith already retired for the evening and I don't want to bother her, but I couldn't get either Brett or Ryan on the phone—they must be out of range— and I don't want them to come back to find us all gone. Would you stay here and tell them what's happening? You can drive over with Brett."

"Of course." She made to hug Big J, but he was too jittery to hold still. The minute they heard the sound of a truck, he seemed to forget about her existence.

Hannah set the tray and the envelope on a step and followed him to the edge of the driveway. She gave a small wave to Jack, who was behind the wheel of a big black truck. "I'll be praying for your mom."

Jack's lips were a thin line as he nodded.

Hugging herself, she watched their taillights disappear along the long road leading off the property. That was it. She was alone again at night on the ranch, exactly in the position she'd promised Brett not to get in. The breeze kicked up, splattering her with the first raindrops of the storm that had been threatening all afternoon.

Lights shone from the bunkhouse, reminding her that she wasn't actually alone. The ranch had lots of people on it at any given time. And somewhere out there in the night, Brett and Ryan were patrolling for the express purpose of keeping everyone safe. Time to call them and give them the tough news about their mom.

She turned back toward the house, picked up the

tray and envelope, and walked the rest of the way to the house. From the phone in the kitchen, she dialed Brett's cell phone. It flipped to voice mail without ringing. So did Ryan's, which probably meant they were out of range.

She closed her eyes and said a quick prayer for Abra, then reached for the envelope. She'd get that hidden behind the vanity, then keep trying to reach Brett. A roar of thunder shifted her focus to the window. The rain was really coming down now. Poor Brett and Ryan.

With a heart heavy with worry, she turned toward the stairs. She was halfway up them when the lights flickered once, twice. The house went dark.

Hannah gripped the rail, startling as a flash of lightning strobed through the house. No two ways around it—it was going to be a long, troubled night and she had a sinking feeling about how it was going to end.

Brett was miserable. The last time it'd rained this hard, he'd found himself in the backcountry, that time chasing pregnant cows. What a wet July this had been. Great for local farmers, but not so good for a rancher trying to keep his family and his livestock safe.

Tonight's storm had arrived earlier than the weather forecasters had predicted, but at least Brett and Ryan had reached the hunting blind before the rain hit, for all the good it'd done them. All they'd done is determine that there was no new evidence to find. No more photographs lodged in the scrub bushes or grass and no unusual footprints or tracks indicating how the arsonist had traveled so far into the backcountry—bicycle or truck or horse. Nothing.

Soaked to the bone, Brett hunched into his jacket and pulled his cell phone from his pocket. It'd been more than an hour since he'd checked it last, not wanting it to short-circuit from the rain.

He'd missed nearly twenty phone calls. A handful from his dad and the rest from Hannah.

"Ryan, something's not right."

He dialed Hannah's number. "Hannah called a lot. Dad, too."

Ryan pulled his own phone out as Hannah's voice mail message kicked on.

"Damn it." Brett's hands were trembling now, but he was afraid to get the horses moving, lest they lose the signal.

"I missed a bunch of calls from them, too. Them and Jack," Ryan said.

"Hannah didn't answer her cell phone," Brett said. "I'm trying the house."

The answering machine didn't even answer the phone at the house. It merely rang and rang until Brett grew impatient.

"Nothing?" Ryan asked.

Brett shook his head.

Ryan frowned. "I'm calling Dad now. It's dial— Hey, Dad. Is everything okay? Looks like we missed some calls." Ryan paused, listening. "Just a sec, Dad. Brett's here, too. Let me get this on speakerphone."

When the speakerphone clicked through, Ryan gave Brett a thumbs-up.

"Hey, Pops, it's Brett. How's Mom?"

"Hannah didn't tell you?" He sounded absolutely defeated.

"She's not with you?" Brett asked.

"No. I asked her to stay at the ranch so she could tell you about your mom. The docs think it might be time for us all to say goodbye to her." His voice hitched.

Brett's and Ryan's gazes met. Brett's own dread and heartache reflected back at him in his brother's eyes.

In all of this time, since she'd been attacked, worry of her death had been distant. Once the doctors stabilized her condition and brain scans revealed that she still had a lot of healthy brain activity, he'd pushed the idea of her dying to the back of his mind. But now, what if she really did die before the two of them could make amends? What if he was about to lose his mother forever?

It was too much. Brett closed his eyes. "Tell me Mom's not dying. Please."

He barely recognized his voice for the strain in it. Suddenly, he was back to being a kid again, watching his mother stack luggage in the trunk of a taxi and driving away. This was how abandonment felt. *As though you should have done more, you should have been better or sweeter. You shouldn't have back-talked, then maybe she would've stayed home instead of taking another extended trip abroad.* Maybe she would've fought harder to live, to come out of the coma, if they'd all been more understanding of her depression...

A squeeze on his shoulder had him opening his eyes to find Ryan next to him, sharing his strength. Probably he was going through his own emotional roller coaster of bitter memories and what-ifs about their mother.

"Oh, son. I'm so sorry," Dad said.

"Hang in there, Dad," Ryan said, his voice strained. "We're out in the backcountry on patrol, but we're on our way. We'll be there as soon as we can."

"I love you, Pops," Brett said. "Hang in there, okay?"

"Love you both, too, Brett, Ryan. See you soon."

They galloped at full speed back to the ranch, neither attempting to talk over the wind and rain and their own troubled thoughts and feelings. All was quiet around the homestead. The Big House was lit, a golden beacon in the bleak night as it ever was.

"I'll take care of the horses after I figure out where Hannah is," Brett said, dismounting. "You go on and we'll meet you at the hospital."

"Roger that. Thanks."

They embraced, sharing each other's strength.

"See you in a few," Ryan said. Then he jogged to his car and took off like a bullet down the road.

Brett left the horses tethered in the grooming stall inside the stable and strode toward the house. Normally, caring for the horses was his top priority, no matter what. But he needed to see for himself that Hannah was safe and sound, and figure out why she hadn't answered the phone.

When he passed by the darkened office, a movement caught his eye. The door was ajar and fluttering open and closed with the wind. He climbed the steps and pulled the door open. Then he gasped.

Even in the darkness, he could tell that the place

was a disaster. Something was written on the side wall, though he couldn't tell what, given the angle. What he could make out was the sign of the cross done in dripping spray paint on the back wall. Eyes on that, he reached in and flipped on the light.

A curse escaped his lips. The office had been trashed. Every file drawer was open and papers were scattered all over the desk and floor. The computer had fallen over, its screen smashed. He took another step into the room and slid on something slippery. He windmilled his hands, catching his balance.

"Hannah?" he called.

A book sat open on the desk. From it protruded the hilt of a knife. He walked the rest of the way into the room, straight to the desk. His first glance was under the desk, in case Hannah was there, but all he found were more scattered papers. The book on the desk was a Bible.

With one hand on the desecrated text, he lifted his focus and scanned the rest of the room. The words painted on the side of the room that he'd noticed before entering sent a fresh wave of sickening fear skittering over his skin.

God's watching you and so am I.

"Hannah!" he tried to shout, though the word caught in his throat.

What if she'd been here when this had happened? What if she'd been taken? Kidnapped? She'd tried to call him nearly twenty times and now she wouldn't pick up her phone. He'd never been so scared in his life. For all he knew, she was being held for ransom somewhere by whatever twisted scumbag had stolen money from their family. Unless…

What if his mother's attacker had returned for another victim?

A strangled noise bubbled up from his throat that sounded foreign to his ears, and he took off running.

Chapter 16

Brett flew through the house and up to Hannah's suite, calling her name the whole way. The door was locked.

He pounded on it. "Hannah? You in there?"

He'd never been so sick with worry in his life. After knocking again, he gave her two more seconds before shouldering it open. The trim around the door frame splintered as he ripped it from the hinges off. He heard a yelp from inside. As the broken door clattered to the ground, Hannah appeared in the bathroom, clutching a towel and shaking from head to toe.

"You scared the snot out of me!" she cried. "I thought you were Abra's attacker coming back."

Infinitely relieved to find her unharmed, Brett bridged the distance between them and grasped her shoulders. "Are you okay?"

"Other than almost having a heart attack out of fear, yes. Why in heavens did you break the door down?"

He pulled her into a giant hug. "Thank God you're all right. You almost gave me a heart attack, too."

She pushed against his chest until he backed up enough for her to look him in the eye. "Is this because I called you so many times? Why didn't you answer?"

"With the storm, I didn't hear it ringing in my jacket pocket. Are you okay?"

"Yes. The power went out, but Edith got it back on without much hassle. I called because your mom's not doing well. She took a turn for the worse, but I've since heard from your dad that she's stabilized again."

"I know. Ryan and I talked to him, too."

She clutched the towel around her more snugly. "Then why are you so freaked out? About your mom?"

"I'm sick about her, too, but someone wrecked the office. I thought something might have happened to you."

She brushed past him and strode to her bedroom. "What do you mean 'someone wrecked the office'? I was just there a couple hours ago, and I locked up when I left."

She grabbed a pair of black pants from the bed and pulled them on.

"The computer was smashed and there's graffiti on the wall, papers everywhere. Someone left a Bible on the desk with a knife stabbed into it."

She pulled a green sweater over her head. "A Bible? Oh, heck, no."

Just like that, she took off out of the room. With Brett

in tow, she jogged down the stairs and out the front door, paying no mind to the rain.

"Hannah, there's nothing you need to see."

"Like hell there is."

She threw the office door open and gasped.

"It's got to be the person who's skimming money, doesn't it?" Brett said. "He's sending you a message that he's onto you."

"Not a he, a she," Hannah said. She walked into the room and touched one of the dripping red crosses on the wall, her finger coming away with the wet paint. She whirled to face Brett and shoved her trembling hands in her pockets, but not before Brett noticed that they were shaking. Angry tears flooded her eyes. "I know who did it. It was Mavis Turnbolt."

"You think Mavis the laundry maid has something to do with it?"

Hannah shook her head. "She's not the laundress anymore. She quit after I confronted her about her leaving a Bible in my room with passages circled about the devil and sin and murder."

All Brett could do was blink, he was so ticked off at her for not being forthright about her problems around the ranch. "She planted a marked-up Bible in your room? I told you to let me know if she gave you trouble. Between her and Rafe and the possible embezzlement, you've been keeping a lot of secrets from me. Is there anything else you haven't told me?"

"No, and I'm sorry. I didn't want to add to your burden."

"Hannah, you've got a target on your back. How can I keep you safe if you don't tell me what's going on?"

"I hadn't thought about it like that, but I think you might be right." She fingered the edge of the Bible on the desk, then, after another shiver, wrapped her arms around herself in a hug. "Maybe it'd be safer for me and the baby if I left the ranch for a while. Until the danger's passed. Someone's out there who has it in for this place and the people in it, not just me. The hunting-blind fire, the damaged fences, Abra's jewelry showing up at the hospital. And now this. I love it here, but I can't be selfish right now. I've got to think of the baby first."

She was right and it pissed Brett off something fierce that some unknown perpetrator was threatening his woman and unborn baby so much that they had to seriously consider fleeing from the home he was trying to provide them.

Not wanting to take his frustration out on Hannah any more than he already had, he stalked out of the office, so spitting mad that he couldn't see straight.

He got Ryan on the phone. "Turn around. I need you at the ranch."

"Whoa, there, bro. What's going on?"

He got Ryan up to speed on the office break-in.

"I'm turning around. I'm about fifteen minutes away, though."

Brett climbed the steps to the Big House and stood on the porch, looking out over his domain, his family's legacy that was being destroyed before his eyes. Enough was enough. "It's time for a reckoning, Ryan. I'm sick and tired of standing around watching my family get hurt. Mom's dying, Tracy was the target of a hit man last month and now somebody's threatening Hannah. And I have a pretty good idea of who it is."

"You have a new lead?"

"Two possible leads. It's either Mavis Turnbolt, who's a member of Hannah's parents' cult, which is Hannah's theory given the religious symbols on the office walls, or it's whoever has been embezzling money out of the ranch's accounts. It's time to start knocking heads around until we get the answers we're looking for."

"What? Slow down and tell me what you're talking about. Embezzlement?"

Brett took a breath, trying to think past his fury so he could speak coherently. "Hannah just told me about the embezzlement this afternoon. She says she's been documenting it since she started working here and she was getting ready to lay it all out for us because she has proof that someone's been skimming from our accounts to the tune of twenty-three thousand dollars over the past year."

"Well, hell," Ryan said. "Could the embezzlement and vandalism perp be one and the same?"

"That's one theory. And another question is, could it be the same person who robbed Mom and beat her within an inch of her life?"

"That thought crossed my mind, as well," Ryan said. "Sounds like we need to figure out who had access to the ranch's ledgers and accounts. That'll narrow the list down."

"You don't sound angry enough for my taste," Brett snapped.

"One of us has to keep a cool head, and it sure as hell ain't you right now."

"I'm trying to make things right with the mother of my child. Do you understand me? I'm trying to show her that it's safe here for her and the baby, or else she's going to walk away. And then what? What the hell would I do without her?"

He flattened against the side wall of the house and squeezed his eyes closed while he got a grip on his spiraling fear. Until he'd voiced it, he hadn't processed how desperately he needed Hannah and their baby in his life. And not just on the periphery of his life, with occasional visits until the danger on the ranch passed— that was, if the police were ever able to catch the assailant. Beyond the Colton code of honor, beyond duty, he needed Hannah by his side. Forever.

"We're going to get this guy, Brett. Whoever did this, we're going to make him pay. I promise you that."

"We keep throwing that line around, about how we're going to get this guy, but this is the second month in a row that our women and our ranch are in imminent danger as we stand by and watch, helpless."

Ryan let out a heavy sigh that seeped to well up from the depths of his bones. "Hang in there and don't do anything stupid. I'm on my way."

Brett ended the call, cursing. He swabbed a hand over his face and girded himself to face Hannah again, even though he had no answers for her, nor any real hope to offer. He'd promised to take care of her, to be a man deserving of her, but he couldn't even do something as basic as provide her with a safe home for their baby. He gritted his teeth, riding out a wave of anguish. He had let her down; he'd failed her and their baby in a fundamental way.

Forcing himself to go numb, he walked back to the office, dialing his dad's cell number again as he moved.

When his dad answered, Brett said, "I'm sorry to bother you again, but I have to ask you something, and I know this is the worst possible time, but you're going to have to forgive me."

"Are you on your way?"

He couldn't decide if his father's dementia was kicking in or if he was purposefully ignoring Brett's words. "Not yet."

"Her situation isn't so dire anymore. She's still fighting and the doctors were able to stabilize her. They're trying a new medication."

"Thank God." A rush of relief battled with his frustration. He fought for numbness again.

"What do you need to ask me?"

"I need to know if, over the last year, you've given anybody access to the ranch's finances and accounts other than Jack and me." Brett's voice was tight with harnessed emotions.

"Huh? It's the middle of the night and I'm at the hospital with my wife who's in a coma."

Brett stood at the base of the office stairs and closed his eyes. "I know, Dad. And I'm sorry. But someone broke into the office tonight and vandalized it. We're trying to fit all the puzzle pieces together to figure out what happened and if we're in any immediate danger here. Have you let anyone else have access to the accounts? Maybe someone to make bank deposits for you?"

Dad huffed. "Only Rafe, and he wouldn't break in and mess with the office. Why would he? He loves the ranch like it's his own."

"Rafe?" As in the man who'd been getting too friendly with Hannah since she arrived at the ranch. A storm of fury started to build in Brett as the pieces clicked together in his mind. The religious symbols didn't make sense if Rafe was the vandal, but there were too many coincidences for Brett to overlook.

Dad sighed. "Yes, Rafe. I didn't want to admit it to you kids, but I just wasn't cut out for the job anymore. My eyes got tired, and Rafe was a big help. I asked him not to say anything to anybody. And then Hannah came, and Rafe and I were both off the hook. But I'm telling you, Brett, he'd never vandalize the office."

Brett bit his tongue, refusing to disagree with his father or chide him while he was in such a vulnerable state of mind. He did his best to modulate his voice and asked, "Was Rafe the only other person you gave access to the ledgers and account information?"

"Yes, besides you and Jack."

"Brett?" It was Hannah, standing in the office doorway, as pale as a ghost. "I found something you're going to want to see."

Phone still to his ear, he followed Hannah into the office.

She pulled a small black camera from the bookshelf against the office's back wall, from behind one of the plants she'd decorated the room with. It had been aimed at the desk.

"That's not what I think it is, is it?" Brett said. He couldn't take any more new discoveries tonight.

"Looks like it's digital and wireless and…" She trailed a finger over the top of it, leaving a clear path through the dust. "It also looks like it's been here a while. Someone was filming me." Her gaze roved to the desk before locking with Brett's once more. "Filming us."

Brett's stomach turned. *God is watching you and so am I.*

He could feel his palm start to sweat and had to grip the phone hard to hang on to it. "Dad, did you have security cameras put in the office?"

"Huh? No. We've never needed to take precautions like that. If we didn't trust someone then we wouldn't hire them. I don't think I'd know how to operate one of those new whiz-bang contraptions, anyhow."

Hannah touched Brett's arm, her gaze imploring.

He shook his head. "It wasn't Dad's doing," he said under his breath.

A firestorm started inside Brett, tensing his muscles, making his breathing shallow. Some psychopathic pervert had been secretly taping Hannah, which meant that, somewhere, there existed a recording of Brett pleasuring her that afternoon—violating their privacy, violating Hannah. Whoever had done this to her, they were going to pay.

"I've got to go, Dad." He didn't wait for a reply. The rage inside him was too all-consuming for pleasantries.

He pocketed the phone.

Hannah's hand flew over her mouth, her eyes going wide all over again. "The jam," she whispered. "That's how he knew I eat jam straight from the jar in my bedroom suite." Her body shivered. She stumbled back against the wall, dropping the camera.

"What? Who?"

"Rafe," she said. "He made a comment last week about me eating jam from the jar and I wondered how he knew because the only place I've done that is when I'm alone in my suite. I figured that he'd seen me on the balcony or something, but what if…"

Only two coherent thoughts broke through the rage pounding through Brett. One, that his .22 was still fully loaded from his patrol that night and, two, that Rafe Sinclair had better be praying that the police caught up with him before Brett did.

Chapter 17

Brett's mind screamed louder than the keening of a tornado siren. If there was a camera, then there was a set of recordings somewhere either in Rafe's bunk or in his phone. Whatever Brett found first—the recordings or Rafe—he had only one plan: destroy.

He barreled out of the office and flew down the steps, over the road to the stable.

He supposed it was raining still, but he couldn't even feel it. He didn't realize Hannah had followed him until he was inside the stable, lifting his .22 from Outlaw's saddle.

"Let the police handle this. Brett, please." She stood in the stable doorway, and he bet she meant to block him from passing, but he wasn't letting anything or anyone stand in his way.

The police would probably want to save the footage as evidence, but the thought of explicit recordings of Hannah being passed around a police precinct or presented in court made Brett's stomach turn.

"Like hell I will."

Rather than try to get past her, he pivoted on his boot heel and strode along the center of the stable to the door on the opposite end. He was nearly there when Hannah grabbed his sleeve.

"Damn it, Brett. This is not the way. I don't want you to get hurt."

He yanked his arm out of her grasp. "Go in the house and wait for the police. This ends now."

She took hold of his shirt again, pulling hard until he stopped walking. Moving around the side of his body, she clamped a hand on his jaw and forced him to look at her. "I'm not going to let you do this. Ryan's on his way and for all we know, Rafe is armed."

"I don't care if he's armed. I'm going to find him and I'm going to destroy those recordings if I have to burn the whole bunkhouse down." He didn't recognize his own voice, it was so even and quiet with restraint. "Do as I said and get in the house. Or better yet, take my truck and go to town. I won't have you in danger any longer."

"No. I'm not leaving. You need to stay with me and keep me safe."

Nice try. "Fine, then stay here. But swear to me that you're not going to put our baby in danger by following me any farther than this barn."

She looked furious with him, but she held her tongue.

Clearly, she knew he was right. "Don't do this," she repeated from behind clenched teeth. "I love you. I need you to be safe."

Her words just brought it home to him what he had to do. She loved him, and he loved her, too. And he wouldn't stand by and let her be violated by some greedy psychopathic scumbag.

"We're wasting time. Let go of my shirt and get out of my way. It's time for justice to be served."

Hannah stood in the barn, alone. In shock.

Brett was going to get himself killed. Or he was going to kill a man and get sent to prison. Either way, the life of the most magnificent man she'd ever met was about to change forever and she couldn't simply stand by and watch it happen. But he'd been right about her not putting the baby in danger. She was a strong, brave woman who'd risk almost anything to save her man, but her hands were tied. Tonight, being strong meant sacrificing what she wanted to do for the safety of her baby. There was nothing left except prayer for the police and Ryan to arrive in time. Or maybe, if God saw fit, for Rafe to be long gone from the ranch.

She walked to Outlaw and stroked a hand over his mane. "He'll stay safe, right? He knows how much I need him, doesn't he?"

Outlaw's ear twitched. He pushed his nose into her chest.

She nodded and stroked the top of his nose. "I'm going to take that as a yes."

The odor of smoke hit her nostrils. Wood burning.

She lifted her nose, confirming her suspicion, which was how she spotted the first tendrils of dark smoke crowding the ceiling of the barn.

She didn't think; she didn't have time to be afraid. She untethered Outlaw and the still-saddled horse next to him and pulled them out the door. They ambled, not getting the direness of the situation. They stood just outside the stable, looking around and not paying any mind to the danger.

She swatted Outlaw's rear, trying to get him to run away, and it was at that moment that she spotted movement out of the corner of her eye. She did a double take and saw a flash of white clothing worn by someone small in stature, the size of a woman, headed west. She shook her head and blinked. Was she hallucinating again or was that the ghost? More likely, it was whoever had started the fire—and they were headed straight toward the bunkhouse. *Brett.*

Every fiber of her being wanted to go after him, but running headfirst into this new danger was yet another risk she couldn't take. Besides that, there was a fire nearby, with smoke pouring into the stable.

She didn't see flames from where she stood, so she backed up and, shielding her face from rain with a hand on her forehead, took a close look at the building. The rain made the smoke hard to see, but it seemed to be coming from the east side. If the stable was on fire, then so many lives were at stake. There were at least ten other horses in the stable that she knew of. She turned a spigot on and, grabbing the water hose that was attached to it, ran around the building.

What she saw when she rounded the corner was the most horrific sight she'd ever witnessed. Worse than the ransacked office.

The fire licked up from the grassy earth in a straight line, as though someone had poured gasoline along a crease. The treated wood of the stable was burning, too, but slowly. Above the flames, pinned to the outside wall of the stable, were dozens of photographs. In each one, every person in the picture had their eyes gouged out, much like the engagement photo Greta had shown her a couple weeks earlier. Above the photographs, carved into the wood siding, were the words *ALL LIES*.

Hannah shook away her horror. There would be time to figure out who'd left such a message, but right now, all she needed to worry about was keeping the horses and other livestock safe. She angled the hose at the flames and sprayed, keeping her mind on the task at hand instead of the dark thoughts threatening to buckle her knees in fear.

She didn't hear the car approaching until it was right up on her. Ryan leaped out and ran her way, his clothes still damp from patrol and a pistol in his hand. "What's going on? Where's Brett? Who set the fire?"

"I don't know. I saw a woman dressed in white, running toward the bunkhouse, but I don't know if she did this," she said.

"Give me that hose. You shouldn't be breathing these fumes."

He tried to take it from her, but she wouldn't relinquish it. "The fire's almost out. I've got this. You've got to stop Brett. He has a gun and he went after Rafe."

Ryan's mouth fell open. His face whipped sideways to regard her. "Rafe, as in the Lucky C employee? Brett thinks he's the one who vandalized the office? I thought we were worried about your parents' church or whoever is embezzling money."

"Brett called your dad. He said he was having Rafe help him with the ranch's finances this past year."

Ryan's shoulders fell. He shook his head. "That doesn't explain why Brett went after the guy with a gun in the middle of the night."

"There's more. We found a secret video camera in the office. Someone's been recording me. Recording me and Brett this afternoon and recording me in my bedroom suite. And it's Rafe. I know it is, given some private things he knew about me."

Ryan cursed. He pressed a switch on his pistol and the magazine dropped out. He gave it a good look, then slid it back into place and cocked it.

Hannah aimed the hose at the last remaining flames. "You've got to go stop Brett before he does something he can't take back or gets himself killed."

"Where are they now?"

Hannah nodded toward the west. "The bunkhouse. And hurry."

Ryan got on his phone. "I need backup at my family's ranch. A fire engine, too. We've got at least one suspect on the loose, possibly armed and dangerous, and a minor structure fire."

"You're not going to wait for backup to get here, are you?" Hannah asked.

"Hell, no. Come with me." He turned off the hose and tugged Hannah's arm. "Let's get you in the house first."

"I've got to get this fire out. You go stop them and bring Brett back to me safely."

"Hannah, I've got to make sure you're safe first."

Hannah threw the hose down and set her hands on her hips. "There's only one violent criminal on this ranch and right now the father of my baby is trying to single-handedly take him on. I'm safe enough. Just go. Now!"

He rotated his jaw, a battle waging in his eyes. Then, with a terse nod, he took off running.

Brett stood over the sniveling, pathetic excuse for a man that was Rafe Sinclair while the other ranch hands stood watch at the door. As soon as Brett had clued them in about Rafe's crimes, they'd let him pass and blocked the hall against Rafe's escape.

"Tell me," Brett roared, backhanding him across the cheek with a fistful of his mother's jewelry that he'd found hidden in the bastard's mattress. "Have the guts to admit that you attacked my mother."

"I didn't. I swear. She was already unconscious when I found her."

"Like hell she was."

"I'm telling you the truth. I'd never hurt nobody. I swear on my father's grave. I just needed the money is all. With that party y'all were throwing, I saw it as my chance to slip a little jewelry out of her room. That's it. You were all distracted and so I made my move. And I found her on the floor, lying in a puddle of blood."

Brett hit him again. "And you did nothing?"

"I thought she was already dead, so I figured there was nothing I could do for her."

Brett was nothing but fury. Rage. "She wasn't dead, you son of a bitch."

"I know that now."

"So what did you do?" Brett said. "You walked around her and riffled through her dresser for things to steal?"

He licked at the blood on his split lower lip. "That's it. That's exactly right. I stuffed my pockets full of gold and diamonds and other pretty stones from the jewelry case, which was already open, I might add, and I got the heck out of there before you all came running in to find her."

"What about the photo albums?" came another voice at the door.

Brett paused, his fist in the air, ready to lay more pain on Rafe, and looked to the door. Ryan stood in the doorway, his entrance blocked by a ranch hand holding a shotgun. "Get out of here, Ryan. I'm not ready to turn this scum over to the police yet. Not until I get the answers I need."

"Don't you think that's what I want, too?"

Brett ground his molars together. "Your hands are tied by the law."

"Not tonight, they're not." He shoved past the ranch hand barring his entrance and stumbled into the room.

Rafe turned his sniveling expression to Ryan, trying to crawl toward him, but Brett kicked him in the ribs and knocked him to the ground.

"Answer Ryan's question," Brett barked. "Why did you take the family albums?"

"I didn't. I have no idea what you're talking about. I just wanted some jewelry to sell."

This time, Ryan grabbed Rafe's hair and wrenched his pathetic face up. "You didn't take the albums?"

"I swear. I'm broke. Gambling debts. The forged checks, the jewelry, it's because they're going to kill me if I don't pay back the money I borrowed. But I didn't want no trouble."

"Then why did you set fire to the hunting blind?" Ryan said.

"I didn't! I was as surprised as you were when that happened."

Brett caught him around the throat and raised him up. "How do we know you're not lying to us?"

He pulled at Brett's wrist, trying to free himself. "I don't know. I can give you the name of the guy I owe money to."

"And the jewelry you dropped outside the hospital? The locket?"

"I didn't take no lockets. Not enough street value."

Brett gave Ryan a sidelong look. Brett's gut was telling him that Rafe was speaking the truth. Which meant that whoever had attacked their mother and set fire to the hunting blind was still on the loose, and was taunting them with a trail of mutilated family photos.

Time to move on to the most pressing matter, now that he had Rafe all primed and scared.

He got both hands gripping Rafe's shirt and shook

him hard until he heard Rafe's teeth rattle. "Where is the video footage of Hannah?"

Rafe raised a weak hand and pointed to his desk. "In my laptop. But I didn't mean no harm with it."

"You gonna stand here and tell me you didn't watch us making love? You didn't watch her in any compromising states?"

Despite his bloody, raw face, one corner of his lips kicked up in a smile. "Of course, but only because I had to make sure she didn't tell you about the money skimming."

With nothing in his mind except red-hot rage, Brett slammed Rafe's head against the footboard of his bed, then grabbed him by the hair and wrenched his head back. "You violated her, you sick prick, and believe me, if it was just you and me in a room with no witnesses, I'd find a way to erase your memory."

Then Ryan was behind Brett, pulling him away. "Easy, bro. I'll take it from here."

But Brett wasn't quite done. He shoved at Ryan until he released him. Leaving Rafe in a heap on the floor, Brett strode to the desk and yanked the cord from the laptop. He raised it over his head, ready to crush it on the ground under his boot.

Ryan grabbed his arm. "Stop. We need that. Evidence."

"Nobody else gets to violate Hannah like this bastard did. Not the police. Not a judge. I've got to destroy it."

Ryan's grip was an unrelenting vise. "Remember Susie? Susie Howard. I'm going to give this to her to process. She'll handle it with discretion. Nobody's going to violate Hannah again. You have my word, but we need this so we can make sure Rafe never sees the outside of a prison again."

Breathing hard, and so conflicted about the right move to make, he let Ryan take the laptop from him. If this meant Hannah's peace of mind by putting Rafe in prison for the rest of his life, then they could endure the existence of footage of them making love.

With his gaze locked with Brett's, Rafe stood and brushed his knees off. Brett's fists twitched with the urge to knock him back down, so he took a step away, then another, backing out of the room.

Rafe wiped his nose with a handkerchief, then found Brett in the doorway and sneered, as though his sniveling had been nothing but an act. "Pregnant women don't usually get my blood pumping, but that sweet little Hannah is a hot number."

Brett snapped again. He lunged for Rafe, but was stopped midair when Ryan shoved against his chest and grabbed his arm. Someone else grabbed hold of the other.

"Let me at him," Brett roared. For the first time in his life, he felt capable of murder.

Ryan and the ranch hand dragged Brett screaming and thrashing into the hallway. Try as he might, Brett couldn't wrench his arms out of their grip.

The sound of breaking glass cut through their shouts. They turned back toward the room to see Rafe's legs disappearing through the broken window.

Ryan lifted his gun up. "Oh, it's on now."

Chapter 18

The fire was out in no time, as Hannah had predicted, though her mind remained fixed on Brett and Ryan and the battle they were waging. Her stomach twisted into knots in fear for them. Straining her ears listening for police sirens, though hearing none, she pushed all the doors and windows of the stable open, airing the interior out the best she could.

She couldn't find a switch for the vent fans inside the stable, but the moment she stepped outside in search of one, she was shoved off-balance.

She braced her arms out, cushioning her fall. But Rafe was above her, screaming obscenities. His face was a bloody mess, with both eyes swollen and a split lip. His nose looked broken. *Brett did that.*

Rafe's hands tightened around her throat. "You bitch. You ruined my life."

She kicked at him and swung her arms. She clamped down on his forearm and sank her teeth in. He howled and released her neck. She gasped for air, but there was no time to recover. This might be her one window of opportunity to escape safely. She got her knee up and kicked out, catching him somewhere in his midsection. He stumbled back, smiling.

"I do love fighting women, but it's time for me to scram."

Then he turned tail and ran toward the saddled horse that Ryan had used for patrol that night.

The horse was jittery, but Rafe had caught his lead rope before the beast could skitter out of reach. Rafe hooked a boot into the stirrup and swung on, then took off southwest into the prairie.

"Are you hurt?" Brett dropped to his knees next to her, his expression bald with fear. "Hannah, talk to me."

"I'm okay. Just a little roughed up. Rafe took off on Ryan's horse."

He cradled her face in his hand. "I don't care. I need to know you're okay."

She clamped a hand on his wrist. "I'm okay. And I'm so glad you are, too. I was out of my mind with worry."

Ryan dropped to her other side. "Is she all right?"

"I'm fine," Hannah said. "Rafe took off on your horse, headed southwest."

"The police will never catch him in that direction. He's long gone."

"I could catch him," Brett said.

Hannah grabbed a fistful of his shirt. "Don't. Please. Who cares what happens to him now?"

Brett's jaw rippled. "I do."

"I'll stay with Hannah. You go get him," Ryan said. He handed him a pair of handcuffs. "Just don't kill him. I'd get a lot of pleasure out of watching him rot in jail for the rest of his life."

Brett stood. He set his top teeth on his lower lip and whistled.

Hannah pushed herself up to her knees, then stood and took hold of Brett's hand. "Brett, I'm begging you. Just stay here with me. Safe. Our baby needs a father."

He shook his hand away and stroked her hair. "Hannah, I love you so much. I have to do this. I won't live the rest of our lives in fear of him coming back."

Outlaw appeared at Brett's side. Brett brushed a kiss across Hannah's lips, then mounted the horse. Brett nodded to Ryan, then took off, man and beast flying over the countryside. Hannah stepped in their direction, drinking in the sight of him until he disappeared from view in the darkness.

Spying on Hannah was a personal violation of the worst order, but there was no greater sin on this earth, in Brett's mind, than a man laying hurtful hands on the woman that he loved. Outlaw knew this prairie from memory, every scrub bush, every tree, every rock. With only the occasional lightning strike to illuminate their path, they flew through the outback—straight in the direction of Vulture Ridge.

He and Outlaw caught up to Rafe and Tumbleweed long before they reached the ridge. Though Brett was the only man armed with a gun, he didn't dare chance a shot that might accidentally hit the horse.

"Freeze, Sinclair. This is it. You're going down."

Rafe looked over his shoulder. "Go to hell."

"Not tonight. But my horse is faster than yours and more experienced in this backcountry than yours. You've got no hope of getting away tonight."

"Stop flapping your lips and shoot me if you're gonna. I ain't got nothin' to live for anyhow. And if you're not gonna shoot me, then just leave me be because the only way I'm going back to that ranch is dead."

They rode neck and neck through the night. Outlaw could've run faster if Brett had commanded him to, but pacing Tumbleweed would preserve his energy if necessary. All they needed to do now was trap Rafe against the ledge of Vulture Ridge, their best chance of cornering him.

When the ridge came into view, Tumbleweed slowed. Rafe dug his heels into the horse's flank, but Tumbleweed was undeterred.

Brett reached into his saddlebag for a lasso. When the ridge was no more than a football field away, he let the rope go. It fell over Tumbleweed's head. Rafe sprang into action, pushing the rope, trying to free the horse, but Brett clicked his tongue and gave a tug on the lasso. On cue, Tumbleweed ground to a stop.

But Rafe wasn't ready to surrender. He swung off the horse and took off running. Brett stayed on Outlaw, crowding Rafe against the ridge of the gully. Now that Brett was close to the edge, he could see that the gully was rapidly filling with water.

"Déjà vu, Outlaw. I don't like the way this is going."

The next time Brett looked at Rafe, he'd taken a running jump over the ledge.

Cursing, Brett pulled Outlaw to a stop and looked over the edge.

Rafe stood in the middle of the gully, looking dazed. His arm swung at a funny angle, one that made Brett wonder if he'd broken it in his fall.

Gun in hand, Brett slid down the mud wall into the gully. He took aim.

"Now will you freeze?"

Rafe limped toward Brett. "I hate to sound repetitive, but go to hell."

Brett put his finger on the trigger. "You have no idea how badly I want to kill you right now."

Rafe panted, his nose and lip bleeding again. He limped toward Brett, but Brett held his ground.

Rafe bumped his chest right into the rifle barrel. "So do it. I won't go to jail. I won't. And if I don't pay back the money I owe, I'm dead, anyway. Just kill me and get it over with."

There had been a time that Brett was as impetuous as to do exactly that. When he was a hot-blooded, hot-tempered young punk. But now he understood the value of mercy. He understood the value in watching Rafe get handed justice by the courts. He straightened his trigger finger and rested it along the side of the rifle.

"I'm not going to give you that kind of mercy, Rafe. I've heard that committing murder changes a man. And I'm not willing to go down that road for a pathetic excuse of a human being like you. It's over, Rafe. I'm taking you in."

A roar sounded behind them, a sound Brett remembered all too well. A wall of water in the gully bore down on them. They had to get out of the gully immediately if they wanted to live.

"I know that sound, Rafe, and it's all kind of bad. We need to get out of this gully." Dropping the gun to his side, he grabbed hold of Rafe's shirt, but Rafe shoved at him, then stumbled back, out of reach.

He limped away from Brett, toward the roar. "This is God's way," he said.

There was no more time to spare or else they were both going to lose their lives that night. Brett took one last look at Rafe, then started his climb up the cliff face, digging his boots into the earth and clawing at the muddy wall with his fingers, blinking out rainwater and bits of mud as he used every last ounce of his strength to save himself.

He had his torso on the top of the ridge when water hit his boots, sucking at his legs. He clawed at the ground, fighting for a grip as water pushed him with the force of thousands of tons of pressure. Growling with the effort, he pulled as hard as he could, but made no progress. His muscles burned with the effort to keep from succumbing to the raging flood.

Outlaw nudged Brett's forehead with his nose.

"Not now, buddy," he said through gritted teeth as he clung to the lip of the ridge.

Outlaw's rein smacked him in the cheek. In a moment of perfect clarity, Brett knew what Outlaw was up to. Keeping one hand on the ground in the meager grip he'd created, he said a quick prayer, then let go with one hand and grabbed hold of Outlaw's rein.

Outlaw stamped the ground and tossed his head, scooting backward. Brett slid up an inch, then another, until his boot cleared the water and he could swing it onto solid ground.

He rolled away from the edge of Vulture Ridge and stood, then threw both arms around Outlaw. Breathing hard, his legs turned to jelly, he rubbed his face against Outlaw's cheek. "Thank you, buddy. Thank you."

With one arm still hugging Outlaw, he turned and looked at the raging flood.

"What a waste, Outlaw. But it's over now. Hannah's going to be safe."

When Brett got back to the homestead, he'd tell the police to start a search for Rafe and clue them in to the direction that the Lucky C's new mama cow's body was recovered a month earlier, but he had no doubt that all they'd find was the broken body of a broken man once the floodwaters receded after the storm had passed.

Chapter 19

"I think this shade of green is your color. Brings out the different shades of black in your hair." From his seat next to the examination chair Hannah sat in, Brett fingered the edge of the paper hospital cover-up she wore.

"My hair doesn't have different shades. Black is black."

He winked at her. "Just testing to see if you're paying attention."

She took his hand. "I can't wait to find out which color hair the baby inherits, yours or mine."

"We've got a few more months before we learn that, unless it's bald and then we have even longer. Either way, as long as it has your features, it's going to be one beautiful kid."

Though Hannah's original ultrasound appointment

was scheduled for the following day, Brett had insisted that she have a full medical workup the morning after her attack at the ranch to make sure she and the baby were healthy and hale.

Hannah knew in her heart that the baby was fine. If anything, it was even more active inside her belly, having shifted from playing soccer to learning acrobatics. But Hannah didn't mind Brett's concern or having her appointment moved up. She was eager to find out if she was going to be a mother to Faith Elizabeth Colton or John William Colton. And she couldn't wait to share the news with the rest of Brett's family—her family now, too—beginning with Abra.

Brett had talked to Eric that morning, who'd assured him that their mother had stabilized since last night's scare. The cardiologist thought her code blue had been the result of a bad reaction to a new medication. Now that they'd switched her meds up, she was back to a quiet, stable state and her doctors gave her 70 percent odds of pulling through and waking up. Thank the Lord.

"You look a million miles away. What are you thinking about?" Brett asked.

She took his hand. "Just how twisty a road we traveled to get here. But I wouldn't trade it for anything. Not one moment of it."

He tightened his grip on her hand and brought it to his lips for a kiss. "I love you, Hannah. You know that, right?"

She did know that. Even more, she felt it in her heart. Having Brett by her side, with motherhood only a few short months away, her life was close to being perfect.

Before she could answer, the ultrasound technician strode into the room, her head bent over Hannah's chart. "Hey, Mom and Dad. Are you ready to meet your little one for the first time?"

Hannah's eyes crowded with tears. Oh, how she loved the sound of that. "We're ready. More than ready."

The technician prepped Hannah's stomach with a thick drizzle of cold gel that made Hannah jump, then squished the ultrasound wand right into the goop, pressing hard on her belly.

"You hear that, Mom and Dad? That's your baby's heartbeat. You can see it, too. There it is, right there on the screen. That flutter."

Hannah didn't think she'd ever seen a more amazing sight as the scratchy black-and-white image on the screen. "Hi, baby," she breathed.

In her periphery, she saw Brett dab at his eye.

"And that's our baby's face," he said, his voice thick with emotion.

"And two perfect arms, and two perfect legs," the technician said, pointing to various parts on the screen. "I have to take some measurements, and while I'm busy with that, how about you two count fingers and toes."

Hannah and Brett were riveted by the sight. Neither spoke, neither moved, unlike the baby waving its arms and bucking for them. For the first time, Hannah was able to put a visual with the movements she'd been feeling for weeks and weeks.

"Active little jelly bean, isn't it?" the technician said with a smile. "And perfectly healthy, by all accounts."

A tear jarred loose and traveled over Hannah's cheek. "Our little star."

Brett dropped his head to Hannah's shoulder. "We've had so much bad news lately. This, right here, is more than a star. It's our little miracle."

"Are you two ready to find out if you're having a girl or a boy?"

Brett took a deep breath. "Ready. I can't wait."

The technician slid the ultrasound wand over Hannah's belly. Grays, whites and blacks undulated on the screen, then refocused. "There it is," she said.

Hannah narrowed her eyes in concentration. If only she'd brought her reading glasses. "What?"

"You see that little thing between the legs?" the technician said.

Hannah's mouth dropped open. She was filled with a joy and love so powerful, she'd never experienced anything quite like it. "I see it."

Brett stood up, his eyes glued to the sight of his son. "Well, hello, John William Colton. I can't wait to meet you." His swabbed the back of his hand over his wet eyes. "But I'm glad you're here to watch me do this."

Confused, Hannah wrenched her gaze from the screen to study Brett. From his pocket, he pulled a little black velvet box.

This wasn't the life she'd been meticulously plotting and planning; this, with Brett and their son, was beyond her wildest dreams, and here he'd gone and made the moment even more perfect.

"We agreed when I found out you were pregnant that we wouldn't marry for the wrong reasons. We both agreed that love was the only reason for two people to spend the rest of their lives together."

"We did say that, didn't we?"

"Hannah Elizabeth Grayson, I'm in love with you. With everything about you. I can't imagine my life without you by my side, and I need to know if you love me, too."

"I do, Brett. I love you so much. It was impossible odds, wasn't it? Me falling for the man I met in a club one night. Impossible, but just like this little baby, the impossible can happen. We've proved that."

Nodding like crazy, tears on his cheeks, he opened the box, revealing a gorgeous solitaire diamond ring set in platinum.

Hannah sniffled at the sight. "When did you have time to buy that, with everything that's been happening?"

"The day after we first made love and I told you that I was going to fight for you, for us. I knew that morning when we were lying in bed that I'd fallen hard for you. There's nothing I want more than to be a family with you and our children."

"Children?"

He gave her a watery grin. "We have to give John some siblings, right?"

"Yes, we do."

"So I guess there's only one question left to ask. Will you marry me?"

There was nothing in Hannah's heart or mind except love for the most amazing man she'd ever known. "Yes, Brett. It would be my honor."

He slid the ring on her finger, then wrapped his arms

around her and kissed her. She poured her heart into the kiss, all the while feeling little John kicking and celebrating inside her. Had there ever been a woman as lucky as she?

"Let's finish this appointment, then go tell my mom," Brett said. "She's going to want to hear all about her new grandson. And after that, what do you say we take the long way back home and find ourselves some twisty roads to explore?"

Over the past five months, she'd discovered the joy of the long and windy road, not so unlike the path to forever that she and Brett had forged. She took the hand of the man she loved, the father of her baby—her hero. "As long as I'm with you, that sounds just exactly perfect."

* * * * *

Don't miss the next book in the
COLTONS OF OKLAHOMA *series,*
THE TEMPTATION OF DR. COLTON
by Karen Whiddon, available August 2015
from Romantic Suspense.

And if you loved this novel, don't miss other
suspenseful titles by Melissa Cutler:

HOT ON THE HUNT
SECRET AGENT SECRETARY
TEMPTED INTO DANGER
SEDUCTION UNDER FIRE

MILLS & BOON®

It Started With...Collection!

**Don't miss Sarah Morgan's
next Puffin Island story**

Some Kind
of Wonderful

Brittany Forrest has stayed away from Puffin Island
since her relationship with Zach Flynn went bad.
They were married for ten days and only just
managed not to kill each other by the
end of the honeymoon.

But, when a broken arm means she must return,
Brittany moves back to her Puffin Island home.
Only to discover that Zac is there as well.

Will a summer together help two lovers reunite or
will their stormy relationship crash on to the
rocks of Puffin Island?

Some Kind of Wonderful
COMING JULY 2015
Pre-order your copy today

315/MB507

MILLS & BOON®

INTRIGUE
Romantic Suspense

A SEDUCTIVE COMBINATION OF DANGER AND DESIRE

A sneak peek at next month's titles...

In stores from 17th July 2015:

- **A Lawman's Justice** – Delores Fossen *and*
  Lock, Stock and McCullen – Rita Herron

- **Kansas City Secrets** – Julie Miller *and*
  The Pregnancy Plot – Carol Ericson

- **Tamed** – HelenKay Dimon *and*
  Colorado Bodyguard – Cindi Myers

Romantic Suspense

- **Playing with Fire** – Rachel Lee
- **The Temptation of Dr Colton** – Karen Whiddon

Available at WHSmith, Tesco, Asda, Eason, Amazon and Apple

Just can't wait?
Buy our books online a month before they hit the shops!
visit www.millsandboon.co.uk

These books are also available in eBook format!

715/46